STEELTOWN MAGNOLIA

A MAISY FARLEY MYSTERY

MELISSA F. MILLER

Copyright © 2023 by Melissa F. Miller

This book is a work of fiction. Names, characters, places, and incidents either are the product of the author's imagination or are used fictitiously. Any resemblance to actual persons, living or dead, is entirely coincidental.

All rights reserved.

No part of this book may be reproduced in any form or by any electronic or mechanical means, including information storage and retrieval systems, without written permission from the author, except for the use of brief quotations in a book review.

Published by Brown Street Books.

steel magnolia (*noun*). (chiefly Southern US) A woman who exemplifies both traditional femininity and an uncommon fortitude.

Steeltown (*noun*). Nickname for Pittsburgh and the surrounding area, once one of the largest steel producers in the world. *See also, Steel City, Iron City.*

Steeltown Magnolia (*noun*). Maisy Farley, Georgia native transplanted to Pittsburgh. Warm and sweet exterior with an inner core of pure metal. Intrepid investigative journalist, embodying softness as a strength.

CHAPTER ONE

Thursday, December 22
Pittsburgh, PA

MAISY FARLEY STROLLED along the sidewalk, humming a Christmas carol and keeping an eye out for icy patches. Christmas was in just three days, but she sensed very little holiday spirit in the air. Despite the garlands, twinkling lights, festive wreaths, and gleaming menorahs that dotted the front windows and doors of the houses she passed, it felt as if the city had already hunkered down and settled into the long, grumpy wait for winter to end and for spring to show a glimpse of itself.

She didn't blame her neighbors. She blamed the stores that rolled out their Christmas goodies before

Halloween had come and gone and then filled their shelves with Valentine's Day cards and heart-shaped candy boxes in late December. The accelerated retail pace of the holidays was out of sync with the calendar, not to mention Mother Nature's rhythms. It made folks testy, tired, and short-tempered all season long.

But not Maisy.

After fifteen long Pittsburgh winters, the sight of snow still filled her with a wonder that made her breath catch in her throat. She didn't much enjoy the cold that seemed to seep into her bones, but she accepted it as the tradeoff for the beauty of ice-laced trees, fresh white snow, and frosty whitecaps dotting the gray rivers. She raised her face to the sky and darted her tongue out to capture a soft snowflake as it fell.

Growing up in Spanish Oak, a sleepy town on the southeast coast of Georgia, Maisy had never seen snow—not once. Each Christmas Eve, Maisy and her parents piled into the minivan for the drive out to Aunt Alice's place. Maisy would swim in the lake with her cousins before they all ate a big barbecue meal followed by peach pie and a bonfire on the shore.

The memory of Spanish Oak hit her chest like an icicle. The cold stabbing sensation was one she knew all too well: guilt. She'd missed the last fifteen Christmases, staying in Pittsburgh to work instead of making the trek south to see her family.

Well, as her mama always said, the best time to make amends is before you need to, and the second best time is now. Like most of her mama's sayings, it sounded good after a few vodka tonics but made little, if any, sense to Maisy. All the same, she should call home.

She jogged up the stairs to the tall skinny red brick building that housed her favorite coffee shop and her lawyers' offices. She hurried inside and stopped in the hallway just outside the entrance to Jake's Coffee to pull out her phone. As she waited for one of her parents to pick up the call, she stamped the snow off her boots.

"Hello?"

"Hi, Mama, it's me."

"My lands, Maisy, your daddy and I were just talking about you. Are your ears burning?"

She laughed. "Yes, ma'am, they sure are, but I think it's because I forgot to wear a warm hat this morning."

"Oh, is it cold there?"

She shook her head at her mother's perpetual surprise that Pittsburgh had four seasons. "It's not too bad. Low thirties. I wish you could see the snow."

"No thank you, darling. No snow for me. In fact, your daddy and I were just packing up our swimsuits when the phone rang."

Her mother's voice grew muffled, and Maisy pictured her covering the receiver and turning toward the den from the telephone table in the entrance hall.

"Percy! Maisy's on the phone. Come on out and talk to her."

"Swimsuits? Since when do you two swim at Aunt Alice's?" Maisy stifled a laugh at the image of her parents splashing around in the lake and playing Marco Polo with her cousins' kids.

Her mother made no effort to hold back her laughter. "Saints alive, could you imagine?" Once she'd caught her breath, she clarified, "We're not going to Aunt Alice's for Christmas Eve."

"You're not? But you always—"

"Percy, how's this speaker phone work? Oh, here we go. Maisy, can you hear us?"

"Hello, sweet peach." Her father's slow drawl, warm as honey, trickled down the line.

"Hi, Daddy. Yes, I can hear you both. Now, what's this about you skipping Christmas with Aunt Alice and all the kids?"

"Gosh, Maisy, we haven't had the Christmas Eve barbecue out at Alice's place for … what, at least five or six years, isn't that right, Bunny?"

"Seven. The last year was when Laura Lynn's youngest got engaged to that fella from Canada."

"Canada, now that's cold," her dad observed.

"Wait. I don't understand. What do you do for Christmas, then?"

Maisy's cheeks burned. In part from the steam heat hissing up from the radiator along the wall, but in larger part from shame at the fact that she had no idea how her parents spent the holiday.

"We usually get together with Alice and her flavor of the month for brunch after church. It just became too unwieldy once all your cousins started popping out babies," her mother explained.

"Mama!"

"Well, they do. They pop 'em out like biscuits. I swear there've gotta be over a dozen now."

A dozen? She'd missed a dozen baby showers, christenings, and first birthday parties? Her face flamed brighter.

"Your mama's not lying. Babies and toddlers running all over the place. It got to be too chaotic. Christmas brunch with Aunt Alice is quiet. Peaceful, even."

She shook her head at the notion, then screwed up her face. "Why do you need your swimsuits to have brunch with Aunt Alice and her latest boyfriend?"

Her mother's laughter—like the tinkling of ice in a Mason jar full of sweet tea—pealed in her ear. "You're a hoot. This year we're doing something different. Alice and her beau, Jerome or Jethro or—"

"—Jared, Bunny. His name's Jared. Unless she's already traded him in."

"This year, your father and I and Alice and *Jared* are taking a holiday cruise."

"A cruise?" Maisy repeated.

"A ten-day Caribbean cruise through the tropics. We'll celebrate Christmas in Mexico and ring in the new year in Panama."

She couldn't help but smile at the girlish excitement in her mother's voice. "Oh, that sounds great, Mama." She infused her voice with as much enthusiasm as she could muster.

Her dad wasn't fooled. But then, he never was.

"You weren't fixin' to come home now, were ya?" His voice oozed concern.

"Of course she's not, Percy. She can't get away from work. You know that. Besides, she's already shipped all the gifts. Alice told me the little ones are bursting to see what's in all those packages."

Maisy swallowed around the lump in her throat and lied. "Mama's right. I'm swamped. I was hoping I could come for a visit next month, though. Y'all can tell me all about the cruise."

"Well, that'd be a real joy. It's been too long since you've been home."

She blinked back tears. "It has. Let's plan on it."

"We'd love to see you, sugar," her mama said in a sweet voice. "And feel free to bring along your flavor of the month, too."

She forced a laugh. The family joked that Maisy took after Alice in her rapid catch-and-release approach to dating. But Maisy and Aunt Alice both knew it wasn't true. Alice ran through beaus like tissues because she'd already had and lost the love of her life. God rest Uncle Ray's soul. Maisy ran through them because she was still searching for her Uncle Ray.

"Well, I best be going. I have a meeting with my lawyers."

"Love you, peach."

"Love you too, Daddy. And you too, Mama."

"Merry Christmas, darlin'."

"Bon voyage," she told them.

She ended the call, took a breath, and pushed open the door to Jake's cafe. She needed a big old glass of sweet tea, extra sugar. But she'd have to settle for a gingerbread latte.

AFTER A FROZEN MOMENT, Maisy carefully placed her latte on the white marble coaster in front of her. She shook her head, and her blonde curls bobbed against her shoulders. She blew back the long tendrils that danced forward and tried to fall over her face. Then she gave her head a slow shake and stared at her attorneys.

"I don't understand."

The lawyers, who also happened to be two of her best friends on the planet, exchanged a look that Maisy couldn't read. The silence stretched over McCandless, Volmer & Andrews' sleek, minimalist conference room and hung heavy in the air.

"Naya?" she prompted.

Maisy had known Naya Andrews for more than a decade. When they'd met, Naya'd been working as a legal assistant, keeping their mutual friend Sasha on her toes, and dodging her long-suffering boyfriend Carl's hints about marriage.

Now, a dozen years later, Naya was a corporate law partner with the shiny luxury car to prove it. And she was still giving Sasha hell and still evading Carl's attempts at proposing. Naya'd changed plenty over the years, but her forthright, no-nonsense attitude hadn't.

Maisy held her gaze and waited for her to explain.

So, when Naya mumbled "Mac" and cut her eyes toward Sasha, demurring to the not-quite-five-foot dynamo, Maisy's confusion ticked up a notch and turned to worry.

Sasha McCandless-Connelly reached across the table and patted Maisy's hand. "Oh, that's a pretty color. What's it called?" she asked, as if she were intensely interested in Maisy's manicure.

Maisy narrowed her eyes. "Pomegranate punch, and since when do you care about nail polish? You two are freaking me out. Just tell me the station finally ponied up my money, and it'll be in my account before the year-end."

Sasha took a long sip of her steaming hot coffee before answering. "Here's the thing. You *will* get your payout—"

Maisy exhaled and managed a shaky laugh. "Good gravy, but you two were making me nervous. So, when do I get it?"

"You'll get it," Sasha repeated. Then she drew her brows together and sighed. "But we're gonna have to fight for it."

"Fight for it? My contract said ..." she trailed off and gave Naya a long look. "You told me my contract said if the station fired me—for *any* reason—I'd get a million-dollar payout. Were you wrong?"

"It's not that," Sasha hurried to assure her. "Naya was right. Naya *is* right. You're entitled to a one-million-dollar lump sum payment."

"So what's the holdup? It's been months already."

"The holdup is that Leith Delone is one of the

richest people in the world, and he just happens to own the station now," Naya explained.

Sasha jumped in before Maisy could sputter a protest. "And you *did* go on live television and accuse him of interfering in a federal court case. So you can see how he might not be eager to pay you, right?"

Maisy felt a hot flower of anger bloom in her chest and struggled to keep a calm tone. "He doesn't have to be happy about it; he's contractually obligated to pay me."

Her statement sounded strong and reasonable to her, but it was met with silence.

She gnawed at her lower lip. "I mean, he is, right?"

"That's right. He is," Naya agreed. "But he's playing hardball."

Maisy caught the sidelong glance Naya shot toward Sasha.

"What?"

"Did you offer Jocelyn a job?"

She blinked at Naya's question. "Well, yeah. I mean, I'll need a camera operator. Why?"

"The station's threatening to sue her for violating her non-compete if she leaves to work for you."

"That's not fair."

"It may not be fair, and, frankly, a non-competition agreement with someone other than on-air talent is unlikely to hold up in court. But its existence is just gonna drag this out further. Wait until you get your payout, then start hiring away the station's employees," Naya suggested.

"Y'all, I'm running out of money. I need to start

generating content before I'm out on the street. How can I do that without Jocelyn?"

The silence stretched on just a beat too long.

Then Naya asked, "Are things that dire? You know, you can always stay with me. Or I'm sure Sasha'd let you stay at her place, But Carl's not as noisy as the twins—at least, not usually."

"And I'll bet he's less likely to pour syrup on a dog to see if it's really that sticky," Sasha deadpanned.

For a heartbeat, Maisy forgot her troubles. She gasped. "They didn't."

"Oh, but they did. Well, Finn did. Fiona was the evil mastermind, though. She convinced him that Mocha, like all chocolate labs, has a syrup-repelling coat."

Maisy laughed at the image of the poor syrup-drenched dog, and the tension in her chest eased a bit. She turned to Naya. "It's sweet of you to offer. And, no, my financial picture's not *that* bleak. Yet. But I do need that money. Starting an independent news station is expensive."

"Why don't you just do a podcast?" A clear voice rang out from the end of the conference room.

They all turned toward Jordana. The legal intern had slipped in without their noticing and was gathering up the dregs of an earlier breakfast meeting.

"You're sneaky," Naya told her. "Like a cat."

"Sorry. I didn't want to interrupt. But Maisy should look into podcasting. Minimal start-up costs, low production costs, and she'll reach a whole new audience."

Sasha twisted her mouth into a skeptical knot, but

before she could knock down the college student's idea, Maisy raised a hand to stop her.

"What kinda audience, sugar?"

To her credit, Jordana—currently experimenting with a neo-goth look that included a black and red split dye of her long glossy hair and an all-black wardrobe—didn't flinch at the term of endearment.

"A younger one. Nobody watches the local news anymore."

"Plenty of people watch the news," Naya corrected her.

"*Old* people watch the news. Everyone listens to podcasts."

"Maisy's a local celebrity. People will tune in to an internet broadcast that features her," Sasha insisted.

Jordana shrugged. "A lot more people will subscribe to a podcast, especially if she's got a juicy story."

"How would that earn money?" Maisy wondered. "Isn't it free to listen to a podcast?"

"It's the same financial model as the local news. The advertisers pay, the audience doesn't."

Maisy tilted her head and considered the idea. Her plan was to offer her internet news broadcast as a paid subscription. It was the only way to cover the costs of professional filming, editing, and production. She had big dreams. But, from the sound of it, she also had—at least for the foreseeable future—a shoestring budget.

"Interesting." Excitement stirred in her chest for the first time in a long while. She turned to Sasha and Naya. "May I take your intern out to lunch and pick her brain?"

Naya waved a hand. "She's all yours. She's not even supposed to be working today. She's hiding out here to avoid a Hanukkah party at her grandmother's place tonight."

At that, Jordana lost her business-like composure and rolled her eyes. "I can't spend the entire long weekend in Maryland. I have things to do. And working for the law firm is the one excuse Bubbie will always accept. She thinks I'm going to be an attorney."

"She's right, isn't she?"

Maisy caught the look that passed between Naya and the younger woman at Sasha's question.

Leaving it unanswered, Jordana quickly hefted the catering tray and turned toward Maisy. "Let me dump this in the kitchen and grab my bag. I'll meet you at the elevator."

They watched her leave the room.

Once the door swung closed, Sasha remarked. "She's a smart kid. She's gonna make a great attorney."

Naya tilted her head, thinking. "Maybe a podcast is just the thing, Maisy. At least for now."

"Maybe," Maisy agreed. "Now all I need is a story."

"A *juicy* story," Naya corrected.

Juicy, dried-up, or something in between would suit Maisy just fine. She just needed to find something to sink her investigative teeth into. She'd turn it into podcasting gold.

Sasha interrupted her musing. "When are you leaving for the holiday?"

Maisy let out a small sigh. "Turns out my folks are going on a cruise. So, I'll be sticking around."

"Then you'll come to Christmas Eve dinner at my parents' place," Sasha informed her.

"Oh. I—"

"And then brunch with Carl and me on Christmas Day," Naya insisted. "Don't worry. It's a small get-together, nothing like the McCandless crowd."

"This'll be a small one by McCandless standards. Only nineteen. Twenty with Maisy."

"Listen, y'all are sweet. But I'm not crashing your Christmases. I'll be fine. Besides, I haven't celebrated Christmas in years."

It was true. She always worked the holiday broadcasts. At first, it was because she lacked seniority, and in the news business, like most businesses, everything rolled downhill. But even after she'd clawed her way to the anchor desk, she kept working them. She didn't have any family in town, and she hated for anyone to miss out on that time with their loved ones. Even Chet, her self-satisfied, bloviating former co-anchor, deserved to be with his kids on Christmas.

"Sure, but this year, you can't exactly show up at the midnight potluck and karaoke bash at the station," Sasha told her. "Come on, it'll be fun."

Jordana stuck her head into the conference room and saved her from answering. "Are we doing this or what?"

Maisy gathered her things and fled from the room before the dynamic duo could twist her arm any further.

CHAPTER TWO

San Francisco International Airport
Flight 220, nonstop from San Francisco to Pittsburgh
11:00 PM Pacific Time

DEANNE LEWIS HUGGED her tote bag close to her body and sidled past a college kid trying to shove an entirely too-large duffel bag into the overhead compartment. Ordinarily, she would have murmured 'excuse me' or at least offered an apology. In this case, it would have been an exercise in futility. For one thing, the young man was fully engrossed in his struggle with the overstuffed bag. For another, his music blared so loudly that she could hear the bass through his earbuds.

She shuffled forward as a flight attendant bustled over to tell the student he'd have to check his bag. She paused alongside a row of seats, pulled out her phone to check her boarding pass, and confirmed that this was her row.

She mustered up an apologetic smile and cleared her throat. "Hi. I've got the middle."

The woman in the aisle seat glared up from under a red Santa cap. The glow of her laptop screen illuminated her scowling face. She huffed and stood. Instead of stepping out into the aisle to let Deanne through, she dumped her laptop on her seat and planted herself in front of it, arms crossed, as though Deanne were personally responsible for the seat assignments or, perhaps, for the existence of middle seats themselves.

Nice holiday spirit, Deanne thought crossly as she squeezed by.

Not that she had room to talk. She was cranky, too. But at least *she* wasn't dressed to mislead people into thinking she was bursting with goodwill and itching to break out into a carol. She plopped into her narrow seat and plunked her bag down on her lap. She dug through it to unearth her weighted eye mask and matching travel blanket. Then she shoved the bag under her seat. She'd just gotten her lap belt buckled when a flight attendant stopped in the aisle and smiled down at Deanne's seatmate.

"Ms. Collins, I have good news. Your standby upgrade came through after all. Would you still care to move to the first-class cabin?"

"What do you think?" The woman shot to her feet, tossed her electronics into her laptop bag, and followed the flight attendant toward the front of the plane against the tide of the crowd.

Deanne nestled against her seatback with a sigh of relief. She was a nervous air traveler under the best of circumstances, and sitting next to a grumpy Grinch of a business traveler for a five-hour-long overnight flight was not the best of circumstances.

Maybe she'd get lucky and have the row to herself. She slipped the eye mask on, leaving it perched on the top of her head like a tiara so she could pull it down over her eyes as soon as her fellow passengers were all seated, seatbelts were checked and emergency instructions given before takeoff, and the cabin lights were dimmed. The melatonin she'd gulped down with an overpriced bottle of water from the airport newsstand would work its magic, and she'd sleep all the way to the godforsaken city on the other side of the country.

As she was powering down her phone, a shadow fell over the row and her dreams were dashed. The student in the Santa Clara University sweatshirt who'd lost his battle with his duffle bag popped out his earbuds and smiled. "I'm the window."

She smiled back and undid the lap belt. He stepped back, and she stepped out into the aisle like a normal human to let him through. Then she settled herself in the aisle seat.

"The woman on the aisle got bumped up to first class," she explained as she reached under the middle seat for her bag. "Maybe they won't put anyone there."

"That would rock. Early Christmas present." He

laughed at himself. "Of course, I don't celebrate it. But my girlfriend's family does. So, I'm flying out to Pittsburgh to meet them and spend the holidays."

"That's nice." She said, striving for a tone somewhere between polite and uninterested. The only thing worse than suffering through a red-eye flight next to an unpleasant, Santa-hat-wearing road warrior might be a talkative college student.

"What about you? You headed home for the holidays?" he asked.

"No."

He waited with an expectant expression, but she didn't elaborate.

How, exactly, would she explain her trip? *No, see, I'm on my way to spend the holidays clearing out my dead ex-husband's apartment and office space because he didn't have the courtesy to change his will and name a new executor before plummeting out of a window to his death.*

"Oh," her new seatmate said in an abashed tone. "Sorry. Rosa—that's my girlfriend—says I'm too nebby."

"Nebby?" Deanne couldn't stop herself from asking.

"Ha, yeah. It means nosy. It's Pittsburghese."

She drew her eyebrows together in a question.

"Regional dialect," he explained. Then, "Hey, can I get your opinion?"

She suppressed a sigh. "Sure."

There was no reason to be a grouch. It wasn't this kid's fault Landon had ruined her holiday plans. She'd make chitchat until the plane took off, then she'd gracefully excuse herself to curl up under her blanket, pull down her eye mask, and sleep.

"Thanks." He stuck out his hand. "I'm Salim, by the way."

"Deanne." She shook his proffered hand, then said, "So, Salim, what's your question?"

"Do Christians really eat anchovies and eels for dinner on Christmas Eve? I think Rosa's pranking me."

She blinked at him, then realization dawned. "Is your girlfriend's family Italian, by chance?"

"Yeah, they are."

"Well, I hope you like seafood. Some Catholic Italian-Americans celebrate Christmas Eve by having the Feast of Seven Fishes."

"Seven?"

"Yep, seven, often, but not always, including anchovies and eels." Salim was looking a bit green, so she hurried to reassure him, "But if memory serves, there are lots of other dishes—not all of them are fish. You can probably just take a nibble or fill your plate with other foods."

He gave her a sidelong look. "And Mrs. Esposito won't be offended?"

"If the Espositos have a big family or a lot of guests, she probably won't even notice if you aren't a seafood lover."

He exhaled loudly. "I hope you're right." Then his relief dissipated and his face clouded. "I didn't offend you, did I? I mean, if you eat that."

"No, you didn't offend me. And I don't regularly eat

the Feast of Seven Fishes. But I did once, a long, long time ago." She shook her head and gave a small laugh. "I dated a guy in college—Nino Russo. I spent one Christmas with his family in New Jersey. The fish dishes weren't that bad, honest."

Salim's eyes flicked toward her bare left hand. "What happened? Between you and Nino, I mean?"

"I fell in love with someone else."

Someone brilliant, and funny, and gentle. Someone who promised me a happily ever after. And we had that. Until we didn't. We married, had a child, raised him, and loved him with all our hearts. But after Josh was murdered, our fairy tale fell apart. So now I'm flying across the country to settle Landon's affairs and take his ashes off the county morgue's hands so they'll stop calling me.

She stared down at her ringless hands, and Salim fell silent. After a long moment, he cleared his throat and reinserted his earbuds. She pulled her blanket up over her shoulders, rested her head on her seatback, and settled the mask in place over her eyes. She pretended to sleep and held back the hot tears that pricked at her eyes.

CHAPTER THREE

Home of Zane and Jenna Novak
Pittsburgh
Almost midnight

SOME JAGOFF WAS LEANING on the doorbell. Zane kept his eyes glued to the TV. The chiming continued.

"Babe, get the door, would ya'? I'm tryna watch something," he shouted.

A moment later, Jenna emerged from the kitchen and swiveled her head toward the screen. Then she rolled her eyes and snapped her dish towel at him.

"Spoiler alert: Muhammed Ali wins. That fight's older than you are," she snarked over her shoulder on her way through the room to the door.

He shook his head. She didn't get it. The Rumble in the Jungle was a classic. Ali's defeat of the unbeaten champ was a thing of beauty. Zane was four years old the first time his grandad had perched him on his knee and shown him the recording of Muhammed Ali knocking out George Foreman. And he must've watched the tape at least two hundred times in the twenty years since that first viewing. He dreamed about it, copied Ali's shuffle, and tried out his moves at the gym. The other gym rats laughed at him, but Zane had been the one laughing after he used the rope-a-dope to beat DeShawn Anderson into a pulp.

He kept one eye on the screen as he craned his neck to get a glimpse of the front hallway. The multicolored lights strung around the door cast Jenna in an eerie light as they blinked red, green, blue, red, green, blue. Her muffled voice was strained and unnaturally high. He shifted on the couch but couldn't see their late-night visitor. Given the tension in her voice, he'd bet it was her sister. Amber was always turning up on their doorstep, crying about her latest loser boyfriend.

"Who is it?" he called.

The door thudded closed, and Jenna walked into the room trailed, not by her sister, mascara streaking her face and snot bubbles clogging her nose, but by an even more disturbing sight.

"I asked if he had a warrant, and he said he doesn't need one. Said this is a *social call.*" Jenna jerked her thumb toward the hulking plainclothes detective and arched a brow just in case Zane hadn't picked up on her skepticism.

He thumbed the remote, and the television blinked off. He half-rose from the couch. "Come on in. You want a beer?"

"No thanks, Zane. Like I said, this isn't official police business, but I am on duty. I need to talk to you. It won't take long." Detective Colchis paused, and his eyes flicked toward Jenna. She'd crossed her arms and was leaning against the wall, eyeballing him hard. "Alone."

Zane cocked his head to the kitchen. "Give us a minute, babe."

Jenna shook her head, but pushed away from the wall and left the room, slowing to paint the detective with a look of disgust as she passed him.

"She seems nice," Colchis cracked.

Zane ignored the jab. "Why are you here?"

The cop's expression flattened. "That job you did last summer. You did what I told you, right? After it was done?"

"Yeah, of course." Zane shot a worried look toward the kitchen. "And keep your voice down. Jenna doesn't know."

"She'd better not know."

"She doesn't." He frowned, thinking. "Why are you asking about that now? It's been five months."

"Reasons. You don't need to know them."

His gut twisted. He didn't like that answer, not one bit. "I think I do."

"You don't think. You just do what I tell you."

"Uh-uh. No. I *did* what you *told* me. That was a one-time thing. We're square now."

Colchis shoved his face so close that Zane could smell the old coffee on his breath. "We're square when I say we're square."

Zane reared his head back. The ugly truth was Colchis owned him. He knew it, and Colchis knew it. Zane should have told the cop to screw himself back in July. But when Colchis threatened to pop him for felony assault after Zane kicked León Hernandez's ass in the parking lot of Dogs 'n' Brews, Zane panicked. León never would've cooperated with the cops. But Zane couldn't risk a collar, not with the promise he'd made to Jenna.

He'd done the job. It had gone south. And now Colchis had him by the balls.

"Whatever, man. I did what you said."

The detective grabbed a fistful of Zane's t-shirt in his freckled hands and yanked him close. "You got rid of the phone."

It was a statement, not a question. But Zane answered it. "Yeah. I pulled out the SIM card and stomped on it, then I threw the phone into the river. Like I told you."

He pulled his neck back and eyed Colchis. One good thrust, and Zane's rock-hard forehead would connect with the cop's nose. He imagined the satisfying crack of bone, the hot spurt of blood, and exhaled through his nostrils.

Something in his expression must have given Colchis a hint of what he was thinking. Colchis released his grip and smoothed the thin material of the worn t-shirt over Zane's bunched-up shoulders.

"Good. Just had to hear you say it. Now, how 'bout that beer? 'Tis the season, after all."

Zane took pleasure in the detective's too-cheerful tone. The other man was hiding his fear with jolly bullshit. He recognized the strength in Zane's eyes and feared him. Zane curved his mouth into a smile.

He turned toward the kitchen, "Hey, Jenna, bring us a couple of Irons. And a plate of your Aunt Tina's cookies, huh? Midnight snack."

The only response was the sound of beer bottles slamming down on the counter and the banging of the cabinet doors where the cookie tins were stored.

LATER, much later, after Colchis had drunk Zane's beer and shoveled handfuls of Aunt Tina's delicate crescent cookies and perfectly shaped Linzer stars into his mouth, he finally stumbled out of the house and down the stoop. Zane, bleary-eyed from staying up so late but too keyed-up to sleep, retreated to the basement.

He snaked his hand behind the hot water tank and patted the cold, damp stone wall until he felt the lid of his granddad's old metal lunch pail. He twisted at the elbow, contorting his arm at an unnatural angle, and yanked the box out from its hiding space. Squatting, resting his butt on his heels, he popped the pail open and pawed through the old undercard programs, fight flyers, and crumpled baseball cards until he found it. He unwound the thick rubber band that secured the butcher paper and unfolded the squares to reveal his insurance policy.

He turned the red iPhone over in his hand, a cool rectangle of promise. He studied it, wondering, not for the first time, what had come over him to make him keep it. He hadn't planned to. He'd intended to do what Colchis had told him to do—what he'd just told the bent detective he had done.

He'd stood on the Hot Metal Bridge and stared down into the silty water. As he'd moved his hand toward the bars that bisected the railing the sun had hit the glossy red phone at just the right angle. Light flared, like a starburst, and Zane's hand hovered over the water's edge. It felt like a sign, and the next thing he knew, he shoved the phone into his pants pocket and jogged across the bridge to the bus stop.

He had destroyed the SIM card, though. Not by stomping on it, the way he'd told Colchis. Instead, he'd tossed it in the garbage compactor at his mom's place. He figured he'd sell the phone to make a little fast, easy money. But when the news of the guy's apparent suicide hit the local media, he thought better of it and tucked the phone away in the basement instead. One day, he might need it.

He carefully refolded the brown waxed paper around the phone and secured it with the rubber band. He returned it to the pail and covered it with the old memorabilia. He was latching the lid when the bare bulb at the top of the cellar stairs flared to life.

"Zane? You down there?" Jenna yelled down the stairs.

Her voice echoed off the stone.

"Yeah." He eased the lunch pail back into its hiding spot. "I'm comin' up."

He loped up the steep wooden stairs and flicked off the light. Jenna backed into the kitchen, hugging her sweater around her middle, and he pulled the door shut.

"Did your scuzzy cop friend finally leave?"

"Colchis is no friend of mine. But, yeah, he took off."

"Took his time about it. What are you looking for down there at this hour?" She jutted her chin toward the basement door.

Zane searched for a believable lie and landed on one guaranteed to take her focus off the basement. "I thought we should hang up that little stocking you made last year. Just in case."

She pressed her lips together in a frown, and furrows in her brow mirrored the downturn. "That's not ... that's bad luck." Unconsciously, one hand fell to her flat belly.

He pulled her toward him and wrapped his thick arms around her. "We don't need luck, Jenn. We have science. Isn't that what the fertility doctors keep saying? The tests all show we can make a kid—all we need is time."

"And money," she added in a tight, defeated voice.

"Forget about the money. I have a good feeling about the last round of in vitro."

She tilted her chin up and met his gaze. "Yeah?"

"Yeah. So, let's put up the stocking."

Her face softened. "Yeah, okay. But it's not with the extra decorations in the basement. It's in the ... upstairs."

She eased out of his embrace and headed for the stairs to the second floor. The hinge on the door to the little unused room squeaked. He could picture her, pausing in the doorway to square her shoulders before going into the pink and green nursery she'd set up before that first miscarriage, almost three years ago now.

A wave of shame rolled over him for using her baby fever as a distraction. He batted it away. Hadn't he taken the money from that job and used it on their in vitro treatments? She'd never asked where he got it, had told her family he'd cashed in some treasury bonds or some crap. But she knew Zane didn't have any bonds. She didn't want to know where the money had come from. And she didn't need to know about the phone.

He heard the nursery door click shut, then her light footsteps tapping down the stairs. He made his way into the narrow living room and stood in the doorway to watch her hang the tiny knit stocking between their two larger ones—his made from the red silk of a pair of boxing trunks, hers a deep emerald color, a piece of fabric from the dress she'd worn to their senior prom. The white Christmas lights on the tall narrow tree jammed into the corner twinkled across her face as she carefully positioned the stocking from the hook in the center of the mantle.

She straightened the stocking, then craned her neck to flash him a smile. "There."

"Looks great, babe."

He held out his arms, and she crossed the room to burrow into his chest.

"What did that cop want, anyway?" Her sleepy voice was muffled against his shirt.

Zane took a beat to answer. "Just to bust my balls, I guess."

He hoped she couldn't feel the rapid thrum of his heartbeat. Truth was, he didn't know why Colchis had turned up now, asking questions about a job from last summer. But he'd been around long enough to know it couldn't mean anything good.

CHAPTER FOUR

Pittsburgh International Airport
Friday, December 23
7:30 AM

DEANNE STUMBLED onto the moving walkway and through the overly bright, nearly deserted airport. Her neck and back protested each step, making sure she knew her body had determined it was too old for this red-eye bullcrap.

It's okay, she reassured herself. She'd scheduled a full day to decompress and adjust to the time change. The management office at Landon's building had promised to leave a key for her at the security desk. She'd get into his place and crash until she woke naturally. Then after a workout and a visit to the sauna at Landon's overpriced gym, she'd figure out her next moves.

Following the signs on autopilot, she trudged to the

ground transportation exit and shivered as she stepped out into the cold gray morning to join the line for a ride into the city.

She was mid-yawn when a whoop caught her attention. A curvy dark-haired girl was squealing at the sight of Deanne's seatmate. Despite her exhaustion and general crankiness, Deanne couldn't help but smile at the young lovers' reunion.

As Salim whirled his laughing girlfriend in a circle, he caught Deanne's eye. A moment later, he was dragging the young woman over to the cab line.

"Deanne! I want you to meet—"

"You must be Rosa," Deanne said to the giggling girl. "Salim couldn't stop talking about you."

Rosa Esposito pressed her lips into a pout and shook her head. "Don't believe a thing he says."

"It was all very sweet," Deanne assured her.

"Where are you headed?" Salim asked quickly, eager to change the subject. "If it's on our way, we can drop you off. Right, Rosa?"

"Oh, no, I wouldn't—"

Rosa cut off Deanne's attempt to demure with a wave of her hand. "If you had to suffer through Salim babbling about me for an entire cross-country flight, it's literally the least I can do. Please. Where are you staying?"

"Downtown, at a building called Kaufmann's Grand. Do you know it?"

Rosa whistled. "I've never been inside, but it's

supposed to be gorgeous. And that's totally on our way. My parents live in Highland Park. It's no trouble."

Ordinarily, Deanne wouldn't get into a car with a pair of strangers. But then, again, isn't that what using rideshares and taxis entailed when you got right down to it?

She hesitated and eyed the cab line. It was long and moving at a snail's pace. And she *was* exhausted. "Are you sure?"

"Positive," Rosa assured her, while Salim bent and swooped her bag up with one hand.

Deanne reminded herself that she'd spent years trying to convince Landon to be more trusting and less paranoid, to no avail. And look at how much good his trauma-induced hypervigilance had done him: she suspected his distrust of the world played no small part in having driven him to suicide.

"Thanks. That's really kind of you," she said with a smile before trotting off toward the parking garage behind the couple, stifling yet another yawn.

SHE DOZED, half-asleep, in the back seat of Rosa's little Mazda. In part, to avoid making forced small talk, and, in part, because her eyelids were so heavy she had no choice. She jerked awake when Salim excitedly pointed out the view of Downtown Pittsburgh that popped into existence as they emerged from a tunnel onto a bridge.

"Cool, huh?" he enthused, twisting around to see her reaction.

"Um, wow." She blinked her eyes open and caught a blurry glimpse of buildings and water.

"Is this your first visit to the city?" Rosa asked.

"Yeah." *And, I hope, last.*

Rosa muttered under her breath as she joined the flow of early-morning commuters, all of whom evidently needed to switch lanes urgently. A few harrowing moments later, she brought the car to a stop in front of a massive building and turned on her hazards.

"This is it?" Deanne asked, craning her neck to look up at the structure.

"Sure is," the younger woman confirmed. "It used to be a department store, more like *the* department store, in the city. You should hear the stories my parents tell about Kaufmann's."

"Well, I appreciate the lift. And I hope you have a wonderful holiday visit. Both of you." She leaned over the console and offered Salim and Rosa her hand.

After a quick shake, Rosa narrowed her eyes. "So are you visiting family for Christmas, Deanne?"

So much for evading the chitchat. Deanne sighed softly as she reached for the door handle.

"No. I'm Jewish, so ..."

"So, you're in town for Hanukkah?" Salim guessed.

She could have lied. Should have lied. But her jet-lagged brain was fuzzy and fatigued, and she blurted the truth. "No, I'm in town to wrap up my late ex-husband's affairs."

The words, and their meaning, took a moment to sink in, but once they did, Rosa turned to face her full-on.

"Your late ex-husband. So he's dead?"

It was too late to do damage control, so she answered simply, "Yes."

"How'd he die?" Salim asked.

"Salim!" His girlfriend shot him a fierce, dismayed look.

"It's okay. He ... apparently he committed suicide. Jumped out the window."

In unison, the young couple's eyes traveled skyward to the top of the imposing building.

"Not here," she clarified. "He was at his office."

"And there's nobody else who can take care of things? Or at least help you do it?" Salim asked in a soft voice.

"No."

"You don't have any kids?"

She was beginning to see why Rosa told her boyfriend he was nebby. But in for a dime, in for a dollar. "No. We had a son, Josh. He died a long time ago."

Rosa screwed up her face as if she were in pain. Then she spoke in a brisk tone, "Well, you'll spend Christmas Eve with us. My mom's motto is the more, the merrier."

"Oh, no, I—"

"C'mon. The bigger the crowd, the less attention there will be on whether I eat all the F-I-S-H," Salim stage-whispered.

Rosa giggled and slapped his forearm. "Stop. Seriously, please say you'll come?"

Deanne studied the girl's bright eyes and earnest expression. She could explain that Christmas was just another day. Or she could mumble some weak excuse. But Rosa and Salim seemed like good kids, and she didn't want to repay their kindness with sourness. So she cleared her throat. "Let me think about it, okay?"

Rosa held out her cell phone. "Program your number in, so I can call and harass you into coming tomorrow night. Actually, I'll just give my Aunt Marisa that job. She's relentless."

Deanne laughed softly and punched her mobile number into Rosa's contacts. "It's a kind offer, and I *will* give it some thought, but I'm not sure I'd be great company because of ... the time change, the circumstances, just ... everything." She handed the phone back and waved her hand as if to encompass everything.

The couple nodded their understanding. A bus driver behind them laid on his horn and gestured angrily for the car to move.

Deanne hoisted her bag from the seat and opened the car door as a rush of cold air swirled inside. She hurried out onto the sidewalk, bobbed her head in an apology to the aggrieved bus driver, and waved goodbye to Rosa and Salim as the little car sped away from the curb and into the morning rush hour traffic. Then she filled her lungs with the bracing morning air, pushed back her shoulders, and walked into the lobby of Landon's building.

CHAPTER FIVE

December 23, evening

MAISY PROWLED THROUGH HER TOO-QUIET, too-tidy townhouse like a restless panther. Her stomach growled loudly. Good thing she wasn't a predator cat seeking a meal on the savanna. Her hunger would give her away in a heartbeat. She needed a story—or, at a bare minimum, a lead and a snack.

As she paced through the kitchen, the light glinting off the highly polished copper tea kettle on her stovetop caught her eye. The kettle—a birthday gift from her pal Bodhi—was intended to be utilitarian. But as far as she was concerned, it was strictly decorative. Only a Buddhist could take the time to wait for water to boil on the stove. She lived by the microwaved rhythms of the modern newsroom, and so did her tea. Still, the copper kettle *was* pretty.

Copper kettle. Copper.

Synapses fired, fast and furious, under the mass of blonde curls that hid Maisy's introspection and intellection. She let out a whoop that echoed across her sparkling, empty kitchen. She knew where to find a lead, a meal, *and* the perfect Moscow mule in one fell swoop. What more did an intrepid investigative reporter need?

Propelled forward by a goal, she raced to her front hallway, sliding along the floor in her socks, and grabbed her oversized purse from the stand by the door. She dug a tube of deep maroon lipstick out from the depths of the tote, slicked the color over her mouth, and jammed her feet into her high-heeled boots. She blotted her lips on the back of her hand as a twinge of excitement coursed through her like an arrow leaving a bow.

She pulled up the ride-share app on her phone with one hand while she shrugged into her snowy white winter coat. Then she tugged her cherry red knit cap over her head and hurried out the door and down the stairs to the street, leaving her little hybrid car snug and warm in its stall in the garage.

SEVEN-AND-A-HALF MINUTES LATER, she was perched on a stool at St. Clair Social, a neighborhood bar situated on the corner of two quiet residential streets on the edge of East Liberty. It was a haunt for locals, kitchen industry workers, and Zone Five police officers stopping in for a pint after their shift ended. It was a little-known spot and, in recent years, her secret weapon. She never shared the location with anyone from the station, letting the rest of the reporters elbow each other at the crowded bars of more established, better-known locations for working sources. Now, she shoved her hat into her coat pocket and raked her fingers through her hair, not bothering to hide her smile.

"Knock me over with a feather. Can it be? Is it really you?" The bartender studied Maisy, head to toe as if she might be an imposter.

"Come on, Gia. It hasn't been *that* long."

The bartender arched one pierced eyebrow. "Hasn't it?"

Maisy sighed and spread her hands wide. "I'm unemployed. Cut me some slack."

Gia's face softened, and she slid a coaster along the bar. It came to a stop directly in front of Maisy.

"Yeah, I heard." She dropped into a squat and retrieved a shiny hammered copper mug from beneath the blond wood bar. "Mule?"

Maisy nodded. As far as she was concerned nothing beat a good Moscow mule. And Gia's was excellent. She used a light hand with the vodka and balanced the ginger beer and lime juice perfectly.

As Gia prepared the drink, Maisy scanned the room. "Sparse crowd."

Gia placed the mug on the coaster. "Well, it *is* Christmas Eve Eve."

Maisy paused with the mug at her lips. "Is that even a thing?"

The bartender swept her arms through the air, gesturing at all the empty seats. "Evidently."

After one sweet, cold sip, Maisy parted her lips and sighed. "Ah, you haven't lost your touch."

Gia made a face as if offended by the mere thought that she might've.

Maisy laughed. "Any cops around?"

"Look at you, out of work, and you're still a workaholic." Gia barked her raspy laugh, then jerked her chin toward the back of the room. "Bass and Evans are in the last booth, splitting a plate of fries and kvetching about office politics."

Maisy slid her a twenty and a wide smile. "Thanks, Gia."

"No tab for you tonight? Wow, unemployment must be rough."

"Yeah, start a tab. The twenty's for you. Early Christmas present."

"I celebrate Kwanzaa, Mais."

"Well, then, it's Kwanzaa Eve Eve Eve, right? Too early to ask what the news is, so instead of *Habari Gani*, I'll just say Joyous Kwanzaa."

The bartender tucked the bill into her apron pocket with a chuckle. "And how do you know Swahili, girl?"

"I dated a guy."

"Evergreen response," Gia snarked.

Maisy laughed a real, open-mouthed laugh, and slid off the stool, taking her copper mug with her. "Will you send their server over in a few minutes, darlin'? I'll put a round on my tab."

"Anything for you, darlin'," Gia mimicked her accent good-naturedly. Then her hazel eyes grew serious. "But, if you're gonna work them, why don't you switch to my nonalcoholic apple cider mule?"

Maisy wrinkled her nose.

"It's good, I swear. It's gonna be on the menu for Dry January."

She considered for a beat. "Yeah, that's smart. Gotta stay sharp. Thanks."

"And skip the fries!" Gia called after her.

She headed toward the back of the gastropub as if she were on her way to the ladies' room then paused by the last booth on the right and did a double take. "Hey, Ilsa. And Oswald Bass."

Ilsa Evans looked up from her beer and gave Maisy a flat smile. "Maisy."

Sergeant Bass' smile was more genuine. "Well, I'll be. Maisy Farley."

"The one and only." She widened her eyes. "Mind if I join you?" she chirped.

"Actually, we were—"

"Not at all. Scoot over and make some room, Evans," Bass directed.

The patrolwoman's face was an impassive mask as she pulled her beer across the table and edged up against the wall.

"Thanks, Ilsa." Maisy infused her voice with warmth. "Are you ready for the holidays?"

Ilsa Evans studied her for a long moment before giving her a grudging answer. "Almost. Still need to do my grocery shopping."

Maisy nodded. "You having a crowd?"

"No. I'm just taking a side dish to my sister's place. Probably making candied yams." Evans waited for a beat, then asked, "What about you?"

Maisy evaded the question with the wave of a hand. "Oh, you know, the usual."

It was a response without a meaning, but Evans didn't press her.

Maisy turned her attention to Bass. "How about you, Oswald? Do you still dress up as Santa for the FOP party for the kids?"

Bass belly-laughed a hearty 'ho-ho-ho' and then shook his head. "Now, how did you remember that? It's gotta be, what, five or six years since you covered that party?"

"Something like that."

A lanky server with a shock of purple hair approached the table. "Can I get you folks anything else?"

Before either of the police officers could answer, Maisy spoke up, "Another round of boilermakers for them. And one more of these." She raised the copper mug.

"You got it." He turned and headed back toward the bar.

"Shoot, Maisy. You don't have to buy a round. We know about your ... situation," Bass clucked at her.

Her situation. She tried not to cringe.

"Oh? What situation is that?" Evans asked, all wide-eyed innocence.

Her boss frowned. "Come on, you must've heard. Maisy left the station."

"Ooooh, *that*. Yeah, my grandmother mentioned something about that." A smile flashed across Evans' face. "She was a faithful viewer."

Maisy's throat tightened at the well-aimed zinger, but when she spoke, her voice was at its most syrupy. "Ah, isn't that sweet? Well, you tell your grandma I'm startin' up a podcast. She should tune in."

Evans blinked. "Huh. Didn't figure you for a podcast. Is it gonna be one of those true crime deals?"

"It's fluid right now. I'd love to start off with a story that'll really grab the listeners' interest, you know? I don't suppose either of you has any ideas. Maybe a cold case?"

The purple-haired server returned and placed a shot and a beer in front of each police officer and traded Maisy's empty mug for a new one. "Gia wants to know how the mule is."

She took a sweet, cold sip. "It's perfect," she purred.

He winked at her as he gathered the empty beer mugs and shot glasses.

Evans and Bass threw back their shots, then chased them with the beers. Then, Bass leaned across the table and said, "There *is* something you might want to look into."

She widened her eyes. "Oh? Tell me."

Bass swallowed a burp, then leaned back against the booth. "Nah, maybe I better not."

To Maisy's surprise, Evans urged him on. "No, sarge, if it's the thing with the jumper, tell her. Maybe she can dig something up."

Bass scrubbed his hand over his face. "Uh, I dunno. I should just keep my mouth shut. Go along to get along and all that."

Evans bobbed her head, and her low ponytail bounced against the small of her back. "Screw that. He's a jagoff."

"Who?"

Evans turned toward her. "Some detective on the freaking nuisance bar task force."

Maisy pretended she knew what Evans was talking about. "Sure, okay. What's that have to do with a jumper?"

"Nothing. That's the thing." Ilsa Evans pounded her hand against the table hard enough to rattle the beer mugs.

But she didn't elaborate. Instead, she thinned her lips into a frown, lowered her chin, and stared at her supervising officer. Maisy followed her lead and pinned her clear, unblinking gaze on Bass as well.

After a heartbeat, he crumbled. "Oh, to hell with it."

He grabbed a gravy- and curd-laden French fry from the platter in the middle of the table and paused, letting it hover near his mouth. He pointed at Maisy with his free hand. "This is off the record, understand?"

"No attribution. I got it."

Satisfied, he swallowed the fry. "At the end of the summer, there was a startup guy who took a header out of his office window, remember? Over in Bakery Square."

"Sure, I remember. Landon Lewis. I was still at the station when he died."

That wasn't the only reason she remembered, but Ilsa and Oswald didn't need to know that.

"Yeah, him. Suicide. Open and shut case," Evans said. "Or it shoulda been."

"But it's not?" A whisper of interest stirred in Maisy's chest like a feather tumbling through the air.

"It is," Bass insisted.

She sipped her apple cider ginger beer concoction and waited.

"It was, at least." He gave the platter of congealed poutine a sour look and pushed it away.

She knew better than to ask what had happened. They'd tell her, in their own time. Pushing a source was a rookie reporter's mistake, and Maisy was no rookie.

Evans broke first. "The county coroner's been chasing after the next-of-kin to come and claim the body for months."

"Wife?" Maisy asked.

"Ex. But there's nobody else, at least not according to that Strike Force guy," the policewoman explained.

"Strike Force? Never heard of it." Maisy frowned.

"Unit," the sergeant corrected. "The guy who ID'd the body was an agent with some super-secret specialized federal Strike Unit."

"Huh. The feds were investigating Lewis' death?" Maybe there was something to the story.

Evans popped the bubble of excitement before it had fully formed. "Nah. This agent was taking a walk with his wife and wandered by the scene—turns out, he just happened to know the guy."

"That's quite a coincidence." Maisy twisted her mouth into a skeptical knot.

"Ah, not really. You know what they say—Pittsburgh's a small town disguised as a big city." Bass dismissed her suspicions.

But Evans arched an eyebrow. "*And* his wife just happened to know the guy, too."

"What, is she a federal agent, too?" Maisy snorted.

"No. Some kind of lawyer."

Maisy managed to keep her face completely blank. A federal agent for a made-up agency and a lawyer? Gee, maybe Bass was right about it being a small world. But, she couldn't resist asking the question.

"This lawyer, she didn't happen to be, like, child-sized, did she?"

"She did, in fact," Evans confirmed.

"Huh." Maisy felt Bass's curious gaze on her face and changed the subject before he could probe her. "So, the county morgue wants to free up some space. That makes sense if the case is closed. I mean, right?"

"Sure," Bass agreed. "Anyway, the morgue finally gets the ex-wife to agree to come and claim the ashes because they can't just freakin' ship them via overnight delivery, I guess. She calls the station to set up a meeting with the officers who investigated the suicide while she's in town. You know, closure."

"Mmm-hmm."

"She's coming in to see us this weekend. So Evans goes to pull the file. Give us a chance to refresh our recollections before we talk to her."

"Sure."

"Only thing is, it's gone."

"Gone?" Maisy blinked.

"Gone. Signed out by some overachiever with the nuisance bar task force." Evans said, her voice oozing with disgust.

"So, I call the task force. Figure it's just a mix-up," Bass picked up the story.

Maisy stared at a Bass for twenty seconds, waiting. Finally, her curiosity won out. "And?"

"And this jag-off tells me don't worry about it. Then he lets it slip he knows my cousin Ed."

"Okay?"

"Ed owns a bar in Greenfield," Evans explained. "He was letting Oswald know that if he kept asking questions about the file, the task force would make life hard for Ed. Random visits, pulling his licenses, checking that he's not serving anyone underaged or anyone who appears to be inebriated. You know, petty crap."

Maisy wrinkled her nose. "Gross."

"Sonofa—," Bass swore under his breath.

"So we can't ask any questions," Evans said, spelling it out in case Maisy somehow missed the point, "but *you* can."

It wasn't much of a story, not a long-dormant cold case that she could break open and get national recognition for. But a cop using his badge to intimidate a small business owner was a solid local angle. And it was better than what she currently had, which was a big, fat goose egg.

She shrugged. "Sure, what's his name—this guy on the task force?"

Bass shook his head. "No, Maisy. Can't go there."

"Can you put me in touch with your cousin?"

"Can't do that either."

Maisy blew out an exasperated breath. "Well, who do you want me to talk to?" she demanded.

"You're the investigative reporter," Evans told her. "So, investigate."

Bass checked the time on his phone. "Ah, hell. I gotta go. Muriel's parents are coming in for the weekend."

He tossed some bills on the table, slid out of the booth, and plucked his coat from the hook. Evans made a motion for Maisy to move so she could get out, too. Maisy obliged.

As the pair of cops started to amble away, she called after them. "Hey."

Evans twisted her head to look back. "What?"

"When are you meeting Lewis' ex-wife?"

Evans screwed her face up in a sickly expression that made her look like she smelled something foul. "In the morning. Helluva way to spend the holidays, huh?" She turned away without waiting for an answer.

Maisy reached absently for the cold fries, then wrinkled her nose, and searched out the purple-haired server. He hurried over to clear away the detritus. As he scooped up the cash, he nodded toward her mug.

"You want another one?"

"Please. A real one, this time. And a grilled cheese."

"You got it."

She propped her chin on her hand and pondered her next move while she waited for her fresh drink. As far as she could figure, it was going to have to involve Sasha and Leo. She didn't see a way around it.

CHAPTER SIX

Saturday, December 24

DEANNE STOOD on the sidewalk outside the Zone 5 Police Station, staring up at the long tan brick building and gathering herself. She'd shaken off her jet lag and had adjusted to the time zone change with little difficulty, but she still didn't feel quite right. As a counselor, she understood intellectually that her unease was more the product of sleeping in her dead ex-husband's bed in his luxury apartment than anything else. And, as a counselor, she thought she really ought to have the tools to cope with the situation, but despite her efforts, a thick, mournful haze had settled around her.

Her stomach was queasy, and her nerves were fraying. It wasn't as if being in Landon's apartment had brought a wave of memories rushing back. It might have, if he'd displayed a single personal touch in the immaculate, light-filled space. But, Landon being Landon, the rooms were devoid of photographs, postcards, souvenirs from travel, or virtually any other item that might hint at the occupant's personality. It, like her ex-husband, was utilitarian and joyless. Sterile to a fault.

She rolled her shoulders, easing the tension that made them bunch up to her ears, and told herself she wasn't being fair. Her ex hadn't always been an emotionless automaton. Before Josh's death, Landon had been lively and empathetic. But their son's murder had broken his spirit—more than that, it had broken *him*. She hadn't seen him in years, but she had no reason to think that the man who'd moved to Pittsburgh to pursue his obsession with preventing crimes before they happened was anything other than a shell of a person.

She shuddered and jammed her hands into her coat pockets. She told herself that her shiver was a reaction to the December chill, but in her heart, she knew it was more than that.

You left him because he turned into a living ghost and it was sucking the life out of you. It would be the height of irony to let him finish the job now that he truly is nothing but a ghost. Put on your big girl panties, meet with the police, and move on.

The only way out, after all, was through. She had a million loose ends to tie up before she could go home. It was time to start tying.

She pushed through the red-framed glass doors and

entered the lobby. A uniformed officer eyed her. "Can I help you, ma'am?"

She forced a smile. "Yes, I have a meeting with Sergeant Bass and Officer Evans."

"Name?" He asked, already clicking away at his keyboard.

"Deanne Lewis."

He nodded and picked up the handset of an old-style desk phone. He punched in a number and then spoke in a low voice. A moment later, he lifted his eyes to meet hers. "Officer Evans'll be down to get you. You can wait over there." He pointed toward a long metal bench shoved up against the wall.

She situated herself on the end of the bench closest to the door and crossed her ankles, balancing the toes of her shoes on the floor. She recognized her posture for what it was—an attempt to distance herself physically from her surroundings by positioning herself so that she could flee at any moment.

But that was ridiculous. She wasn't going to run out of the building. She was going to meet with the officers, ask her questions, and get her answers. She could do this. She *would* do this. She set her chin and stared at the peeling paint on the wall opposite her until she heard footsteps. A female officer, her hair long and secured in a neat ponytail, strode over to her.

"Mrs. Lewis? I'm Ilsa Evans." She extended her hand.

Deanne hurried to her feet. "Thanks for agreeing to

meet with me, Officer Evans. I know you must be very busy, and on Christmas Eve, no less."

Officer Evans scoffed. "Criminals don't take the weekends or the holidays off, ma'am. So neither do we. Sergeant Bass and I are happy to answer any questions you have about your late ex-husband's suicide. You don't have any weapons on you, do you?"

"No, no weapons."

Officer Evans nodded to the desk officer, who pulled a sticker sheet from the small desktop printer at his elbow and handed her a visitor's name tag with her name printed on it in capital letters.

Officer Evans waited while Deanne peeled it off the sheet and stuck it on her coat. Then the two women weaved their way through a maze of narrow hallways and open cubicles. The HVAC system pumped out stifling hot air, and Deanne unwound the scarf looped around her neck and stuffed it into her handbag.

Finally, the officer stopped in front of a metal door and knocked once, then pushed it open. She ushered Deanne inside, where a portly older man stood beside a small round table. Four chairs surrounded the table, their backs nearly touching the walls of the cramped room.

"Mrs. Lewis, I'm Sergeant Oswald Bass. I'm very sorry for your loss." He had a deep voice that matched his surname, and the rumbled condolence struck a chord with Deanne.

"Thank you." She shook his outstretched hand. "It's strange being the ex-wife widow. I'm not even sure if I am a widow. I suppose not. Anyway, it's been odd. So I appreciate that you and Officer Evans were willing to meet with me."

"Of course." He gestured toward the closest of the chairs. "Sorry for the accommodations, but this is better than an interrogation room. Please, sit."

Deanne sat. Officer Evans squeezed past Deanne and pulled out the chair next to hers. Then, she paused before her bottom hit the seat. "Does anyone want a cup of coffee or a glass of water before we get started?"

Deanne shook her head. "No, thank you."

"How 'bout you, sarge?"

"No thanks, Evans."

The niceties out of the way, the two officers sank into their chairs. Deanne folded her hands on the table and pinned her eyes on the senior officer.

He tapped a red cardboard file folder that rested on the table in front of him. "Rather than subject you to unpleasant details that might not interest you, why don't you tell us what you'd like to know."

She cleared her throat. "Sure, that makes sense. I guess I.... Well, are you sure he killed himself?"

The police officers exchanged a loaded glance. After a moment, Evans said, "Do you think he didn't?"

"I have no idea. The officer who called to notify me said Landon had jumped from his office window. There's no chance it was an accident?"

Evans sucked in a breath and wrinkled her brow. "The way the windows in his office worked, it's hard to imagine someone falling out."

"But it was the end of July, right? Hot and humid?" Deanne pressed.

"Sure, it was a muggy night. And the windows didn't have screens. But ..." he paused as if a thought had struck him. "Have you been to his office?"

She shook her head. "Not yet. It's on my list. He prepaid his rent through the end of the year, so I have a week to clear out his things and give the key back to the landlord. Why?"

Bass scratched his chin. "You'll see when you go there. The windows are tall and skinny. Casement windows, they call them."

"The kind you crank open sideways?" she asked.

"Right," Evans confirmed. "Only one window was open. But it had been cranked wide open. Which is how he fit through it. You'd expect a person to crack all the windows to get a cross breeze, not open one all the way."

Deanne bobbed her head, conceding the point.

"And the building has air conditioning. Your ex controlled the temperature in his space, and the AC was pumping," Bass added.

She frowned. "Landon wouldn't waste energy by using the air conditioning if he had the window open."

The police nodded, letting her draw her own conclusion. After a beat, Bass said, "And he did leave a note."

Deanne's eyes widened. "A suicide note? Nobody mentioned that to me."

Bass flipped the folder open and slid a linen notecard across the table. She stared down at Landon's precise, elegant handwriting. She reached for the sheet so she could read it but stopped herself before she touched it.

"Is it okay to pick it up? It's not evidence or something?"

Evans rubbed her forehead. Bass shot the junior officer a frown before answering Deanne's question.

"There's not an active investigation, Mrs. Lewis. Your ex-husband's death has been ruled a suicide. I believe the medical examiner released his body. It's been cremated, hasn't it?" Bass said in a low voice.

"Well, yes. That's true." Deanne heard the tremor in her voice and tried, but failed, to steady it. "The county morgue liaison told me there wasn't ... that he was ..."

"He jumped from quite a height. You wouldn't have wanted to see him," Evans told her with a somber expression.

A wild thought burst into Deanne's mind and escaped her mouth before she could censor it. "Are you sure it was Landon? I mean, if he wasn't recognizable, maybe it wasn't him. Someone else was in his office and fell. Or jumped."

She noticed her hands shaking and clenched them together, bowing her head over them. She knew her theory bordered on the ridiculous. If the dead man wasn't Landon, then where exactly had he been for the past five months?

Officer Evans rested a gentle hand on Deanne's shoulder. "Ma'am, a man who knew your late ex-husband was able to identify him. His wife is the one who gave us your name. The remains in the morgue *are* your ex-husband's. And the note makes it clear that he was full of regret, to say the least. Why don't you read it?"

Deanne gripped the notecard, trying to focus on the words that were blurred by the tears swimming in her eyes:

> *I have made mistakes in my life. Lord knows I have. But I have always tried to do the right thing. I didn't always succeed, but I tried. That's why I have to find a way to make amends for my recent errors of judgment.*
>
> *It may be too late, but all I can do is try. It's better than being haunted by the unknown, better than always wondering if there was more I could have done.*
>
> *Everything I did, I did in Josh's memory, as an effort to honor him. Please bear that in mind when you judge me.*

The tone was Landon's. Formal, unsparing, and just the tiniest bit defensive. And, although the message was unsigned, the handwriting was unmistakably his. But something was off. She screwed up her forehead.

"What?" Bass asked, studying her expression.

"He doesn't say he's ending his life. He says the opposite—he screwed something up, and he wants to try to fix it. He couldn't do that if he was dead. It doesn't make sense."

The police officers nodded in unison. Bass took the lead in responding.

"The man who identified your husband had seen him earlier that day. He told us Mr. Lewis was in a highly agitated state."

She dragged her eyes away from the note. "What? He had a business meeting with him?"

"No, ma'am. Your husband spotted him from the window and raced down to the alley and engaged him in conversation."

"What? What kind of conversation?"

"Well, Agent Connelly didn't go into detail. He mentioned the encounter during a follow-up interview. I got the sense he wished he'd realized the state your ex was in. Kinda blamed himself, I think."

"Agent Connelly? What kind of agent is he?"

"He's in law enforcement," Bass told her.

"Did he have some sort of business relationship with Landon? With The Joshua Group?"

Bass shifted uncomfortably in his stiff chair. Evans gave him a look that clearly said, this one is all you.

"What?" Deanne demanded. "What aren't you telling me?"

The sergeant coughed into his fist. "You probably know the name because of Agent Connelly's wife. Sasha McCandless-Connelly. The lawyer?"

Understanding clicked into place in Deanne's brain like a gear turning. "The lawyer he abducted after she exposed the flaws in his Cesare Program. The lawyer who sued the Milltown Police and got the feds to impose a consent decree on Landon. *That* Sasha McCandless-Connelly?"

Evans mumbled something indistinct.

But Bass spoke clearly. "That's the one."

"And you don't think that's odd? Two people who were very much antagonistic to Landon's work just happened to find his body? And the husband was the last person to see him alive? Maybe they killed him and staged it to look like a suicide!" Disbelief and outrage forced Deanne's voice up an octave.

"Hang on, now," Bass cautioned. "It's a strange coincidence. No doubt about that. But, they live in the area, so they had plenty of business being there. And the wife told us your ex-husband had agreed to testify on her side in the case against the Milltown prosecutor. So, it actually hurt her case that he died."

Deanne was struggling to bring her breathing under control when Ilsa Evans leaned over and caught her eye.

The police officer took both of Deanne's hands in her own. She spoke slowly and clearly, "Listen, Mrs. Lewis, I don't have children. But I can imagine that losing a kid would do a number on any parent. And losing your only son in a vicious murder—that'd mess a person up good. I understand you became a grief counselor, but it's clear your husband never really dealt with Josh's death. It's tempting to spin out all sorts of scenarios about his death, but isn't the most likely explanation that his demons simply caught up with him?"

Deanne's voice caught in her throat. But the woman was right. Landon had been tormented by Josh's murder.

She knew that better than anyone. And his life had deteriorated at an alarming rate in recent years. His note was proof of that.

Her ludicrous theories were just an attempt to protect her own psyche. Maybe she should have stayed in touch with Landon. She might have seen the signs, might have been able to get him some help.

She managed to speak in a hoarse voice. "You're right. I'm sorry for wasting your time. Can I keep this?" She pointed a finger at Landon's final note.

"Sure," Bass told her. Relief that she'd come to her senses was splashed all over his face. "In fact, we have a package of his personal effects that the coroner's office sent over. We'll get that for you."

He jerked his chin at Evans, who fled from the room like Deanne might try to stop her.

Bass drummed his fingers on the table while they waited for her to return. Deanne broke the awkward silence with a lame question. "Do you have plans for the holiday weekend?"

"My wife's parents are in town. We'll celebrate with them and then get together with our kids and grandkids in January. Easier that way. How about you?" He asked the question with a sickly expression as if he feared the answer.

She laughed. "Well, I celebrate Hanukkah, but a nice young man who sat next to me on the flight somehow wrangled me an invitation to his girlfriend's parents' house for Christmas Eve dinner tonight. They're having the Feast of the Seven Fishes."

That got a chuckle out of the sergeant. "That's Pittsburgh for ya," he told her with unabashed pride. "You gonna go?"

"I think I will," she said to her own surprise.

After this meeting and the looming appointment with the county coroner's office, it would do her good to spend the evening with other people. Even—no, especially—a bunch of strangers who didn't know about her, and Landon, and Josh. She'd ask Rosa and Salim to keep her history private in exchange for providing Salim cover to not eat his fish.

She was smiling to herself when Officer Bass returned with a clear plastic bag that held Landon's meager belongings.

CHAPTER SEVEN

Lobby of the US Steel Tower

TIM COLCHIS POPPED the collar of his leather overcoat and tried to slump lower into the bright orange leather seat of his chair. But the chair hadn't been designed with slouching in mind—or, as far as he could tell, the comfort of adult humans. The white leather back of the two-toned chair hit him smack in the small of his back, forcing him to sit upright despite his best efforts.

He eyed the bustling lobby with no small measure of disgust. Who in their right mind would arrange a meeting like this in such a busy public place? A civilian, that's who.

He cracked his knuckles and rolled his neck from side to side, studiously avoiding making eye contact with any of the last-minute shoppers and harried office workers scurrying through the lobby. He checked the time on his old Casio wristwatch. And on top of everything else, the fool was late. Tim told himself he'd wait five more minutes, then head out. He didn't have time to screw around like this. He didn't give a crap who this guy worked for. He had things to do.

He stretched his legs out long and let his booted feet fall with a thud onto the light wood donut-shaped coffee table. If anything, the table was less useful than the blasted chair. Why would anyone cut a hole in the middle of a freaking table?

As he was processing his displeasure with the recent lobby renovations, a woman slid onto the couch opposite him and deposited an oversized handbag on the seat next to her. He glanced over at her. Middle-aged, and well-kept. Her shoulder-length blonde hair was streaked with white, but even Tim could tell the streaks were courtesy of a pricy salon, not Mother Nature. Everything about this chick screamed 'money.' Not high-powered business-woman rich, not like the female attorneys, engineers, and consultants who strode through the lobby during the week, with their tall heels clicking against the polished floor, their glossy hair pulled back in sleek buns or cut in short wispy styles, their bodies encased in tailored suits, and their shiny black leather bags swinging from their hands.

No, this woman was a different breed altogether. Her purse was a bright purple color. She wore a pair of over-sized sunglasses perched on the crown of her head. Her skin had a healthy glow, like she spent a lot of time outside. He imagined her tending an herb garden or something. She was well put together and sturdy-looking. She looked like clean country living. Horsey, his mom would've said.

She was probably a housewife married to a banker or some titan of industry. A Martha Stewart wannabe. who spent her time decorating her mansion in Fox Chapel or Sewickley, serving complicated appetizers and throwback cocktails at dinner parties, and asking questions like, 'so what are you reading currently?'

She watched him assess and dismiss her, then smiled tightly and nodded toward his feet. "Do you mind?"

He eyed her for a moment longer. Then he dropped his feet, one at a time, to the floor. Two distinct thunks. "I'm leaving anyway."

"I don't think so," she told him.

He laughed. "Uh, yeah, I am. The guy I'm meeting is late, and I have better things to do than hang around here." He leaned forward and started to raise himself out of the chair.

"Sit down, Mr. Colchis."

Her tone reminded him of a humorless librarian or a strict piano teacher. Someone who expected immediate compliance. But it was her use of his name that made his jaw drop open for a moment.

He clamped his mouth shut and shook his head. Then he said slowly, "You're my contact?"

"Bravo, detective."

"I'm supposed to be meeting a guy. Rudy or something like that."

"Randy," she corrected. "And Randolph wasn't performing to our employer's satisfaction. He's no longer with us."

"And *you're* his replacement?"

"Mr. Colchis, I haven't the time to indulge your performative display of macho disbelief. It is, after all, Christmas Eve, and I have appointments with both my florist and my caterer this morning, so let's get on with it, shall we?"

He couldn't hide his grin. "I had you pegged as a society lady," he told her.

"Bully for you," she told him as if he were an underperforming student. "Now. Have you confirmed that nothing exists in the police records that would tie your man to our employer?"

"First off, lady, *my* employer is the Pittsburgh Police. And, second, Zane Nov—"

"No names. Not here." She raised her hand sharply, and her large diamond and emerald ring glinted in the sunlight pouring in through the glass walls.

"Fine, whatever. The guy isn't my guy, alright? He's a, uh, freelancer."

"We don't care what he is, Mr. Colchis. We care that he was thorough and careful and that you've confirmed as much."

Tim shifted in the hard seat. "Yeah, I went to see him. He told me the same thing he said last summer. He cleaned everything up. And I took a peek at the file.

Nothing jumped out at me. You can tell your employer, whoever he is, that he's got his shorts in a bunch over nothin'." He grinned.

"Certainly not," she snapped. "I'll say no such thing. And I do hope you're correct in your assessment because my employer abhors loose ends. Randolph is proof of that."

He spread his hands wide. "I don't know what to say other than you both need to relax. Are we good or what?"

She unclasped her purple purse and withdrew a thick, cream-colored envelope. She dropped it on the table between them, then leaned toward him. Her light blue eyes sparkled like ice. "This a small token of my employer's appreciation. A holiday bonus, if you like."

He reached for the envelope, calculating how much cash might be inside. She snaked out a cold hand and stopped his. "Deanne Lewis has a meeting with your employer later this morning. We'd like her to leave the meeting assured that her late ex-husband tragically ended his life by jumping from his window. Please see to it."

He lost control of his jaw again and gaped at her. "How do you know she's meeting with the police?"

"That's not your concern."

He clamped his free hand over hers and tightened his grasp. "Uh, yeah, it is. If you have a source in the department, I'd sure like to know who it is."

Her lips turned up, but he wouldn't call the effect a smile. She dug her sharp fingernails into the underside of his wrist. "Get your hand off me this instant, Mr. Colchis."

He released his grip, and she did the same. He turned over his arm and rubbed at the bloody scratches on his wrist. "Jeez, lady."

"I trust you don't want me to share your name with anyone, correct?"

"Well, yeah."

"And I obviously provide the same discretion for any others who may be helping us. Now, will you do what I've asked?"

He eyed the thick envelope on the table. "Yeah, I'll try. I'm not scheduled to talk to the ex-wife, though."

"We're aware. Her meeting with Sergeant Bass and Officer Evans is at ten-thirty. You could easily arrange to run into her afterward and engage her in casual conversation, could you not?"

He shrugged. "Maybe. I don't have any reason to be at the Zone Five building, though. Especially not on the weekend. Like, that's not where I'm stationed. I guess I could—"

"Mr. Colchis, if I gave the impression that I care about the mundane details of your job, I apologize. I certainly didn't intend to. Because I don't. Care, that is. Just make it happen. Now, if you'll excuse me, the children's choir is about to perform, and off-key, high-pitched singing gives me a headache." She swept away toward the elevator without a backward glance.

Tim watched her vanish into the crowd. Then he shook himself out of his daze. He snatched the envelope and shoved it into his pocket just as a group of preteens in white gowns clomped up onto a set of temporary risers he hadn't noticed when he'd arrived. He ducked his head as a microphone screeched feedback. Then he checked the time and started to speed-walk to the doors. He'd have to haul ass to Washington Boulevard if he wanted to catch Deanne Lewis before she left the station.

CHAPTER EIGHT

MAISY FINISHED her workout and headed for the ladies' locker room. The day before a major holiday, the cavernous fitness center was, not surprisingly, nearly deserted. Aside from Maisy, there were the hardcore gym rats, a handle of single, childless twenty-somethings, and a group of Chinese seniors who'd moved their daily qi gong practice from a nearby park to the gym after the season's first snowfall.

She took her time showering and dressing, enjoying having the space to herself. But eventually, her hair was dried, her face was done, and she'd run out of delay tactics. She checked the time. Assuming Sasha had kept to her own morning routine of running to Daniel's Krav Maga studio for a class and then running home, she'd also be dressed and ready to head out the door for the short walk from her home to her office right about now. And if Maisy timed her route correctly, she'd run into

Sasha on the corner of Ellsworth and Bellefonte, or thereabouts.

As she hurried outside and bent her head against the wind and swirling snow, she allowed that it was possible even Sasha would take off the Saturday before Christmas. But she had to walk home one way or another, so she figured it was worth the chance to bump into her friend accidentally on purpose.

Several blustery minutes later, her gamble paid off when she spotted a small woman mincing across the ice, her gloved hands clutching an oversized travel coffee mug. Maisy pushed back the hood of her puffy coat and waved. Sasha returned the greeting with a head bob.

"Good morning, sunshine," Maisy drawled as they drew close to one another.

"If you say so," Sasha deadpanned. "Coming back from the gym?"

"Yep. Please tell me you didn't run this morning in this weather."

A small shrug. "It wasn't too bad."

"On your way to the office?"

"Just for a few hours. If I can get all the year-end admin done this morning, I'm taking off all of next week."

"Nice. Well, I'm glad I bumped into you. Do you have a minute?"

"I do if you want to tell me you're coming to my parents' tonight." Sasha grinned.

Maisy hesitated for a heartbeat. The McCandless clan was loud and boisterous. But the truth was, she didn't have anywhere else to be, and spending the entire night alone felt unnecessarily grim.

"I was thinking I could come for dessert?" she ventured.

"Not a chance. If I have to suffer through the entire meal, so do you."

"Suffer through?"

"Poor choice of words. Please come for dinner. Everyone will be hustling the kids home to put them to bed, and my parents don't stay up for Midnight Mass anymore. They'll kick the stragglers out by eight, so they can make it to the nine o'clock service. It'll be an early night."

She relented. "Sure, I'd love to. Will you ask Valentina what I can bring?"

"Wine," Sasha replied instantly.

"You already checked with her?"

"No, but she's bound to assign you something complicated with three thousand ingredients if I do. Wine always works." She took a sip of her coffee and arched an eyebrow. "Unless you *want* to spend the day making some elaborate dish that I guarantee won't meet her standard?"

"Wine sounds good," she said in a hurry.

"Great, see you tonight."

As her friend started to walk away, Maisy fell into step alongside her. Sasha threw her a sidelong look.

"I know, I'm going the wrong way. I'm fixin' to stop by Jake's and get a coffee or something."

"You've been frequenting Jake's a lot." Sasha's voice

was amused and teasing. "I think he's got a thing for you. Is it mutual?"

Maisy shook her head. "You don't have to act like a seventh grader just because you're the size of one. You know that, right?"

"Hit a nerve, huh?"

They both giggled at their silliness, then Maisy said, "Actually, I wanted to talk to you about something more serious than dinner—or a crush."

"Ah, so there *is* a crush."

"Sorry, counselor, I meant alleged crush. Anyway, I was at St. Clair Social last night and ran into some cops I know. I think I might have a lead on a story."

Interest sparked in Sasha's bright green eyes. "Ooooh, what is it?"

Maisy wrinkled her nose. "I think it's gonna turn out to be about abuse of authority."

"By the police? You can't be serious."

She let Sasha's sarcasm go without comment. The little lawyer had had more than her share of run-ins with local law enforcement in the past few years, so Maisy overlooked her cynicism.

Instead, she asked, "Did you know there's an interagency, interdepartmental Nuisance Bar Task Force?"

Sasha let out a little snort. "No, but I'm not surprised. My tax bill goes up every year; they must be getting more creative with ways to spend the money."

"Mmm. Well, it sounds like one of the detectives assigned to the task force used the threat of harassing a bar owner to gain unauthorized access to a closed case file."

"A closed case about the bar?"

As they waited for the light to change so they could cross the street, Maisy clarified, "No. The bar owner has a cousin who's a cop—Oswald Bass, he's a sergeant working out of Zone Five. This nuisance bar guy signed out of one of the Bass' files. Bass asked why he was looking at it, and this charmer told him not to worry about it. He threatened to give the cousin a hard time if Bass didn't drop it. Follow?"

"Yeah. It's nasty behavior, but I'm not sure interdepartmental squabbling is gonna set the podcasting world on fire. Unless you have a unique angle. Is the cousin a particularly sympathetic character?"

"I don't know. Bass doesn't want me to involve his cousin."

Sasha frowned. "Then do you even have a story?"

Maisy exhaled. Her hot breath was visible in the cold air. "The closed case is—well, it's Landon Lewis' suicide."

Sasha gave her a pained look and groaned. "Please tell me the Milltown PD isn't mixed up in this."

"I don't know. I don't *think* so. The cousin's bar is in Greenfield, so I'm not sure how Milltown would factor into it."

"Well, be careful. You know as well as I do that Landon Lewis was nothing but trouble when he was alive. No reason it'd be different now that he's dead."

"Mmm. His death *was* a suicide, right?"

"That's what the coroner's office said."

Maisy noted that she hadn't answered the question. She stopped walking. "You were there that night."

Sasha stiffened and turned toward her. "What?"

"The responding officers said a federal agent identified Lewis' body. The agent gave them a fake agency name, by the way. I don't think they realized it, but I checked it out this morning. There's no such thing as the HRS Strike Unit."

Sasha laughed. "You can't think Connelly's the only federal agent who likes to fly under the radar. I mean, look at Hank."

"Yeah, but Hank isn't married to a petite lawyer who was working on a case where Lewis was going to be a witness. I mean, not unless his life circumstances have changed since the last time I saw him."

Sasha mumbled something Maisy couldn't quite catch.

"What was that?"

"I said, 'son of a gun.'"

"Still trying to clean up Fiona's language?" Maisy smiled despite the tension she sensed in her friend.

"Sure am. Mainly because I don't want the blame for my daughter's proclivity for profanity."

"There's that famous Sasha McCandless self-preservation instinct."

Sasha narrowed her eyes and studied Maisy for a moment as if she was trying to decide whether Maisy was taking a shot at her. Maisy looked back at her with her patented innocent expression.

Finally, Sasha sighed. "Enough with the doe eyes, Bambi. You don't fool me. Come on, it's too cold to do this on the street corner. Let's go get you your ridiculous coffee confection."

They hurried the rest of the way in silence.

CHAPTER NINE

DEANNE WAITED inside the police station doors until the car service app on her phone chimed to let her know her car was just minutes away. Then, she braced for the cold and exited the dingy, depressing building. But the feeling of dingy depression clung to her.

She moved closer to the parking lot, clutching the drawstring bag filled with her ex-husband's things and scanning Washington Boulevard for her car service. After a moment, determined to shake herself out of her funk, she pulled out her phone and thumbed a quick text to Rosa Esposito:

> If the invite still stands, would love to join your family tonight.

Rosa's response was immediate:

> 🎉 Yay, yay, yay! Salim and I will pick you up at 6:30.

Deanne was smiling down at the screen when a large guy in a leather coat walked around from the corner of the building at high speed and bumped into her, jostling the bag and the phone.

"Oh!" she exclaimed, startled by the contact. She managed to keep a grip on both items.

"I'm sorry, ma'am," he said in a gruff voice. "I didn't see you there. Head in the clouds, I guess." He flashed her a contrite smile.

"It's okay," she assured him. "I wasn't paying attention either."

"You sure you're all right, Ms. Lewis?"

She gaped at him. "Do I know you? I'm sorry ..."

He grinned at her confusion and jabbed a thumb at the name tag stuck to her coat. "I *am* a detective, but the case of your identity wasn't the toughest nut to crack."

She blushed and shifted her phone to her other hand, then peeled the sticker from her lapel, folded it onto itself, and dropped it into her pocket. "Nice work, Columbo."

He guffawed and stuck out his hand. "Detective Tim Colchis."

She shook it. "As you already surmised, I'm Deanne Lewis."

His expression clouded, and his eyes darted to the drawstring bag she was clutching. "You're not related to Landon Lewis, are you?"

"Um. Actually, I'm his—he was my husband. I mean, ex-husband. I'm sorry, detective, did you work on Landon's case?"

Detective Colchis made a face and a vague gesture. "Not officially, no. But I did review the file, and it stuck with me. It's always tragic when someone decides their only option is to end it all."

She nodded.

"His death *was* ruled a suicide last summer, wasn't it? Or am I misremembering?"

"No, your memory is correct."

"So, you just stopped by to pick up his things?" He pointed at the bag.

"Right. I had come into town to wrap up some of Landon's affairs, and the officers who handled his death were kind enough to meet with me."

He nodded as if he knew what had prompted her request for a meeting. "Do you mind if I give you a piece of unsolicited advice?"

She did, but for some reason, she couldn't find the words to say that politely, so instead she smiled. "Of course not."

"The loved ones left behind when a guy offs himself, they can go off the rails. I've seen it a dozen times, they grasp at straws, making up all sorts of out-there scenarios. Maybe it was an accident, maybe someone killed him and staged it. Anything seems easier to handle than the truth, you know? But that's torturing yourself. Better to face the reality, tough as it may be."

He gave her a close look, gauging her reaction.

The fact that this man had accurately described her reaction from just moments ago unnerved and embarrassed her. She was falling apart the way Landon had fallen apart after Josh's death. The detective was right. Inventing a fantasy world to insulate oneself from the pain of the real world was not only foolish, it was dangerous. Landon was proof of that.

She mustered up a genuine smile. "I hear you. I'm a counselor, and there's a lot of truth to what you say. Don't worry, detective. I'm not about to deny the facts. As you say, it's better to face them."

He bit down on his lower lip before responding. "Well, that's good to know. Hope I didn't overstep or anything. Just wouldn't want you to torment yourself."

She shook her head. "No, I appreciate your input."

He jerked his chin toward a red Civic making its way up the long driveway from the street. "That your ride?"

She glanced down at the app on her phone to confirm the make and model. "It is."

The driver parked near a flagpole displaying the American flag, and the detective yanked open the back passenger side door for her.

"Thanks."

"No problem." He leaned into the back seat as she settled in. "And happy holidays." He retracted his head and closed the door, then gave it a little slap as if he were urging a horse to move.

She waved goodbye, and he turned away. He didn't go into the police station but, instead, turned back the way he'd come.

A moment later, her cell phone dinged. She looked down and forgot all about the detective. Her notification was the calendar reminder for her appointment at the morgue. Happy holidays, indeed.

CHAPTER TEN

"HAPPY HOLIDAYS!" the teenager behind the counter at Jake's chirped as Maisy and Sasha stepped up to place their orders.

"Same to you, Tara. I'm surprised to see you working today," Sasha responded, handing over her now-empty travel mug.

Tara refilled it with the fresh dark roast that Jake stocked especially for the lawyer and bobbed her head. "I could say the same for you. This place has been dead all morning."

"It'll pick up once all the shops open," Maisy told her. "The last-minute shoppers will be looking for a caffeine boost."

"I hope so because this is *booooring*. So what can I get you, ma'am?"

Maisy managed not to wince at the teen's use of the honorific. She'd used it all the time herself growing up in

Spanish Oak. Although, there, it was a matter of simple politeness. Up here, it seemed to be code for 'old.'

"How about one of those gingerbread lattes?"

Tara shot Sasha a confused look.

Sasha leaned over and stage whispered, "This is Maisy Farley."

"Oh. Oh! Got it." The barista tittered and turned to assemble the drink.

"What was that all about?" Maisy demanded.

"Jake doesn't have a gingerbread latte on the menu. There *is* a sugarplum latte. But apparently, you asked him for a gingerbread latte, so he made you a gingerbread latte—and left the employees directions for how to make it for you if you came in when he wasn't here."

Maisy felt her cheeks flush. "I feel like a dope."

Sasha waved a hand. "Don't. Lots of coffee shops have secret menu items. Besides, it's cute."

Apparently, Tara thought it was cute, too, because she was still giggling when she delivered the steaming caramel-and-chocolate drizzled drink, complete with a ginger snap wedge nestled on the rim of the mug. "Here you go!"

"Thank you, sugar."

Maisy held out her credit card, and the girl gave her a blank look.

"I don't know how much to charge you. What does it cost?"

"Um, I'm not sure, to be honest. The last one was on the house," she admitted.

Her face burned hotter as Sasha doubled over with

laughter. In desperation, she dug a twenty out of her wallet, pressed it into the girl's hand, and then dragged the still-cackling Sasha to a two-top table in the corner.

"Honestly, will you grow up?"

Sasha wiped her eyes and flung herself into the chair. "I wish you could've seen your face."

Maisy sipped the sweet drink and sniffed. "Well, he should put it on the menu. It's amazing."

Having finally composed herself, Sasha rested her mug on the small wrought-iron table and gave Maisy a serious look. "To answer your question, yes, we happened to walk by the scene the night Lewis died."

Maisy probed, "You and Leo happened to walk by? Was it a coincidence? I mean, really?"

"Yes, really." Then she sighed. "Well, yes and no."

Maisy arched one brow and eyed her over the oversized latte mug. "Which one is it?"

"We'd just dropped the twins off at my parents' for the night so we could have a date night. We got into an intense discussion in the car, and Connelly pulled over so we could talk it through. This beat cop came over and told us to move along." Sasha laughed at the memory. "I think he expected to find a couple of teenagers making out. Not an old married couple. He was in the middle of recommending a Chinese restaurant he thought we'd like when a call came over his radio."

"And it was about Lewis?"

She nodded. "We both recognized his office address, and Connelly knew the code was for a suspected suicide."

She stopped and looked at Maisy as if that explained everything. And, knowing the couple, it more or less did.

"So, instead of getting dinner, you headed over there to see what was going on," she guessed.

"You'd have done the same thing," Sasha countered.

Maisy acknowledged that truth with a shrug. Then she wrinkled her brow. "I don't understand why anyone would check out the file now. The police thought it was a suicide when it happened. It was ruled a suicide. Why go digging around now?"

Sasha shook her head. "It's definitely weird. And the other weird thing is that the reason we'd pulled over that night was to talk about Landon Lewis."

"Wait, what?"

"You remember that I was getting ready for that prosecutorial misconduct trial, right?"

"The one I got myself fired over? Uh, yeah, I remember."

Sasha sucked in her breath. "Right. Anyway, Lewis had been dodging Jordana's calls to set up a time to go over his testimony. So I called him from a restricted number. Ambushed him, you might say."

"That same day?"

Sasha nodded. "He tried to brush me off on the phone. He wouldn't schedule a time to meet. It pissed me off, to be honest. Then Connelly randomly ran into him outside his office about thirty minutes after I talked to him. He said Lewis was acting unhinged."

"Well, he was unhinged, wasn't he?"

"True, he was. But, according to Connelly, he was

way more unhinged than usual. So it was just the strangest timing when we heard his address come over that police radio."

Maisy frowned. "Unhinged enough to kill himself?"

"Evidently."

"But you don't think there's anything hinky about the suicide?" Maisy pressed.

"Hinky? I mean, I don't know. The man was troubled. But neither of us thought he'd do something like ... that. Although I think Connelly blames himself for leaving him in the state he was in."

Sasha fell silent, and Maisy took a moment to imagine how it must feel to know you were the last person to see someone before he killed himself. She was sure she'd be going over the interaction obsessively, wondering if she could have prevented it. She gave a little shudder.

"Exactly," Sasha said as if she were reading Maisy's thoughts.

"And Connelly identified his body?"

"What was left of it."

An uneasy tightness took up residence in Maisy's gut. "Maybe this isn't the story to follow," she said more to herself than to Sasha.

Sasha weighed in anyway. "It's terribly sad. But I don't think there's anything to sink your teeth into. I guess if the nuisance bar task force guy had some history with Lewis, maybe. If he used to work on the Milltown force or something. But, most likely he's just bored with busting underaged drinkers and responding to bar fights.

If I were him, I'd be trolling closed cases looking for something more exciting, too."

"Mmm, yeah, maybe you're right."

"Hey, you'll get a juicy lead. You're Maisy Flippin' Farley. Something'll fall into your lap."

"Yeah, I guess so." She sighed.

Her friend gave her an encouraging smile as she stood. "I know so. And I wish I could hang, but I have to get to the office and my pile of paperwork. See you tonight."

Maisy waved goodbye absently, then dunked the ginger snap into her latte. As she nibbled on the cookie, she reluctantly decided her favorite little lawyer was right. This story wasn't worth chasing. Back to the drawing board—but first, the wine and spirits store.

CHAPTER ELEVEN

The Pittsburgh Crèche
US Steel Tower Plaza
near midnight

DEANNE STOOD ALONE in the courtyard and stared up at the massive Nativity scene. It was lit from within by lights on the ceiling and topped by a replica of the Star of Bethlehem.

The Espositos hadn't oversold the display. Aunt Marisa had insisted that Rosa and Salim drop their guest off at the site after dinner and had even sketched a map for Deanne to follow so she wouldn't get lost on the five-minute walk from the plaza to Landon's apartment. Having glanced at the map, Deanne was certain she could manage the directions, which boiled down to walk straight down Grant Street for three blocks, turn right onto Fifth Avenue, and walk another block and a half.

The full-sized replica of the crèche on display at the Vatican in Rome was well worth the short walk. Deanne found she couldn't quite form the words, even inside her head, to describe the awe that filled her at the sight. The religious figures didn't resonate with her as a matter of faith, but as a matter of pure artistry and craftsmanship, they were astounding. The scene flooded her with a sense of calm and tranquility that had been missing since she'd been here. If she were being honest, that equanimity had been in short supply for months—ever since she'd received the call that Landon had killed himself.

But the noisy, joyful feast with Rosa Esposito's family had sparked happiness in Deanne's chest for the first time in a long time, and, now, this quiet display was sparking peace. Tears of relief and gratitude glistened in her eyes, and she bowed her head.

"May his memory be a blessing," she whispered softly.

The traditional Hebrew phrase was used to comfort mourners after the death of a loved one. The words had been her lifeline after Josh's murder. But they had a second meaning, too—one that she seemed unable to accept when it came to her ex-husband. It was the responsibility of the mourners to honor their dead loved one's memory, to ensure that the good deeds of those no longer with us live on and that their lives continue to have meaning.

After Josh's death, she devoted herself to grief counseling work to honor Josh, to help other grieving parents, and to ease the pain of the loss of his easy, empathetic presence in the world. But with Landon, she was floundering. How could she honor *his* contributions to the world? Why would anyone want *his* deeds to live on? The world was a better place without her ex-husband's work. If anything, his *death* was a blessing because it ended his work. The thought tore a bitter laugh from her chest. The laugh cracked and turned to a hoarse sob.

She knew she dwelled in a dark place when it came to Landon. Her heart was covered in shadow. She had to find a way to accept his death, or this pain would consume her like his obsession had consumed him when he'd been alive. She raised her face to the majestic angel suspended in mid-air over the manger, heralding the baby's arrival, and silently begged it to give her a sign. How could she move on from Landon's death when it made no sense to her?

From behind her, a clear, lilting voice called out, "Ma'am, do you need help?"

Deanne started and turned toward the speaker. Her heart pounded, and tears tracked down her cheeks. "Yes, I think I might."

MAISY MAINTAINED a careful distance from the weeping woman in front of the Nativity, but she couldn't ignore her pain. She'd asked Matthew, Sasha and Leo's eldest nephew, to drop her at the landmark crèche instead of her place because Leo had been talking about the breathtaking display at dinner, recounting the first time he'd seen it.

With his tongue loosened by scotch, she could have sworn he mumbled something about stopping a tragedy there. But Sasha knocked her glass of red wine over on her mother's silver tablecloth and shouted "shit!" at full volume. Maisy had a suspicion both the spilled wine and the curse word that 'slipped' out of Sasha's mouth were intentional, designed to draw attention away from her husband's story. It had worked, too. Valentina had fussed over the spot with a bottle of soda water, and Fiona had led the kids' table in a rousing chorus of 'shits.'

Then Matthew had offered her a lift, and their route through town took them down Grant Street. When Maisy spotted the star shining atop the crèche, it felt like a sign. So she'd asked the young man to let her out at the plaza. He'd protested, but she played the 'I'm old enough to be your much older sister' card, and he'd relented. And now she was sharing the moment with a mentally imbalanced stranger.

Perfect.

Before she called to the crying, shaking woman, she craned her neck to see if, by chance, Matthew had ignored her instructions and stuck around. No dice. The street was as deserted as the plaza.

It was nearly midnight. The temperature hovered near the single digits. And she was alone with a woman who appeared to be having a breakdown. This was not in her evening plans.

Suck it up, buttercup, she ordered herself in her mama's voice. *This gal is in trouble.*

"Ma'am, do you need help?" she called, praying the woman would tell her to buzz off.

But, she didn't. Instead, she jumped and wheeled around, clearly startled. Her eyes were red and swollen, and tears stained her cheeks as she clutched the lapels of her coat together at her throat and croaked, "Yes, I think I do."

Maisy took a slow, cautious step forward.

"Are you hurt?"

The woman shook her head, and then sobbed, "I think I'm losing it."

Maisy was inclined to agree with her, but her Southern training kicked in. "Ah, now, don't feel that way. Lots of people get really emotional looking at the Nativity—especially *this* Nativity. It can be overwhelming."

The woman wasn't having it. "I'm not even Christian," she said, a frantic laugh rising in her voice.

Maisy wasn't sure what to say to that beyond, "Okay."

"I'm sorry. I'm so sorry. I guess I *am* overwhelmed. My former husband died recently, and it just hit me all at once."

Maisy's heart squeezed in sympathy. She risked patting the woman's arm. "Oh, that's terrible. Here, let me see if I have a tissue." She pulled open her bag and started pawing through it.

The woman stopped her. "Forget the tissue. Is there

somewhere around here that'll be open this late on Christmas Eve where I can get a drink? A stiff one."

Maisy thought. "Well, we're about a hot minute away from the William Penn Hotel. One of their lounges might still be open."

The woman wiped her face with the back of her hand and deadpanned, "It's a Christmas miracle."

Maisy couldn't hold back her laugh. "It must be."

"If you'll just point me in the right direction, I'd be grateful."

She studied the other woman for a long moment, then said, "I'd feel better if I walked you over. Might even grab a nightcap myself."

"That's really not necessary."

Maisy silenced her protest with a look. "I've got nowhere else to be. And drinking with a broken-up stranger in a hotel lobby bar would be a step up from drinking alone in my empty, undecorated house."

She nodded. "Okay, that'd be great. I'm Deanne."

Maisy shook Deanne's extended hand. "Maisy. Nice to meet you, Deanne."

They took one last look at the crèche, and then Maisy led Deanne out of the plaza and across the street.

CHAPTER TWELVE

MAISY AND DEANNE hurried through the hushed lobby, past the Tap Room bar (closed), and down a set of stairs that led to the hotel's Speakeasy lounge, tucked under the stairwell. They pulled up short in front of the closed double doors.

"Oh, no," Deanne breathed. "It's closed, too."

Maisy checked the time. "Well, the Palm Court upstairs is probably still serving drinks. But I have a better idea. Wait right there." She flashed the woman a grin and then took off along a corridor that led to the kitchen and service areas.

She returned a few minutes later, accompanied by a hotel employee who brandished an ear-to-ear grin and a ring of keys. He unlocked the doors with a flourish. Then he ushered the women inside, turned on some low lights, and stepped behind the bar.

Deanne gave Maisy a wide-eyed look. "What have

you done? He's gonna get in trouble," she whispered loudly.

Maisy shook her head. "No, he's not. Deanne, meet Titus Brace. Titus, Deanne."

Titus leaned across the bar and pumped Deanne's hand. "It's a pleasure. Any friend of Maisy's is a friend of the William Penn's." He reached beneath the bar and produced two cocktail menus.

"Titus is the overnight manager. He's in charge until morning."

Titus nodded sagely. "And 'tis the night before Christmas. All through the property, not a creature is stirring. Save one little bar mouse." He gave Deanne a broad wink, and she finally relaxed her tense shoulders.

"Now, pick your poison and find a comfy corner. I'll bring your drinks over in a jiffy."

Deanne studied the options. "What are you getting?" she asked Maisy.

Maisy opened her mouth, but before she could speak, Titus answered for her. "Miss Maisy's drinking The Girl with the Golden Curls, of course."

Maisy smiled and fluffed her trademark blonde curls. The concoction of light rum, pineapple juice, maraschino liqueur, and simple syrup satisfied her sweet tooth and Titus' flair for the dramatic.

"The drinks are all period cocktails from when there really was an illegal speakeasy operating right here in this spot," she explained to Deanne.

"Hmm ... okay, I'll try The Informant."

"An excellent choice," Titus assured her before shooing them away from the bar.

Deanne trailed Maisy to a pair of roomy red scarlet leather club chairs situated in a little nook in the wall. A small table sat between the chairs. Maisy dropped into one of the chairs and watched Deanne take in the tin ceiling, the flocked silver and black wall fabrics, and the clubby, intimate vibe.

"First time?" Maisy guessed.

"Yeah. This place is something else," she murmured.

"It's like going back in time," Maisy agreed. "Can you believe the hotel turned it into a storage closet when Prohibition ended?"

"Really?"

"Really."

"So, how do you know Titus?" Deanne wondered.

"You're not from here, are you?"

Deanne shook her head. "No. I live in Carmel-by-the-Sea, near Monterey."

"You're a long way from California."

"Mmm, I suppose I am. Like I said, I just lost my ... ex. He was living here. I had to fly out to wrap up his affairs."

Maisy grimaced. "That's not a fun way to spend the holidays."

The other woman shrugged. "I dragged my feet long enough. But you didn't answer my question. How do you know Titus?"

"Oh, I know everybody," Maisy said simply.

"What are you, some kind of local celebrity?"

"As a matter of fact, yeah, I am. Or I was." She paused as Titus arrived bearing a small silver tray that held their cocktails. He placed the drinks on the table and then waited for them to sample the libations.

Maisy raised the glass and took a long, sweet sip. "Perfection," she told him.

Deanne took a cautious sip, and her face lit up with delight. "It's wonderful."

Titus bowed his head, beaming. "I'll leave you ladies to it. Let me know if you need anything, anything at all."

As he walked away, Deanne said, "This might be the most surreal sixth night ever."

"Sixth night?"

"Of Hanukkah." She checked her watch. "Technically, seventh. Anyway, you're a local celebrity? For real?"

"Until recently, I was the evening news anchor for one of the local stations. I was named Pittsburgh's fan favorite media personality for the past seven years." Maisy recounted her resume in an emotionless tone, then sipped her drink.

Deanne pursed her lips and considered this information. "So, what happened?"

"Pardon?"

"You keep using the past tense. You're not a local celebrity anymore? I think Titus would beg to differ."

That got a laugh out of her. "Over the summer, a new owner took over the station. Management *suggested* that I might want to get some work done if I wanted to stay on the anchor desk."

Deanne blinked. "Plastic surgery?"

"Maybe. Or fillers or Botox. I don't know. I didn't stick around to find out the details."

"You quit?"

"Better. I made them fire me. Which meant a million-dollar payout clause in my contract kicked in."

"I'll drink to that!" Deanne beamed at her and did, in fact, raise her glass to drink.

Maisy eyed the woman. She was terrible at guessing ages, but she suspected Deanne was in her mid- to late fifties. Old enough to have heard the whisper of irrelevance that starts stalking women through their thirties and grows ever louder as the years tick by.

"Thanks."

"What are you doing now?"

"Well, I've been focusing on investigative reporting in recent years, so that's what I'm going to do. I'm starting a podcast first. Eventually, maybe I'll do an independent digital news report."

"Wow."

"So, what do you do in Carmel?"

"I'm a counselor. A grief counselor, if you can stand the irony."

Maisy cocked her head. "What irony?"

"Hmm, maybe the irony that a trained grief counselor fell apart in the middle of a public space to the point that a passerby had to check on my well-being? Thanks for that, by the way."

"I think you're being a bit hard on yourself."

"How so?" Deanne trained her bright eyes on Maisy, curious and intent.

"Well," she said slowly, "you obviously were divorced—or at least estranged—from your husband when he died. I've never been married, but I can't imagine the fact that you weren't currently together makes his death easier. Especially not if it was sudden or something."

She watched Deanne's reaction. The woman took a deep, shaky breath and swallowed hard.

"You're right. I think the fact that our marriage had already died made Landon's actual death worse. Well, that and the fact that he apparently killed himself."

Maisy froze. Her drink hovered an inch from her mouth and sloshed dangerously in the cocktail glass. Her chest tightened and her throat constricted.

"Maisy, are you okay?"

Breathe, sugar, she ordered herself.

Carefully—so very carefully—she placed her drink on the table. Then she lowered her chin and met Deanne's eyes. "You're Landon Lewis' ex-wife?"

CHAPTER THIRTEEN

JENNA OPENED her eyes and squinted at the time on her phone. Just after midnight. She listened to Zane's steady breathing punctuated by the nasal whistle of his thrice-broken nose. He insisted he didn't snore and that the sound was related to his boxing injuries. Regardless of the cause, it was annoying as all get out and had kept Jenna awake more nights than she could count. Zane joked and said she ought to thank him: it was good training for when they had a baby.

"If," she whispered to herself.

As if he'd heard her, Zane muttered, "When."

She froze, then rolled over and propped herself on her elbows to study his face. He was zonked out, talking in his sleep. After a beat, the whistle-snore resumed.

Instead of reaching over and pinching his nose closed, her little trick to interrupt his breathing pattern and stop the noise at least temporarily, she eased herself out of the bed and reached for her fuzzy robe. Then she slid her feet into her slippers and crept out of their bedroom and down the stairs.

She tiptoed through the living room, pausing to take in the lights of the tree twinkling in the darkened room, and then continued through the dining room to the kitchen.

The light over the sink illuminated the small backyard. She smiled at how the soft covering of new snow made even their busted cement and weed-infested yard look fresh and clean.

Then she padded across the floor to the basement door. As she opened it, a gust of cold air rushed up. She tightened the belt of her robe and hit the light switch.

She hurried down the stairs.

She had one more gift for Zane tucked away down here. His big gift, even though it was small in size. She planned to slip it into his stocking, but she didn't want him to catch a glimpse of it before they opened presents, so she'd waited until he'd finally fallen asleep.

Moving quickly, she passed the furnace and hot water tank and came to stand in front of the shelves Zane and his granddad had built for storage. She popped open the sturdy plastic bin labeled 'garden stuff' and shifted the seed packets and planters to one side. There, under her rose-patterned gardening gloves, was the slim package. She'd already wrapped it in striped paper and tied a gold ribbon around it.

She grinned down at it, imagining Zane's excitement when he opened it to see a signed photo of Roscoe Davis hoisting his championship belt. She'd found the picture in a box of papers in the attic and did some research to find out who Roscoe Davis was.

As it turned out, the old boxer was still alive, and when she'd shown up at his nursing home in Mount Oliver, photograph in hand, he'd been tickled to sign it. He'd even written a personal note in his jagged, shaky handwriting: *To Zane, whose granddad was one helluva opponent. Racin' Roscoe Davis.* His nickname, Roscoe had informed Jenna with pride, was a tribute to the speed with which he used to bob and weave.

She and Zane agreed to spend no more than thirty dollars each on gifts so they could sock the rest of their money away in the baby fund. As a result, the priceless picture was encased in a flimsy cheap frame that she'd found on clearance at the home goods store. But the frame didn't matter. Besides, they could always replace it later, when money wasn't so tight. Because the day *would* come when they wouldn't be so strapped. She had to keep the faith.

She replaced the lid and pushed the bin back into its spot on the shelf. She slid the package into her robe pocket and hurried across the cold earthen floor.

As she neared the furnace, a glint of silver leaning against the wall caught her eye, and she frowned. She drew closer, worried that the ancient furnace they'd inherited from Zane's grandfather along with the house had given up the ghost and was finally falling apart. So much for not being cash-strapped.

But when she reached behind it to snap the panel

back in place, she realized the glinting metal wasn't a panel that had somehow shaken loose. She shoved her hand between the furnace and the cold bare wall and retrieved a dented metal lunchbox. She stared at it, her heart thudding as if it were Pandora's box and not an old steelworker's lunch pail.

Zane must've hidden the dusty, dented thing here. But why?

Same reason you hid his gift in with the gardening supplies. So you wouldn't find it.

Classic Zane. He'd probably ignored their agreed-upon gift budget and bought her something outrageous. If he'd gotten her another necklace, so help her, she'd strangle him with it.

She knew she should return the box to its hiding place. But she also knew she was a dyed-in-the-wool, first-class snoop. She wasn't proud of it. But it's who she was.

She was no more able to put the box back without taking a peek than she was able to sprout wings and fly. She glanced around the basement guiltily and then snapped open the latch on the box.

She drew her brows together in consternation at the jumble of papers inside. None of this memorabilia was worth hiding. Keeping, sure. Hiding? Why?

She rifled through the tickets and programs and unearthed a package wrapped in waxed brown butcher paper and secured with a rubber band. She removed the band, unwrapped the paper, and stared in disbelief at a glossy red iPhone. The phone was so far out of their price range that it may as well have been made from platinum.

What was he thinking? She had a perfectly good Samsung phone that had come free with their cell phone contract. This wasn't just extravagant, it was wasteful and stupid.

Easy, tiger, she cautioned herself as anger burned in her tight chest. She shook her head at the device as she realized what he'd probably been thinking.

The iPhone had not one but two amazing cameras that were infinitely better than the cameras on their basic cell phones. Zane always joked that her blurry pictures looked like she'd taken them with a potato. Why a potato, she had no idea. But it was just like Zane to buy this thing so she could take clear, vibrant pictures of their someday baby.

Her eyes filled with tears as she envisioned it. Posing their precious child on a tasteful blanket, propped up in a soft chair, or snuggling with an oversized teddy with one of those 'X month old' signs to document their infant's progress from cooing newborn to smiling, drooling baby to tottering toddler.

Her chest relaxed and her irritation dissipated, melted by the warm glow of the vision. Zane's heart was in the right place. It always was. Even when he was being a complete and total bonehead, which was often. She carefully rewrapped the phone, replaced the band, and tucked the package into the box. Then she closed the lunch pail and wedged it back into its spot behind the furnace.

She promised herself that, in the morning, when Zane surprised her with the iPhone, she'd focus on this feeling and respond with all the love she felt right now.

Then she hurried up the basement stairs, clicked off the light, and closed the door. She slid the framed picture into Zane's stocking, arranging it so that one wrapped corner peeked out of the stocking's top. Then she moved on swift, silent feet back upstairs to return to the bed she shared with Zane before he woke up and found her missing.

She lay awake for a while, staring at the ceiling and listening to Zane's nighttime noises. They weren't perfect, she and Zane. Far from it, to tell the truth. But nobody could deny that they loved each other without restraint. She drifted off with a small smile of anticipation on her lips.

CHAPTER FOURTEEN

MAISY HAD ALWAYS THOUGHT 'TIME STOPPED' was just a saying. But at this moment, she was fairly confident that the laws of the universe were not in effect in the basement of the William Penn hotel. Because she and Deanne were both silent and unmoving, as frozen as if they were in suspended animation.

She didn't know how long the moment would've stretched if two things hadn't happened in close succession. First, an ice cube in Deanne's drink cracked, and Deanne blinked at the noise. Second, Titus materialized and deposited a ramekin holding a small mountain of olives on the table right by Maisy's elbow.

"I know they're your secret vice," he whispered. Then he winked and walked away.

Maisy popped a briny green olive into her mouth and stared at Deanne. Deanne stared back.

Finally, the other woman said, "You knew Landon?"

Maisy rubbed her right hand over her forehead, then picked up her drink. She fortified herself with a long sip before answering. "I knew of him."

Deanne's expression flattened. "Because of the mess with Cesare, right? I'm sure he was as infamous around town as you are famous."

Maisy blew out a breath that ruffled the curls framing her face. "His ... situation ... did make some waves locally, for sure. But it wasn't as big of a story as you might expect. I know the details because Sasha McCandless-Connelly is one of my closest friends."

Deanne pursed her lips. "That name keeps coming up."

"She's the lawyer he abducted. The one who blew the criminal profiling issue wide open, got that policewoman in Milltown charged with manslaughter, and sued the DA's office."

Deanne blinked. "I know. I mean, I know what I read. Landon and I—we weren't close. We didn't talk about what happened out here in any detail. Although he did make it a point to tell me he planned to testify against the district attorney's office. He thought it showed personal growth. Of course, it turns out it was a condition of the consent decree with the Justice Department." She laughed harshly and drained her drink.

Maisy caught Titus' eye and held up two fingers. He nodded his understanding.

"Connelly. The husband identified Landon's body. Something Connelly. I have the police report in here somewhere." She rummaged through her purse.

"Leo," Maisy said quietly.

Deanne raised her head. "What?"

"His name is Leo Connelly."

Deanne flung herself back against the chair. "Nobody thinks it's strange that the lawyer's husband just happened to find Landon's body? How small is this town?"

"It's the smallest big town imaginable," Maisy told her. "Do you think it wasn't a coincidence?"

"I don't know what to think. I met with the officers who responded to the scene this morning. They were adamant that Landon killed himself. And even some random detective I ran into outside the station felt it necessary to weigh in that it was suicide."

"But you have doubts?"

Maisy kept her voice soft and easy, treating the woman like a trapped, feral animal.

"Some things don't make sense."

Titus took their empty glasses and replaced them with fresh drinks. "One Blonde Girl with Curls and one Informant," he announced.

The blonde girl with curls eyed her would-be informant and waited for an answer. Deanne stayed silent until Titus drifted away.

Then she leaned forward and said, "The police gave me Landon's personal effects today. His phone was missing. I asked one of the officers about it, and she said it wasn't recovered at the scene or in his office. I'm staying at his apartment, and I tore it apart looking for it. It's not there, either."

Maisy frowned. "Maybe it was destroyed. Um, on impact."

Deanne told a long drink. "No, Officer Evans was clear. There was no phone."

A long silence stretched between them. After a beat, Maisy ventured, "Maybe whoever called the police rolled him first."

"Rolled him?"

"Oh, sorry. Cop jargon. Some unhoused people live in that alley. If one of them saw Landon jump, they might have checked his pockets and taken anything of value before they called it in."

"Maybe, but I don't think so. His watch was in the bag. The face is smashed, but it's still an expensive piece. Wouldn't someone who stole the phone also take his watch?"

"Yeah, probably. What about his wallet?"

"He left it up in his office. The police retrieved it and gave it to me with the rest of his things. They unsealed the office when they closed the case, but the landlord has it locked up tight. I need to go through whatever's there before the lease is up on New Year's Eve."

As she spoke, Deanne seemed to age before Maisy's eyes. She looked exhausted and hollow.

"I'm sorry you got stuck dealing with this. There was nobody else who could do it?"

Deanne shook her head. "Landon didn't have any friends. Or hobbies. Or a life, really. His work was his life." Anger flared in her eyes. "That's why I can't believe he killed himself. He was obsessed with making a difference."

Maisy recalled her conversation with Sasha at the coffee shop. "Could he have realized that his intentions, while good, were so misguided that he'd just made a total mess of things? Maybe ending his life seemed like taking the high road."

"You don't know Landon." She dismissed the idea out of hand.

"People change, though. You said yourself you weren't close anymore."

"Look, I just know, okay? It's more likely that your friend's husband killed him in a rage to get revenge. Isn't he some kind of federal agent?"

Maisy wasn't sure how serious Deanne was, but she figured she'd nip this idea in the bud. "Leo didn't kill your ex-husband."

"You can't be sure of that."

"I'd wager I know Leo Connelly better than you knew your late husband, at least in recent years," she shot back.

Deanne held Maisy's fiery gaze for a moment and then burst into tears. "I'm sorry. I just … it feels wrong. In my bones, I know he didn't kill himself." Suddenly, she sat up straighter. "Wait, you can help."

Maisy widened her eyes. "Help how?"

"You said you're starting an investigative podcast, right? This can be your first case." Deanne's despair had morphed into excitement. She was nearly vibrating with urgency.

"Hang on—"

"Please say you'll help me."

Maisy appraised the woman sitting across from her. Hadn't Sasha just said a juicy case would fall into her lap? She sipped her drink and popped another olive.

"I have some conditions."

"Sure," Deanne agreed instantly.

"How about you wait until you hear them? One, I'll dig into your ex-husband's death, but I'll follow where the evidence leads. No matter where it leads."

"Okay. Does that include your friend and her husband?"

Maisy raised an eyebrow at the pointed question. "I'm not going to pursue a theory that Leo and Sasha were involved in Landon's death because that'd be a waste of my time. But,"—she held up a hand to stave the objection she saw bubbling up—"if I turn up evidence that points to their involvement, I'll run it down. I'll pursue the truth, no matter where it leads."

Deanne nodded.

Maisy continued listing her conditions. "Two, you have to be completely honest and transparent with me. You can't hold anything back even if it's uncomfortable or embarrassing."

"Understood."

"Three, you don't talk to anybody else about this. If your ex's death wasn't suicide—if it was an accident or intentional or part of a coverup—there's someone out there who's gone to great lengths to make it look like suicide. Presumably, they wouldn't hesitate to go to the same lengths to keep us quiet. Do you understand?"

Deanne faltered. "I don't want to put you in danger …"

"I'm a big girl, and it's not my first time at the rodeo. But you have to understand the risks, too. Okay?"

She swallowed hard, and her chin jutted out. "When I was standing in front of that nativity scene, I broke down because I have an obligation to Landon's soul to make sure his death has meaning. This is the only way I can see to honor him. So, I'm in. Are there any other conditions?"

Maisy thought. She considered mentioning that she had made a personal enemy of the richest man on the planet. But while that little tidbit wasn't relevant to Deanne Lewis, it might make her reconsider forming an alliance.

"No, I think that's it. If you give me the key to Landon's office, I can take care of the rest of this stuff, so you don't have to do it. You can get back to your life and your counseling practice. We'll handle updates and questions by phone. Nothing in writing, though. No texts. No emails."

"You've got a deal."

They shook hands over the little table to make it official. Then Deanne opened her purse and took out her checkbook.

"How much do you want as a retainer?"

Maisy blinked at her. "You can't pay me."

"Why on earth not?"

"Because I'm an independent investigative journalist. Independent means I don't take your money or anyone else's."

Deanne tapped her pen on the checkbook cover. "That million dollars isn't gonna last long if that's your business model."

Maisy snorted. If she only knew. The million dollars was, at best, abstract, seeing as how it was not yet in her bank account. But she didn't waver.

Deanne sighed. "Have it your way. But you know, I'm happy to cover your expenses. I don't know what else I'm going to do with this fortune."

"What fortune?"

"Landon left everything to me. Including a hundred million dollars that was wired into his account the day he died."

"Hold up," Maisy shook her head and wondered just how generous Titus had been with the rum. "Did I hear you correctly? One hundred million dollars?"

"That's what I said," she confirmed.

"The day he died?"

"Yep."

"From whom?"

Deanne screwed up her face. "Now that I can't tell you. My financial people—because I apparently need financial people now—are working with lawyers and accountants in Switzerland and the Caymans to unravel the transfers. But they've only gotten so far. To date, they've tracked it to something called Thor Trust International."

"Thor, like the god?"

"Right. But you see, there's no way Landon would have killed himself at the exact moment he got rich beyond his imagination. He would have used the money to fix his stupid AI program or something."

Maisy stared at her numbly. "What was the money for?"

"Don't know that yet either. The financial people are doing an audit of his assets to see if maybe he invented another new technology or something, seeing as how Cesare turned out to be a dog."

Maisy was barely listening. "Your husband received a windfall the day he allegedly committed suicide."

"Yes."

"A one-hundred-million-dollar windfall."

"Still yes."

She let out a low whistle. "Do the police know?"

"No. As far as I know, nobody knows. Except for me, and now you. Oh, and Thor, I guess."

Maisy finished her drink. "Word to the wise? Definitely don't tell anybody else about the money."

"Who would I tell?"

She shrugged. "I have no idea. Also, just so you know, if you wanted to entice me to look into the case, you should have led with the money. That's the most compelling evidence so far that he didn't off himself."

"Maybe, but it's also the least important. If you'd known Landon, you'd understand."

"If you say so." She raised her glass. "To finding out what really happened."

"To the truth," Deanne replied, clinking her rim against Maisy's.

They finished their drinks, and Deanne got to her feet, not entirely steadily.

"Easy." Maisy hurried to loop an arm under the woman's elbow. "I'll take you home. Where's the apartment?"

"Just down the street. Kaufmann's Grand on Fifth."

"Nice." Maisy reached into her wallet and took out all the bills inside. "Stay," she instructed.

Deanne swayed but stayed.

Maisy found Titus cleaning the already-gleaming prep station. Unsurprisingly, he waved off the money. But he extracted a hug, a holiday greeting, and a promise that she'd be back soon.

Then she bundled Deanne into her coat and guided the woman through the basement, up the stairs, and out into the brisk early morning air.

The day was barely an hour old, but it was already, hands down, the strangest Christmas of Maisy's life.

CHAPTER FIFTEEN

December 25

MAISY HAD JUST DROPPED Deanne off at the departures curb when her cell phone rang. She glanced at the car's radio display. *Naya.*

She pressed the screen to pick up the call and pulled away from the curb as Deanne disappeared inside.

"Hey."

"Hey yourself. Merry Christmas!"

"Oh right, Merry Christmas to you and Carl."

"Are you driving?"

She glanced in her rearview mirror, saw not a single car, and merged onto the exit ramp. She couldn't remember the last time she'd been to the airport when there'd been no traffic. Deanne was right about the benefits of travel on the actual holidays. She filed that tidbit away for future reference, then answered Naya's question.

"Yeah. I just dropped a friend off at the airport."

"Back up," Naya ordered. "You dropped a *friend* at the airport?"

"Mmm-hmm."

"On Christmas morning?"

"My friend is Jewish. Not everyone celebrates Christmas, you know."

"Uh-huh. But you still do, right?"

"Well, yeah."

Naya's amusement oozed through the Bluetooth connection. "Did you just have a Christmas bootie call? A long-distance Christmas bootie call, no less? I can't decide if that puts you on the naughty list or the very nice list." She howled with laughter.

Maisy could hear Carl's deep rumbling laugh faintly in the background.

"Good grief, Naya. My friend is a girl. I mean, a woman."

The speaker went silent for a beat.

"Naya? Did I lose you?"

"No, I'm here. I'm sorry for giving you a hard time, Mais. I didn't realize you had a friend visiting. You could've brought her to brunch."

Maisy flushed. She was a terrible liar, but she could hardly admit that her friend was a total stranger she met at the nativity display and then took drinking. Let alone that she turned out to be Landon Lewis' ex-wife.

She scrambled for a response. "It was a last-minute thing. She just came in for a few days."

"Oh, well maybe we can meet her next time."

"Definitely," Maisy promised without basis. Then she squared her shoulders and plowed forward. "About brunch—"

"Uh-uh. No. Mac told me you came to dinner last night. She also told me about her wine-throwing and cussing. So if you lived through that, you're not begging off a perfectly civilized brunch with well-behaved adult humans."

Maisy knew that voice. It was Naya's brook-no-argument tone, guaranteed to strike fear in the hearts of associate lawyers and middle-aged men named Carl. But Maisy was made of tougher stuff.

She pulled her shoulders back and enunciated her words as she said, "I actually have my first case. I need to work."

Naya 'mmmed' low in her throat. Then, "This isn't an excuse, is it? You really have a case for your podcast?"

"I really do."

"That's fantastic!"

Maisy exhaled a sigh of relief. "Thanks."

"Can you tell me about it?"

"Not yet. But I'll send you the first episode when it's ready to load."

"You'd better."

"Hey, Naya, before I let you go ... would it be okay if I ask Jordana if she wants to work on the podcast with me? She knows a lot about editing, mixing, and producing."

Naya groaned.

"If it's going to cause problems, I won't ask her," she hurried to add.

"Oh, it's gonna cause problems all right, but you should ask her."

"Really?"

"Yeah, really. Jordana has no interest in going to law school, but you know Mac. She's gonna steamroll that poor child right into a legal career. You'll be doing the good Lord's work if you give her a graceful exit."

Maisy's stomach sank. "Okay. I'll … talk to Sasha."

"Woman, don't be a fool. You talk to Jordana and get her on board. I'll deal with Mac."

"Really?"

"Really," Naya said in a grim voice.

"Wow, thanks. I owe you."

"Nope. This is your Christmas gift this year. Enjoy it because it's priceless."

Maisy was still laughing when Carl grabbed the phone to wish her a happy holiday. After a few minutes of chatting, he handed it back to Naya.

"I have to go, Naya. I have some legwork to do before I record my first episode."

"Go, you. I'm happy for you, Maisy. And listen, don't worry about your money. Delone's gonna pay up. It's just gonna take some wrangling."

At the mention of the rotten billionaire who was

holding her payout hostage, Maisy's gut tightened. "How much is that gonna cost? In legal fees, I mean."

"Don't worry about it."

"Naya, no. You have to bill me. I—"

"You're breaking up. You must be going through the tunnel."

"I'm nowhere near a tunnel."

"Can't you hear you. Talk to you soon." Naya ended the call.

Maisy looked at her radio display in disbelief for a second and then laughed a loud, carefree laugh. She switched the music on to let the holiday standards wash over her in a warm wave of familiarity.

She hadn't been lying about the legwork. She had the file the police had given Deanne, the keys to Landon's office and apartment, and an entire day stretched out in front of her to get to work. She drummed her hands against the steering wheel in time with the music. First stop, Landon's apartment.

WALKING through a dead man's apartment, even an absurdly luxe, gorgeous apartment, was decidedly creepy. A little shiver ran along Maisy's spine, and her Aunt Alice's words rang in her head. "Someone just walked over your grave, darlin'."

Maisy took a moment to reflect upon what a morbid thing that was to say to a small child. At that moment, her cell phone rang in her hand, and Aunt Alice's face popped up on her screen. She squealed and nearly dropped the phone on Landon Lewis' foyer floor. A floor, which, if she wasn't mistaken, was made of exotic tiger wood. Evidently, being evil had paid well even before the Norse god of thunder bought Landon's soul for a cool hundred mill.

She shook her head at her musings, gripped her phone tighter, and answered the video call. "Hi, Aunt Alice! I was literally thinking about you when the phone rang."

"Well, isn't that somethin'? We're fixin' to sail off on our adventure, so we thought we'd call to wish you a Merry Christmas before we're out to sea."

Alice hit the button to turn her camera around, and Maisy saw her mom, decked out in a white linen dress and an oversized matching sunhat, and her dad, wearing a candy-cane striped bow tie and a bemused expression as if he didn't quite know how he came to be standing on the deck of this cruise ship. Her parents waved and called to her. She blew them a kiss.

The camera panned wildly. Either Aunt Alice had the worst photo skills in the family or the ship had already hit rough waters. A close-up of half of the face of a tall, tanned man confirmed it was the former.

"This is Jared," her aunt announced. "Say hello to my sweet magnolia, Maisy."

Jared obliged. "Merry Christmas, Maisy. Your aunt talks about you all the dang time. I'm looking forward to meeting you when you visit your parents in the new year."

Well played, Mom. Well played. The more people she told about Maisy's promise to come home, the more pressure there'd be on her to show up for once.

She smiled at poor hapless Jared, who was almost certain to have passed his expiration date by next month. "That'll be lovely."

Her aunt's face filled the screen again. "Where are you? That's not your townhouse."

Her mother trotted across the deck to peer at Maisy over Aunt Alice's shoulder.

For Pete's sake.

"I'm at a friend's place. Just checking on things."

"House sitting?" Her mom asked.

"Something like that."

"Mmm, well, it looks like your friend has a nice view. Take us on a tour."

She had to shut this down before it got further out of hand. "Now, listen, I need to work on my podcast. Y'all enjoy the send-off. Oooh, I think I see a waiter back there with a tray of mimosas!"

Her mother and aunt swiveled their heads in unison, the camera swooped, and she suddenly had a view of the deck floor.

"Bye, darlin'," her dad called as the video feed cut out.

Maisy stowed the phone in her bag and continued her walkthrough of the silent, eerie apartment.

For all its graceful lines, thoughtful details, and high-end touches, the place might as well have been a mid-priced hotel. There wasn't a single lick of personality in the entire home. Nothing that made it feel welcoming or lived in.

Was that by design? Did Landon Lewis present a bland, blank slate to the world so nobody would look twice at him? Or had his son's violent death sucked the life out of him? That latter was Deanne's theory, and Maisy could see how Landon's environment supported that view.

His couch was beige. His chairs were beige. His drapes were dove gray. As was the linen tablecloth that covered his dining table. She walked through the room to the kitchen. Each strike of her heeled boots echoed off the unadorned walls. She realized belatedly that she should have removed her footwear and propped one hand on the wall to take off first her right boot, then her left.

She continued on into the white-on-white kitchen, her boots dangling from one hand. The glass-fronted cabinets revealed stacks of white dishware. She scanned the room. There wasn't a spot of color in the blindingly bright white room. It was as if she'd stepped into the light in an inspirational made-for-TV movie.

She hurried out of the kitchen like someone was chasing her. She followed a short hallway to the back of the apartment. An open door revealed a bedroom had been converted into a home office. It wasn't warm and homey, but at least it was a reprieve from the constant onslaught of light neutrals. She stepped inside. A sleek black lacquered desk sat in the center of the room. Instead of facing the floor-to-ceiling window and the sweeping view of the city, the desk was positioned so that its user looked at the door.

She circled the room. A complicated-looking ergonomic chair was pushed under the desk. The desk itself was spotless. There was a laptop dock but no laptop. The device couldn't have been stowed in a desk drawer because Landon's desk didn't have a single drawer. She made a note to ask Deanne where Landon's laptop was. A pink-veined gray marble vessel that functioned as a pen cup held a pewter fountain pen and a matching letter opener. She reached for the pen and rolled the smooth barrel across her palm. A date was engraved on the pen: 03.11.90. The initials JLL were etched above the digits.

The matching letter opener bore the same inscription. She suspected the set commemorated the birth of Landon and Deanne's only child. She set both pieces on the gleaming black desk and snapped a picture with her cell phone so she could confirm her hypothesis with Deanne later, then she returned them to the marble cup. She put her hands behind her back and paced around that room at a deliberate speed, studying each item as if she were in an art gallery, not a spare bedroom/home office.

A floating shelf on the wall to the left of the door held a set of bronze horses that flanked a handful of leather-bound volumes. She tipped one of the books off the shelf and flipped it open. It was an early edition of Dante's *Divine Comedy,* translated into English. She returned it to its spot on the shelf and ran a finger lightly along the spines of the remaining books. *The Complete Sherlock Holmes,* Dostoevsky's *Crime and Punishment,* Kafka's *Metamorphosis,* and Camus' *The Stranger* rounded out Landon's sad and telling collection. A psychologist could have a field day with this material. All that was missing was Captain Ahab's maniacal quest for vengeance against a white whale.

She narrowed her eyes and peered closer at the bookend on the right side of the shelf. It was askew. She hadn't moved the horse, and she surmised from her tour of Landon's obsessively neat apartment that he would never have left the thing sitting crooked on the shelf. Maybe Deanne had been perusing her ex-husband's reading material.

She reached out to push the bookend into alignment, and a possibility struck her. She picked up the bookend instead, propping *The Stranger* against its neighboring title. She turned the bookend over and, sure enough, a keyhole was set into the base. She returned the horse to its spot and checked the other bookend. It, too, had a storage compartment concealed in its base with an identical keyhole. She pumped her fist at the discovery.

Alas, her triumph was short-lived. Unlike Jason, her boyfriend from sophomore year of high school, who hid his weed in a similar compartment in his bronze fish bookends, Landon had not made the rookie mistake of taping the key to the locked compartment to the bottom of the bookend. Maisy chuckled at the memory of Jason's amazement that his mother had discovered his contraband despite what he considered elite levels of concealment.

She scanned the office. Where would Landon hide the key? Aside from the desk, the chair, and the shelf that held the books, the room was empty. She ran her hand along the underside of the shelf and felt nothing. She repeated the gesture under the desk and came up empty there, too. She peered inside the marble pen cup. No dice. Or key, as the case may be.

"Think," she said aloud.

She perched on the edge of Landon's chair and thought. Assuming the bookends hid something more important than crumbly ditch weed, he would have put the key somewhere safe. And somewhere far from the locked compartments.

"His office," she announced to the empty room.

She nodded to herself. The theory felt right. She'd finish her sweep of the apartment and then head over to the Bakery Square office to test it.

She retrieved her boots from the floor beside the door and moved on to Landon's bedroom. A low platform bed, king-sized with a frame made of distressed wood, sat atop a cream-colored rug, which anchored the room. The walls were painted a soft gray, and the bedding was light blue with gray pinstripes. A snowy white comforter covered the sheets, and a pile of blue, cream, and white decorative pillows sat at attention against the headboard. An enormous framed black-and-white photograph of Alcatraz Island, shot while fog rolled in off the Pacific and enveloped the historic prison, hung on the wall above the bed. She cocked her head and studied the art Landon had selected to display in his bedroom.

"You were a weird dude," she declared to the dead man.

Her eyes fell on the nightstand to the right of Landon's bed, and she snorted. A leather-bound copy of *Moby-Dick* sat beside the reading lamp, a bookmark tassel dangling from within the book. She assumed the bedtime reading was a re-read of the classic and that Landon hadn't died without learning of the captain's tragic fate.

Like his desk, Landon's bedside table lacked drawers. Where the devil did this man stuff his junk if he didn't have any drawers?

The answer was obvious: he didn't have any junk. She eyed the book again and corrected herself. He didn't have any *material* junk. She was willing to wager that his psyche had been an overstuffed junk drawer bursting with revenge fantasies, remorse, and regret.

She walked into the attached bathroom. It was sparkling, tasteful, and devoid of anything of interest. A door behind the glass-enclosed oversized shower led to a walk-in closet. She entered the closet—more of a dressing room, really—and turned on the light.

She made a soft mewl of appreciation at the sight. It was gorgeous. The walls were lined with cedar wood, and a large, low dresser the size of a kitchen island sat in the middle. Next to the dresser, there was a leather bench for Landon to sit on when he put on his shoes, and one wall boasted a multilevel shoe rack that held multiple identical pairs of men's dress shoes and a lone pair of white sneakers.

She sank onto the padded bench and studied the clothes hanging from the rods that ran along three walls. Button-down shirts in a rainbow of hues that ranged from white to off-white hung, crisply starched, next to a row of black, navy, and charcoal gray suits. But most of the space was simply unused. His clothes took up, at most, a quarter of the available real estate. The tie rack was, if anything, even more uninspiring. She sighed, walked over to the dresser, and pulled open the drawers to reveal more monochromatic basics, tidy rolls of socks, checked boxer shorts, and neatly folded white undershirts.

Perhaps nothing depressed her more about Landon Lewis' drab existence than his criminal misuse of this jewel of a closet. She shook her head and left the space. How could she make Landon come alive for her podcast listeners when his soul had evidently shriveled up and died years before his physical death?

CHAPTER SIXTEEN

ZANE EYED JENNA over the sausage and egg casserole. She was unusually quiet.

His glance slid to her sister. Amber was babbling about the gift her latest loser boyfriend had given her. She lifted the chain from her neck to show off the heart-shaped charm.

"It's beautiful," Jenna told her without enthusiasm.

Zane drew his eyebrows together and studied his wife more closely. "Are you feeling okay?"

His concern (and an ardent desire for Amber to quit her yapping) made him talk right over the top of her. Amber pressed her lips together and gave him the stink-eye.

"I'm fine," Jenna told him in that same dull voice. "Just tired."

Zane knew her well enough to know that it was more than fatigue. Maybe the shots she gave herself in the butt were making her feel bad. They'd have to ask the fertility doctors about that.

He turned to her motormouth sister. "Did you see what Jenna gave me? A signed picture of Racin' Roscoe Davis. He even wrote a personal message." He gestured over his shoulder to the china cabinet, where the framed photo sat. "It's the best present I could imagine. And it was a complete surprise."

His enthusiasm about the gift managed to drag a real smile from Jenna. That was something, at least.

"Yeah, she was bursting with excitement to give it to you. She talked about it for, like, weeks. So what did you get her, Zane?"

Jenna answered before he could. "Really nice yarn. It's hand-dyed ombre. It's been on my wishlist forever. He got me two skeins."

"So she can knit her baby stuff," Zane added, feeling oddly defensive about the gift.

He frowned. Was she disappointed? The hard budget cap had been her idea. And that fancy yarn was really expensive. Once he paid for the shipping, he'd only had enough left for a candle and some body lotion from the pharmacy.

"Mmm. Yarn," Amber said, rubbing a finger over her necklace charm.

Zane curled his hands into fists beneath the table. Jenna pushed back her chair and stood. She gathered up the dirty breakfast dishes.

Once she was in the kitchen and out of earshot, Zane turned toward Amber. "Well, I guess it's time for you to go, huh? We'll see you at your mom's place for dinner. Don't let the door hit ya'."

She gaped at him. Their mutual dislike was no secret, but he was usually pretty polite to her—out of respect for Jenna. Sometimes, though, Amber was like a piece of steak stuck between his teeth. A constant irritant. The only way to get rid of the steak was to floss. The only way to get rid of Amber was to kick her out.

She glared at him and huffed off into the kitchen. Zane tipped his chair back and reached for the picture. Then he shifted his weight forward to let the front chair legs fall back to the floor with a thud. He grinned at the photo and the message for a few seconds then took a long pull on his breakfast beer. Jenna didn't stand for him drinking before noon. But she made an exception for Christmas.

He returned the photo to the china cabinet and drained his beer. Then he burped softly and made for the kitchen to get a second bottle and give his sister-in-law the bum's rush because she hadn't taken the hint yet.

As he reached the doorway, he swore he heard Jenna murmur something about an iPhone.

He paused and listened hard, straining to make out their low conversation. It was no use, they were whispering.

He told himself he must've misheard. Jenna didn't know about the iPhone. Nobody did.

He shook off the cold finger of worry that tried to crawl up his spine and walked into the kitchen.

AFTER AMBER LEFT, even more pissed-off than usual at Zane, Jenna finished cleaning up from breakfast. Zane wandered back into the kitchen while she was up to her elbows in soapy water to ask if she wanted to play cards.

She raised one hand, encased up to the elbow in a yellow rubber glove. "Sure, just let me finish washing these dishes first."

"You want me to dry?"

"I've got it. Why don't you go watch football until I'm done?"

He grabbed another beer from the fridge (his third, not that she was counting) and wrapped one arm around her waist. "You're the best, you know that?"

He leaned in to kiss the side of her neck and she willed herself not to stiffen.

"I know." She twisted around to face him and booped him on the nose with a sudsy finger, leaving a soap bubble in her wake.

They both laughed. He ambled out to the living room and turned on the television.

She hurried through the rest of the dishes and wiped down the counters and the stove. She knew it wouldn't take long for him to doze off in front of the pre-game show, and she was right. After a few minutes, she heard the unmistakable whistling buzz of his I'm-not-snoring snore.

She dried her hands on her jeans and tiptoed to the

doorway to confirm that he was asleep. He was. His head lolled back, and his mouth hung open.

She hurried to the basement door. Her pulse raced, and her heart thudded, but she had to know. She'd confided to Amber about the phone she'd found, the one Zane *didn't* give her for Christmas. Amber, whose reaction was the result of her own terrible luck with men and her long-running feud with Zane, immediately suspected an affair. She said Zane obviously had someone on the side, someone who'd given him the phone so they could arrange their trysts in secret.

Jenna had told her sister she was wrong, and Amber said there was an easy way to be sure. If Zane had gotten the phone for Jenna but had, for whatever reason, decided not to give it to her yet, it wouldn't be activated. If, on the other hand, he was sneaking around on her, it would be. "All you have to do is turn it on, and then you'll know," Amber had hissed.

Now, Jenna stood at the top of the basement stairs rationalizing what she was about to do. It wasn't like she was going to go through his messages, if he even had any. Turning on a phone just to see if it turned on wasn't an invasion of privacy. Not really. Besides, she wasn't trying to catch him fooling around, she was trying to *clear* him.

Fortified by her justifications, she hurried down the stairs before she could change her mind. She flew across the basement, shoved her arm behind the furnace, and yanked out the metal box. Her fingers trembled as she fumbled with the latch. She took a shaky breath and tried again.

The latch fell open, and she dug the phone out from the bottom of the pail. She tore off the rubber band and unfolded the paper. She stared down at the phone.

Her heart felt as if it had literally jumped into her throat even though that was a physical impossibility. She swallowed hard and braced herself. One way or the other, she'd know as soon as she pressed the power button.

Do it, she urged herself.

She shook her head. *No, you trust Zane. You don't need to do this.*

If that's true, why did he hide this from you? The cynical voice in her head sounded exactly like Amber's.

I don't know, but I am sure he'd have a logical explanation if I asked him.

Which you can't do, unless you want to admit to snooping, the Amber in her mind pointed out. *And you already snooped, so just finish it. Press the button.*

So she did.

She held her breath and stared at the display. Nothing. Then, an image of a battery with a little red line inside appeared in the middle of the screen. Beneath it, a little lightning bolt and a charger let her know the phone needed to be charged. After a few seconds, she laughed. The iPhone was completely dead. All this drama, and for nothing.

She rewrapped the device, placed it in the lunchbox, and returned the box to its hiding spot. She wiped her tears of relief away with the back of her hand and hurried back upstairs.

CHAPTER SEVENTEEN

MAISY TOOK the stairs to The Joshua Group's office suite. She didn't want to risk getting into the retro caged elevator with some tech employee who'd either chosen or been forced to work the holiday. Ordinarily, she loved finding herself in those situations that most people found annoying: a slow-moving line at the grocery store, a crowded elevator, or a waiting room. Any place that trapped strangers in close quarters was her favorite place. Because it was a truth about humanity that some folks sought out connection in those circumstances, and if there was one thing Maisy loved, it was making human connections. It didn't hurt that people had a habit of confiding in total strangers, provided they expected to never see them again.

But today, she didn't want to field any questions about her visit to Landon's office. So she climbed the stairs, humming under her breath.

When she exited onto the top floor, the hallway was deserted. She hurried to the door to Landon's space and dug out the key Deanne had given her. When she'd first seen it, she'd been surprised to learn that it was an actual key and not a programmed key card. Deanne explained the building management had deactivated Landon's card access after his death and returned it to keyed access until a new tenant took over. The police had asked for a copy of the key, and it was this copy Maisy now gripped in her right fist.

As she turned the key in the lock, the sound of the elevator car lurching to life came from below. She opened the door and rushed inside in case the elevator was destined for this floor.

Safely out of sight, she eased the door closed and re-engaged the lock with a soft click. Her heart raced, and adrenaline coursed through her.

Even though she was authorized to be here, she felt sneaky and subversive. She laughed at the image of herself as a cat burglar that popped into her mind, then looked down at her bright red coat and matching boots. She made a mental note to take a page from Landon's book and invest in a few outfits designed to make her blend in rather than stand out.

For now, she rested her bag on the credenza, peeled off her gloves, and unbuttoned her eye-catching coat. She hung it from the hook on the back of Landon's door and studied his clean, bright office.

The aesthetic echoed that of his home: it was tidy,

minimalistic, and devoted to efficiency rather than any desire to impress.

She walked over to the large casement windows. Before she looked outside, she paused to wonder which window had delivered Landon to his death. Then she looked down.

The view wasn't inspiring. It overlooked a parking lot, an abandoned factory, and the sketchy alley where Landon's body had been found. The windows were uncovered—a design choice that would have made more sense in his apartment or if he'd taken the corner office with a view of the public courtyard. She peered down into the parking lot, where she spotted her little hybrid sitting in a row reserved for electric cars. It was tucked in next to a metallic silver Tesla. She frowned. The Tesla hadn't been there when she'd parked. In fact, the lot had been deserted.

A knot of unease twisted in her belly, and she tried to shrug it off. It wouldn't be the strangest thing if a Tesla-driving overachiever decided to come into the office on the holiday to catch up on paperwork, reset a company's network, or maybe just escape an insufferable uncle.

She turned away from the window and resumed her survey of the office. Landon's style must have been growing on her because she was able to appreciate the elegant simplicity of his tidy workspace.

This office held another sleek desk. Like the one in Landon's home office, this one lacked drawers. This desk also didn't hold a laptop, but then, this one didn't have a laptop dock. There was a wireless cell phone charger (but, as expected, no phone) and another stylish cup that functioned as a pen holder. This one was made of wood—bamboo to match the flooring, with an inlaid jade rim. It held a pewter pen—identical to the fountain pen in the apartment—but no letter opener. She plucked the pen from the cup and examined it. Like the pen at Landon's apartment, this one was engraved with the initials JLL and a date. A different date, though: 10.13.07.

She tapped the pen against her index finger and considered the significance of the date. Just over fifteen years ago. She dropped the pen to the surface of the desk. Had Landon had a pen engraved with his son's date of death? It seemed morbid. If he wanted to bear witness to his son's time on earth, why not add the date to the original pen and letter opener set? And where was the letter opener?

It was possible, Maisy allowed, that Landon hadn't bought a second full set. But he didn't strike her as that sort of guy. No, he'd have duplicated the set. And if he'd lost or broken the letter opener, he'd have replaced it. She nodded, confident in her assessment of the dead man's personality.

She snapped a picture of the pen and returned it to the cup. To the left of the pen cup, a matching bamboo tray held a stack of ecru-colored linen notecards and matching envelopes. For a tech guy, Landon had been a fan of traditional writing implements, stationary, and books.

Was it a matter of personal preference or had Landon favored print because analog materials couldn't be hacked?

She pulled out her phone and dictated a voice note to that effect. Well aware of the irony, she laughed at herself. Well, she was an elder Millennial. It was to be expected.

But Landon was of a different generation. Still, she had an inkling his habit held meaning. Another question for Deanne.

She crossed the room to the long tiger maple credenza that stretched the length of one wall. At long last, she had drawers to rifle through. She pulled the top one open with a fizzy feeling of anticipation. But before she could dig into the files, the sound of a key jiggling in the lock in the hall made her draw up short. She eased the drawer shut silently, grateful that Landon had sprung for dovetail joints and soft-close drawer slides on what was clearly a handcrafted piece.

By the time the door swung open, she was standing on the far side of the room, her purse over her shoulder and the digits 9-1-1 keyed into her phone. Her finger hovered near the send key.

A woman swept into the room. When she spotted Maisy, she gasped and clutched the soft cashmere scarf tied artfully at her throat.

"My goodness, you startled me!" After the exclamation, she took a breath and smoothed a hand over her perfectly coiffed white-streaked hair.

"That makes two of us," Maisy told her.

The older woman frowned and gave Maisy a once-over. Maisy had the distinct feeling she'd been found lacking.

"You're not Ankan Chaudhary."

"No, I'm not," she agreed.

The woman waited. Maisy took in the violet Birkin bag, the styled hair, and the expertly applied makeup and connected the woman to the Tesla in the lot. Then she took a guess. "Are you the listing agent for this office?"

The woman blinked. "Yes, I am. Are you interested in leasing the space? I don't understand how you got in. I have an appointment to show the office to Dr. Chaudhary in twenty minutes, but it should have been locked up tight."

She sidestepped the question. "You scheduled a showing on Christmas Day?"

The realtor sighed. "Ordinarily, I wouldn't. Believe me. I have a house full of people out in Upper Saint Clair who I've had to leave in the hands of my darling husband and our youngest son. He's home from Wharton for the holidays." She delivered the non sequitur about her child's educational pedigree with a dollop of maternal pride.

Maisy smiled her encouragement, and the woman prattled on.

"But Dr. Chaudhary was insistent, and he's flying back to Michigan in the morning, so I sneaked out. I need to be back before the harpist arrives." She gave Maisy a frosty look that suggested she'd thrown a wrench in these carefully laid plans.

Then her eyes widened. "I know you. You're the reporter."

Her cover blown, Maisy stepped forward and extended her hand. "Maisy Farley. Guilty as charged."

"Oh, how rude of me. I'm Bella Steptoe." The real estate agent flashed a smile and pressed a business card into Maisy's palm with a sleight of hand that rivaled the best street magician.

Maisy glanced at the card and tucked it into her purse. "By the way, I love your bag."

Bella smiled warmly and patted her twenty-thousand-dollar Hermes bag. "Thank you."

"Business must be good," Maisy observed mildly.

Bella waved a be-ringed hand. "It's more of a hobby than anything."

"Most hobbies don't drag you away from your guests on Christmas," she countered.

"Well, that's true. This office suite is an unusual situation, though. The lease is up next week, and we haven't been able to show it because the previous occupant's estate hasn't ...." She trailed off and gave Maisy a horrified look. "You're not doing a story on the unfortunate demise of Mr. Lewis, are you?"

"Deanne Lewis is a friend. I offered to clean out the office for her. She gave me the key." Maisy dangled the proof of this statement from her finger.

"Oh, I see. That's kind of you to help her out. I suppose I should have called first. I assumed she wouldn't be in until Monday, at the earliest."

"It's no problem. I have some work to do, so when

your prospective tenant arrives, I'll be happy to camp out in a common space somewhere else in the building if you can direct me to one."

The evident relief on the woman's face seemed to have distracted her from the fact that Maisy hadn't directly answered her question about doing a story. Maisy allowed herself a small moment of triumph while Bella tried to decide where to stick her.

"Well, now, let me see. Most of the office suites have their own meeting spaces, but Mr. Lewis gave up all his space except for this one office after … the controversy."

"Would that be when the Department of Justice shut down his company?"

"I don't know the details," Bella answered primly. "But he let all the employees go and emptied out the factory space. The building owner re-let all The Joshua Group's other offices at a higher price point, so Mr. Lewis was able to renegotiate his rent with no penalty. It was a good result for everyone."

"Well, everyone except Landon Lewis."

Bella sniffed but didn't otherwise respond. Instead, she changed the subject. "There is one room you could use while I show the space."

"Oh?"

"Yes, the building owner isn't local, so he reserves a small office on the first floor for his representatives when they travel into town for meetings or other business."

"That sounds perfect," Maisy told her. "Who owns the building?"

Bella's eyes narrowed to slits. "That information isn't public record," she said stiffly.

Maisy wrinkled her brow at the odd response. "Sure it is. I could go look up the tax records and find it."

"You could, but the ownership group owns the building through a trust, so ... good luck with that."

Maisy hid a smile. Bella didn't need to know that Naya had taught her the rudimentariness of tracing and untangling corporate entities.

She nodded toward the door. "If you don't mind, I'd like to keep working until Dr. Chaudhary arrives. I might even finish up before he gets here. It seems Mr. Lewis was something of a minimalist."

"That's an understatement. Oh, what does Mrs. Lewis want to do about the furniture? They're exquisite pieces. I could see if the new tenant—Dr. Chaudhary or whoever ends up in the space—is interested in purchasing them. For a small finder's fee, of course."

"Of course. I'm sure that would be Deanne's first preference."

"Great. So, don't let me stop you." She gestured for Maisy to continue whatever she'd been doing.

Maisy'd sooner try to saddle a chicken than go through Lewis' files in front of this woman. She smiled her sweetest smile. "I don't suppose Landon had a supply room? I confess I didn't think to bring a box. Can you believe it?" She rolled her eyes at her own silliness.

Bella gave her an unamused look that suggested no, she couldn't believe it. After a moment, though, she jerked her chin toward the door.

"There's a supply closet just outside. It's the door to the immediate right. The same key should work."

Maisy had planned to ask Bella to grab the boxes for her, so she could peek inside those files without an audience. But on closer consideration, she had to admit that she doubted Bella Steptoe fetched anything for anyone. Having backed herself into a corner, all she could do was follow through. So, she headed out the door.

She covered the short distance to the closet in under a minute. As advertised, the key Deanne had given her fit in the lock. She opened the door, flicked on the light, and stepped inside.

CHAPTER EIGHTEEN

TIM WAS HALF-WATCHING the kids build a tower with the magnetic tiles his parents had gotten them and half-watching the football game. The smell of turkey wafted in from the kitchen where his mom, aunts, and sister were gabbing and cooking, and his stomach growled in anticipation. He snagged a cookie from the tray on the coffee table to tide him over.

"When do you have to take them back?" His cousin asked, jerking his chin toward the kids.

"Custody agreement says five PM, but Marlena and her fiancé are taking them to Disney for the week off from school, so I said I'd get them back early. That's why dinner's at two."

Nolan made a sound of disgust. "That's not right, cutting into your time like that."

Tim shrugged. The reality was, this was his year to

have the kids over the winter break. But unlike Marlena's new man, he didn't have a job that would let him take a full week's vacation whenever he pleased and his paycheck sure as heck didn't cover a trip to Disney. So if he'd told her no, he'd end up having to dump the kids on his mom all week. And they'd drive her nuts whining that they were bored. Not that he'd blame them: Disney or magnetic tiles? It wasn't much of a decision.

And, the truth was, Tim liked his kids in small doses. Dinner. A trip to Kennywood. A movie. Fun, time-bounded activities—that's where he shined as a dad. Bedtimes, brushing teeth, homework, doctor's appointments—Marlena was better at that stuff. She had the patience for it.

All he said, though, was, "We agreed to co-parent with the kids' best interests in mind." He silently congratulated himself for managing to get out the word 'co-parent' without gagging.

Nolan nodded. "You're a bigger man than I am."

Tim smiled and reached for another cookie. Just then, his mobile vibrated on the table. He grabbed it instead of the coconut layer bar.

"Colchis."

"Detective, we have a problem." That Martha Stewart wannabe's voice was clear and demanding.

Tim's gut clenched. He stalked out of the room and into the front hallway. He hissed in a dangerous whisper, "What are you doing calling me on my work phone? On Christmas Day, no less?"

"You're the detective. Why don't you venture a guess? Why *would* I violate our agreed communications protocol? Especially on a holiday meant to be spent with family?" She asked coolly.

The answer that sprang to mind was sure to offend. So rather than say it was because she was a crusty bitch, he wrangled control of his temper, tramped out onto the porch, and pulled the door closed behind him with more force than was strictly necessary.

"I assume something urgent has come up. But I don't know what that could be. I did what you wanted." He stomped his feet to keep his circulation up and lowered his head against the cutting wind.

"You intercepted Deanne Lewis at the station?"

"Yeah. Just like you said, she was there meeting with Bass and Evans. I waited for her to come out. Then I went around the corner and bumped into her accidentally on purpose."

"And?"

"And she was already on board with her ex's death being a suicide, but I reinforced the idea, anyway. You do know this is stupid, right? Everyone accepted the suicide angle. The more your employer mucks around pulling strings, the more attention it brings to the case. Ever hear the saying let sleeping dogs lie?"

She ignored most of his rant, zeroing in on one statement. "But does everyone accept the suicide angle? Are you sure?"

He blew out a frustrated breath. "As far as I know

they do. Quit beating around the bush already and say what you have to say."

He knew it was a mistake to show this woman—and by extension her, no, *their,* mystery employer—disrespect. But she'd crossed a line calling him like this, and he wanted to make sure she knew it.

"Mister Colchis," she gritted out as if her teeth were clenched together, "I assure you I'm no happier about this development than you are. But Maisy Farley is snooping around Landon Lewis' office as we speak."

"Maisy Farley?"

"The washed-up news anchor."

"I know who she is. How do you know she's at the office?"

"Because *I'm* at the office. I got a call from a doctor who's interested in renting the space, but he can only meet today. So I drove in. And ran into Ms. Farley, who was already inside when I arrived."

"How'd she get in?"

"She claims to be friends with Deanne Lewis and says she volunteered to clear out Landon's office. She has a key."

It sounded plausible to him. "So? The ex-wife was pretty broken up after she had her meeting at the station and took possession of Lewis' personal effects. Her eyes were all puffy and red. She'd clearly been crying. Listen, I've been divorced for three years, and there's no love lost between me and Marlena. But if she did a header off a building, it would affect me. You know?"

"Leaving aside your dysfunctional relationship and

your insights into the human psyche, the fact that a woman who fancies herself an investigative journalist is poking around is a problem. Especially because our employer has preexisting issues with her."

"That sounds like an ish-you, not an ish-me. Just let her poke. There's nothing to find, right?"

The line went silent while she considered this. He knew he had a point. Her people had been through Landon Lewis' apartment and office with a fine-toothed comb after his death, and they hadn't found a thing.

"What if she stumbles across the missing laptop?"

"How?" he countered. "We looked everywhere. I told you, he probably stashed it in a safe deposit box or an actual safe somewhere. He was paranoid."

"You're certain that your subcontractor didn't take it to pawn?"

Not this bullcrap again. "For the thousandth time, I have Novak on a leash. He didn't steal that MacBook, and he disposed of the freaking phone. You need to let this fever dream die."

"Keep a civil tongue in your mouth when you speak to me, detective. And you should pray that your confidence is warranted. Because if Maisy Farley is investigating Mr. Lewis' death and she finds anything, it'll be on your head. Are we clear?" Her voice was shot through with white-hot anger.

"Crystal."

"Good. I'm getting another call."

She hung up before he could say another word, which was fine by him. He put the phone on Do Not

Disturb mode and went back into the house to enjoy the rest of the afternoon with his kids.

AS MAISY RUMMAGED through Landon's tidy stacks of office supplies, she could hear Bella giving someone what for. She hadn't heard the doctor arrive, so the realtor must be reading the riot act over the phone. Maybe her harpist was running late. She snickered to herself as she tried to imagine employing live musicians for family gatherings, but her imagination fell short. It was another question for Deanne. After all, she was the newly minted multi-millionaire. Maybe she had a cellist on speed dial.

She was still laughing at her own wit when she heard her name through the wall. Or thought she did. She hurried over to the wall the supply closet shared with the office and pressed her ear against the exposed brick. She didn't bother to try to be quiet about it because Bella knew she was in here. She was the one who sent her here, after all.

Bella's agitated tone was muffled, and Maisy sighed. This was fruitless. The realtor was probably just complaining that someone had been in the office when she'd arrived. She turned back to the task at hand: searching for cardboard boxes she could use to cart away Landon's files. In addition to the files, she'd take the phone charger, his pen cup, and the stationary set. She'd tell Bella to have Dr. Chaudhary (or whoever ended up leasing the office) make an offer on the rest of the stuff.

On the bottom shelf, she found three sturdy empty boxes. They were the kind that office supply stores used to ship cases of printer paper. Score. Then she frowned. She hadn't seen a printer in Landon's office. And there wasn't one at his apartment, either. How did a guy with no printer go through twelve thousand sheets of printer paper?

Her list of questions for Deanne was getting long. She checked the time. Deanne's flight would be on the ground in less than two hours. Maisy would get the files, take them back to Landon's place, and go through them until she could talk to Deanne. She grabbed the boxes. They were light but awkward to carry. She balanced two on one hip, and one on the other and tottered toward the door.

The flaw in her plan was revealed when she reached the door and was unable to open it. Shaking her head at herself, she let one box fall to the floor and pulled the door open. Then she kicked the box into the hall and tossed the other two out beside it. She reached for the light switch without looking, and her hand grazed the edge of the metal storage shelf. Something hit the bare floor with a clink. She turned to see what she'd knocked down and bent to pick up a small key ring that held a single key. She turned back to the shelving unit. The wire shelves were affixed to the end posts in such a way that each shelf's wire extended just beyond the post and was covered with a rubber tip. She hung the ring from one of the tips. It dangled but stayed.

She moved to hit the lights, then froze for a second before reaching back to snatch the key ring from the shelf. She studied it more closely, and her heart rate ticked up. Unless she was mistaken—and she knew she wasn't—this little key would grant her access to the hidden compartments in the base of Landon's bookends. She slipped it into her pocket and hurried out into the hallway.

She picked up two of the boxes and kicked the third along the hall. As she reached the door to Landon's office, it opened, and the realtor walked out. She spotted Maisy and held the door open for her.

"Oh, there you are. I just got a text from Dr. Chaudhary. It seems he's not going to be able to come to tour the space today after all. So, it's all yours."

"Thanks. It's too bad you had to leave your party for nothing, though."

Bella sighed heavily, then she brightened. "At least I won't miss the harpist."

Maisy smiled as she kicked the box through the open door. "Always find the silver lining, that's what my mama would say. Enjoy your party."

Bella nodded and began to walk away.

Maisy called after her, "What should I do with the key when I'm done?"

"Just leave it on the desk."

"Thanks, Bella."

The woman was already halfway to the elevator, but

she turned and acknowledged Maisy with a little wave. Maisy watched her enter the elevator car and waited until it had begun its descent. Then she raced into the office, yanked open the credenza, and started tossing files into boxes. The faster she finished up here, the sooner she could see what Landon had hidden in his bronze horses.

CHAPTER NINETEEN

MAISY HAULED the boxes back to Landon's apartment and surveyed the place with her hands fisted on her hips. She liked to spread out when she was working, so she decided to use the living room floor. She grabbed a soft throw blanket from the back of his couch and draped it over her lap, opened her notebook, and removed the lid from the first box.

Despite her eagerness to see what was hiding in Landon's bookends, she decided to wait. She'd called Jordana from the car to talk about the podcast idea. The teenager was plainly regretting her decision to spend her weekend alone in her apartment instead of with her family in Maryland, so Maisy told her to come over. She'd open the bookends after Jordana arrived—the younger woman would either be part of the excitement or bear witness to her very own Geraldo opening Al Capone's vault moment. Her laughter at the most infamous moment in non-news died in her throat when she realized it had happened at least eighteen or twenty years before the intern had been born.

She was halfway through the second box when the building's concierge called up from the lobby to announce she had a visitor. She marked her spot in the file with her pen and hurried over to unlock the door for Jordana.

"I hope you're hungry," the girl said as she walked through the doorway with a large white bag.

Maisy inhaled. "You picked up Chinese food? I'm surprised you found an open restaurant."

"It's the traditional Christmas dinner for most Jews," Jordana told her. "Chinese restaurants are always open on the Christian holidays. I didn't know what you'd want, so I got ... a lot."

Maisy's stomach rumbled in appreciation. "It smells great, and I don't think I remembered to eat today, so let's dig in."

She took the bag of food from Jordana's arms and led her into the sparkling kitchen.

Jordana turned in a slow half-circle. "I've always wondered what these apartments were like inside. This place looks like a hotel."

"That's probably a function of Landon's decorating sensibilities," Maisy said.

Jordana shrugged out of her heavy backpack and slung it over the back of a chair. "I can't believe you ran into his ex-wife at the crèche display. That's *wild*. You never met him, did you?"

"Landon? No." Maisy shook her head.

"He was a quirky dude."

"That seems about right based on what I've learned." She pulled two plates down from Landon's cabinets and placed them on the island. "I'll fill you in while we eat."

They piled the food onto their plates, each taking small portions of all the various dishes (which Jordana noted was effectively a DIY dim sum experience), and carried the plates to the dining room.

Maisy returned to the kitchen to get drinks. "How does mineral water sound?" she called to Jordana after checking Landon's mostly bare fridge.

"Great."

"I'm so glad you thought to pick up food," Maisy said before grasping a dumpling between her chopsticks. "I'm famished."

Jordana nodded. "It's a habit. When Sasha's working through something complicated, sometimes she forgets to eat, too. I always make sure to bring her a sandwich or something."

"Mmm, smart. She's terrifying when she's hangry." Maisy winked, and Jordana snickered.

The gentle jab seemed like a natural lead-in to a more serious discussion about the young woman's future. "You've worked at the law firm for a long time. What's it been? Five or six years now?"

"Almost seven. I was just about to turn thirteen when I spray-painted Sasha and Leo's fence."

She laughed ruefully at her younger self's act of

vandalism, and Maisy remembered what an angry, hurt teen Jordana'd been back then.

"Right, because Sasha and Leo bought your childhood home after your folks divorced."

"I know it wasn't their fault. My parents couldn't afford to keep it. I mean, I understood that even then. I was lashing out."

"You were hurt and confused. And you were being pummeled from the inside by an onslaught of hormones at the same time that your external world was falling apart."

Jordana blinked rapidly a few times as if she was holding back tears, then she looked directly at Maisy. Maisy was impressed. She'd have been even more impressed if she didn't know the five-foot-nothing queen who'd taught them both that trick.

"Yeah. That's basically what Sasha said when it happened. So she waddled her enormously pregnant self over to my mom's apartment and cooked up a plan to have me 'work' at the law firm until I earned enough to cover the cost of repainting. After that, she asked me if I wanted to keep working as an intern to earn some pocket money." She paused to take a bite of her pork. "The first couple of years, I didn't do much. Mainly made copies and ran down to Jake's to get people coffee and snacks."

Maisy considered the self-possessed young woman sitting across the table from her. "Seems like you do quite a bit more than that these days. Everyone raves about you and your work—Will, Caroline, Naya, and, most of all, Sasha."

Instead of reacting with pleasure or even embarrassment at the compliment, Jordana grimaced. She rested her chopsticks on the edge of her plate and sighed. "It's a really great place to work. Nobody in my classes gets to do the kind of stuff I do. They trust me with actual client work. I mean, it's amazing."

"I'll bet."

Jordana sipped her water. "They pay me really well, they accommodate my class schedule ..." her voice dropped, then broke. "Seriously, they're great. And, they're my friends, you know? I babysit their kids. Sasha was the first person I called when I got arrested at that protest. But ..."

"But you don't want to be a lawyer," Maisy said softly.

Jordana's eyes widened with worry. "They don't know," she hurried to explain.

"They know."

"Not Sasha."

Maisy kept her voice gentle. "Sasha sees a lot of promise in you, kid. It might be blinding her to what's obvious to everyone else. But, I think in her heart, she must know. And I'm confident she'd be the first one to tell you the law will eat you alive if you don't really love it. She wouldn't want you to be miserable."

"I can't disappoint her, though. She took a chance on me." She lowered her gaze and twisted her hands in a worried knot.

"Well, I have a proposal for you."

Jordana eyed her from under her lowered lashes. "What is it?"

"Deanne Lewis wants me to look into Landon's death. She thinks—and I agree—that extenuating circumstances make the suicide look fishy. But as you're well aware, I don't know the first thing about podcasting. I need—"

"An intern."

"No, not an intern. A producer," she corrected.

Jordana's eyes were salad plates, or at least saucers. "Are you being serious? I'm still in school."

"So? It's not like there's a degree in podcasting. Oh, mercy, is there? Is that a thing now?"

She laughed. "I'm a Communications major. My concentration's in journalism with an emphasis in digital media. So while there's no podcasting degree, there are relevant elective classes. I've taken almost all of them."

"Are there electives in social media and influencers, or whatever they are?" Maisy felt positively prehistoric, but she had to know.

Jordana eyed her carefully. "Do you really want me to answer that?"

"Nope. Forget I asked."

They both laughed.

Then Jordana asked in a tentative voice, "Could you work around my class schedule? And I'd have to give Sasha plenty of notice."

"First, yes. I'm told podcasting is a very flexible gig, so it wouldn't interfere with school. And second, if you want to come work with me, Naya will take the bullet for you."

"Um ... what?"

"She'll break the news to Sasha."

Maisy expected to see relief break across Jordana's face. Heck, *she*, a full-grown adult who'd taken on a whole entire news station, had nearly wept with relief when Naya told her she didn't have to face Sasha. But Jordana didn't exhale loudly or smile. Instead, she jutted her chin out and leveled her gaze. "No. I'll tell her. It's only right."

And that reaction, that moment, crystalized everything Maisy thought she knew about Jordana Morgan.

"However you want to handle it."

"I'm going to have to tell my Bubbie. Telling Sasha will be *nothing* compared to that conversation."

Maisy laughed and extended her hand over the sesame chicken. "So, do you want to come on board as my producer?"

Jordana eyed Maisy's outstretched hand, then bit her lip. "Um, so, you were telling Sasha and Naya that you're broke. Does that mean ...? I mean ...." She took a breath and tried again. "Are you gonna be able to pay me?"

Maisy smothered her amusement with a cough. "I may have been exaggerating about my financial situation a bit. I'll pay you whatever the law firm is paying you hourly, to start. But even if you work less in the beginning, I'll pay you a guaranteed minimum number of hours so you'll make at least what you're making now at the firm. Then, once Sasha and Naya shake my million out of Leith Delone's pocket, we'll work out a salary and benefits and all that stuff. How's that sound?"

Jordana pushed out her lip and nodded. "Yeah, that's fair." She pumped Maisy's hand.

"Welcome aboard," Maisy told her.

Jordana grinned. Then she cocked her head. "So is this a business dinner?"

"I suppose it is. Why?"

"Can I submit the receipt for reimbursement?"

Maisy cringed at her own cluelessness. How could she have forgotten what it was like to be a broke college student? She hadn't even offered to pay the kid for picking up the food.

"Oh, I'm so sorry, sugar. I wasn't thinking. How much was it?" She popped to her feet, ran into the living room, and grabbed her purse. As she was digging through it for her wallet, her phone rang.

Deanne Lewis.

"It's Deanne returning my call," she shouted as she scrabbled for her notebook and her list of questions.

"Put her on speaker," Jordana called as she came skidding into the room.

The Chinese food sat, forgotten and congealing, in the dining room. As Jordana was about to learn, the law wasn't the only jealous mistress. The news business gave the law a run for her money.

CHAPTER TWENTY

ZANE WOKE up at the end of the first quarter and rubbed his eyes. Jenna was sitting in the rocking chair in the corner of the living room knitting. He stretched, scratched his belly, and leaned forward to look at her. He was bleary-eyed, but she didn't comment on that.

"You using your new yarn?"

She shook her head. "No, I'm finishing up the scarf for my mom. I just have to bind off this edge and put it in a gift bag. Then we can go."

He eyed the TV screen. "Can we wait until half-time?"

"Tell you what, I'll head over in the car when I'm done here. You can watch as much of the game as you want and then walk over. Just don't think she'll hold dinner for you if you're late, 'cause she won't."

He frowned. "Walk over? It's snowing."

"It's only four blocks. Besides, the cold air will clear

your head and sober you up some, which wouldn't be the worst idea."

He bobbed his head back and forth, considering what she'd said. "True. Plus, it'll give your sister less time to poke at me."

She smiled frostily. At least that's how the smile felt on her lips—brittle and insincere. She took a breath and tried again, reminding herself that she loved her husband and she couldn't let the phone in the basement mess with her head. She cast off, cut the tail of her yarn, and then wove it into her final stitch. She held the scarf at arm's length to examine it. Mom would love it.

Then she crossed the room and dropped a kiss on Zane's head. "Please don't fight with Amber anymore today." Before he could start squawking about how Amber antagonized him, she covered his lips with her finger and gave him a serious look. "Please. As a favor to me."

He relented instantly. "Okay, but for you. Not for her." He interlaced his fingers through hers and pulled her onto his lap for a beery kiss.

After a moment, she pulled away. "Thanks, babe." She retrieved the gift bag that Zane had used for the yarn from beneath the tree, then wrapped the scarf in a sheet of colored tissue paper and slid it into the bag. By now, Zane's attention was already back on the action on the gridiron.

She touched up her lipstick in the mirror over the mantle and grabbed the casserole dish from the kitchen counter and the keys from the hook by the door. Then she shrugged into her winter coat.

"See you in a bit," she called as she stepped out onto the front stoop.

"Don't forget to let the car warm up before you pull out," he called. "And be careful."

"I won't, and I will," she responded, and then pulled the door closed behind her.

Seven minutes later, after letting the car warm up as Zane had requested, she pulled into the alley behind her childhood home. Amber's car was already parked on the concrete pad behind the small backyard. She squeezed in perpendicular to Amber's Honda and parked on the grass.

When she banged through the kitchen door, Amber pounced on her before she had a chance to take off her coat.

"Well? Was it activated?" she breathed.

Jenna thrust the green bean casserole into her sister's hands and ignored the question. "Put this on the counter for me, would you?"

She wriggled out of her coat and slung it over her arm.

"Jenna, come on. Did you do it?"

"Would you relax? Just give me a second to hang my coat up and say hi to everyone. I'll be right back."

Amber's eyes bugged out as if they might pop, and Jenna gave her a 'get a grip' look. Then she walked through the house to the den and greeted her mom and aunts. She looked around for all the men and anyone under the age of thirty.

"Where's everyone else?" she asked after dropping a kiss on her mom's cheek.

"In the basement watching the game. Where else? Isn't Zane coming?"

"He'll be over in a bit. I brought that casserole you like. You need any help in the kitchen?"

Her mother waved a hand toward the back of the house. "It's under control, but your sister's been pacing around the kitchen like she's waiting for a bomb to go off."

In a way, she was.

Jenna made her way back to the kitchen, where Amber was waiting with two generous glasses of Prosecco.

"I shouldn't ..."

Amber pushed the glass into her hand. "I thought they said you shouldn't drink after day fourteen of your cycle. Not never."

Jenna had to smile. Amber's own personal life was an unmitigated hot mess, but she was the quintessential protective older sister. She'd been Jenna's rock through the fertility journey and had even helped her inject the intramuscular shots into her buttocks after Zane passed out the first time. Of course, Amber hadn't passed up the chance to poke fun at the tough boxer fainting at the sight of a needle. But, still. She was Jenna's best friend.

"Cheers." Jenna raised her glass toward Amber and then took a fizzy sip.

Amber followed suit. After a moment, she said, "Well?"

Jenna took another swallow of the crisp cold Prosecco before answering. "The battery's dead. Like completely. But to tell the truth, I'm glad. Really, I am. I trust Zane; I don't need to check on him." She laughed shakily.

Amber didn't hear her. She was already in the dining room, rummaging through the corner china cabinet. Jenna and her glass trailed her into the room.

"What are you looking for?"

Amber ignored her, digging through the pile of old electronics that their mom had stowed in the bottom of the hutch.

Jenna looked over her sister's shoulder. "What even is all this stuff?"

"Mostly old cell phones that she doesn't know what to do with. Some of these are so outdated, the recycling places won't even take them."

"The women's shelter will. They'll clean them and then give them to residents so they can make emergency calls. You know, in case their partners violate the restraining orders. You should give them to Aunt Tina. She can take them in the next time she volunteers."

"That's a good idea," Amber said from within the depths of the cabinet. Her voice was muffled.

"But seriously, what are—?"

The question died on Jenna's lips when Amber tossed an old iPad charger over her shoulder.

"Take it. Even if you don't need to satisfy your

curiosity, you need to satisfy mine." She paused. "Or I could just ask Zane why he has a fancy new iPhone in a box in your basement."

Jenna grabbed the charger from the floor and stuffed it into her pocket. "Keep your voice down."

CHAPTER TWENTY-ONE

SWITCHING to a video call with Deanne was Jordana's idea, and it was a good one. Maisy told the tired traveler they'd call her back as soon as they got the computer set up. Then Maisy watched as the college student pulled a jumble of wires, chargers, and USB thingies (to use a technical term) from her backpack and pushed the food containers to one side.

"What should I do?"

Jordana didn't look up from connecting all the peripherals to the laptop. "Just give me a sec."

So Maisy busied herself with taking dishes out to the kitchen and loading Landon's dishwasher. She was searching through the drawers built into the counter for containers to store the leftovers in when Jordana called her back into the dining room. She walked in to see Deanne waving to her.

"Long time, no see," Maisy said.

Deanne yawned. "I was just telling your friend or your tech guru or whatever she is that I am about ten minutes away face planting."

"Cross-country flights are brutal," Maisy commiserated.

Deanne raised an eyebrow. "The hangover didn't help."

They shared a laugh at that, then Maisy said, "Let me introduce Jordana properly, and then I promise to keep this short so you can crash. Jordana Morgan is getting her communications degree at Chatham College and has just come on board as my podcast producer."

"Hi, Ms. Lewis," Jordana said. "My degree will be a Bachelor of Arts in Communications, but my concentration's in journalism. I have a particular interest in digital media."

Deanne smiled. "If Maisy offered you a job, I'm sure you're well qualified." She leaned forward and squinted at the screen. "Oh, you're at the apartment."

"I brought the files from his office back here. I'll explain why in a second," Maisy started.

"I don't care. You can camp out there all week if you want to. The rent's paid through the end of the year. Actually, that's not even right. I had a text from the leasing office when I landed. Apparently, when he paid for twelve months there, he got one month free as part of a promotion. So, while I need to get everything out of the office this coming week, you can use the apartment until the end of January."

"That's helpful. I ran into the realtor for the office

building. She's pretty eager to get his space rented out again. She offered to try to sell the furniture to the next tenant. I assume you want her to, right?"

Deanne threw her head back. "Yes, please," she moaned. "One less thing for me to deal with."

"Great. So, before we start, I have a random question. Does Landon have storage containers? You know, for leftovers? Jordana brought dinner." She gestured toward the takeout boxes.

"I doubt it. Landon didn't cook. As far as I know, he existed on protein bars and regret. What is that—Chinese carryout? What are you doing working on the seventh night of Hanukkah, young lady?" Deanne asked in mock disbelief.

"Told ya it's the traditional Jewish Christmas dinner," Jordana cracked to Maisy. Then, to the screen, "My family's at my grandma's place in Maryland. I was bored, and Maisy said she found something interesting at the office. So here I am."

Maisy gave the budding journalist an approving smile for the deft way she brought the conversation back to its point. She was about to launch into a summary of the day, when Deanne snapped her fingers.

"And wine."

"Pardon?"

"Protein bars, regret, and wine. The good stuff. You know that closet in the corner of the kitchen?"

"The pantry?"

"It was a pantry, but he retrofitted it for temperature-controlled wine storage. Help yourself to whatever you like because I'm not paying to have all those bottles shipped out here. I don't want them."

"Noted, and thanks."

She glanced down at her notes, then Jordana raised her hand to stop her from diving in.

"Before we start, do you mind if we record this?" she asked Deanne.

"No, go ahead."

"Well...," Maisy hesitated. "I don't think that's necessary. This isn't an interview. I'm gathering background."

Jordana gave her a pained look out of Deanne's view.

Maisy twitched her lips to the side and caught herself. "But Jordana's the producer, so I defer to her."

'Thank you,' Jordana mouthed. She hit a button on the screen, and a message popped up to notify them that the session was being recorded.

Maisy reminded herself to ignore the recording light and focus on connecting with the widow. "After I dropped you at the airport, I came here—to the apartment—to get a better sense of the man."

"And?" Deanne's curiosity was genuine.

"And everything is very precise, orderly, and impeccably clean. But I can't say his living space gave me any insights into your ex-husband."

Deanne laughed dryly. "To the contrary, you nailed him—precise, orderly, and impeccable. That was Landon in a nutshell."

"But he wasn't *always* like that, was he? What was he like when your son was alive?"

Deanne's expression softened. "No, Landon was

always brilliant and driven. But when Josh came along, he was also committed to being a good father. He was patient and gentle with Josh. And, to my surprise, Landon had a decent sense of humor and playfulness. I'd never seen that side of him until we had Josh."

Maisy smiled. "Tell me a playful story."

"Oh, let's see. When Josh was seven or so, he was obsessed with pirates—buried treasure, sailing the seas, the whole bit. One long weekend, Landon put together a treasure hunt for the family. He made a hand-drawn map and scattered clues around our house and backyard. It took us the full first day to find the key, and most of the next one to find and unearth the treasure chest. Later, he told me, he buried it in the middle of the night when I was sleeping. He was out there for over an hour with a work light and a shovel! I know you never met him, but it was impossible to picture him doing that."

"I've seen his closet," Maisy offered. "I find the image mind-boggling."

"I actually did—meet him," Jordana interjected.

Deanne cocked her head. "You did?"

"Yeah. Well, the first time I *saw* him was the night I got arrested at the protest over the killing of Vaughn Tabor."

Deanne's smile faded. "That boy in Milltown?"

"Yeah. My boss at the time—well, she's a friend, too. And a lawyer, so she came to the station to get me. He was walking in when we were walking out. It was the middle of the night, and he was dressed—"

"Let me guess. To the nines, in a suit and tie, the whole works?"

"Exactly."

"That was Landon. I used to joke that he'd probably worn a little suit and tie for Halloween growing up, but his mother, rest her soul, told me that he actually had. Which is why the effect Josh had on him was so special. Landon was never going to be relaxed or easygoing, but Josh did loosen him up."

"Where did he hide the key?" Maisy asked.

"What?"

"The key. To the treasure chest."

"Oh, ha. It was in the freezer." She laughed.

Jordana cleared her throat. "In the interest of full disclosure, I also worked on the case against the Milltown prosecutor's office as a legal intern. So I talked to your ex-husband several times about his testimony."

"Wait. Back up. You worked with Sasha McCandless-Connelly? The woman whose husband was the last person to see Landon alive?" Deanne's voice dripped with suspicion.

Jordana threw Maisy a wild, wide-eyed look. Maisy took a breath. "Deanne, we talked about this, right? Sasha's one of my closest friends, so I know Jordana through her. That's not nefarious or suspect. That's just Pittsburgh."

"So you said."

"Hang on," Jordana waded into the icy waters. "Leo? Leo? He is the straightest straight arrow imaginable. I mean, talk about Mr. Law and Order."

"You should've known him before Sasha loosened him up," Maisy told her.

She addressed this next bit to Deanne, "Truthfully, if anyone could have understood your ex-husband's views, it would've been Leo. I mean, within limits. Putting his wife in a cage was probably a bridge too far, but this is a man who met his absentee father because the guy needed a liver donor. Leo found out after the fact that his dad was a murderous gangster, so what did he do?"

Deanne shook her head. "I don't know. What?"

"He underwent the liver donation to save the man's life and then turned him in to the authorities. Dad went straight from the transplant ward to a maximum-security prison. There's no way *that* man killed Landon and staged his suicide."

After several interminable moments of consideration, Deanne nodded. "Yeah, he doesn't seem like the type. But we're in agreement that someone did?"

"It looks that way."

"Why?" Jordana prompted.

"Landon had just come into money—a *lot* of money. The very same day he took a header out that window, one-hundred-million dollars hit his bank account." Maisy told her. "Add in the fact that his phone and laptop were never found, and it's pretty clear someone helped him out that window."

"His laptop's missing, too?" Deanne asked.

"It wasn't at his office. Although, there didn't appear to be a battery or a dock for it there, either. But there's a dock here in his home office. And I don't see a printer in either office, but he had three empty printer paper cases in his supply closet. So, first question, what is his deal with tech?"

Deanne laughed shortly. "Remember, I haven't talked to him much in recent years. So his routine could have changed some. But he was always paranoid about his digital information being stolen. Despite the fact that he spent most of his life working on computer tech projects—or maybe because of it—he didn't trust it."

"What do you mean when you say he didn't trust it? Did he think the computer would crash and his work would be lost or corrupted?"

"Well, yes, that, but also that someone would hack into his work and copy, steal, or change it."

"Did anything like that ever happen? Was his fear founded?"

"Not as far as I know. And I don't know how anyone could've done it. That was the whole point of his routine. He had one laptop that he used in both the office and at home. And once the MacBook hit the market, that was all he used. I remember he bought his first one less than a year before Josh died. So for his Cesare project, it was definitely all MacBooks."

"Is the fact they were Macs meaningful?"

"He thought so. He liked the security features. He didn't keep many files on the laptop. He offloaded everything important to an external drive backup. Please don't ask me for the technical details because my eyes used to glaze over when he talked about that stuff."

"Fair enough. So the laptop traveled back and forth with him."

"Right. It slept where he slept."

"Then it would have been at the office when he died, wouldn't it?" Jordana asked.

"Mmm, not necessarily. He didn't use the computer every day. Or at least he didn't use to. He did a lot of work by hand. Longhand, I mean. Writing in notebooks."

Maisy frowned. "I didn't see any notebooks."

"You know, now that you mention it, neither did I. That's odd because he definitely kept them. He had a whole shelf of them at our old house."

"Could he have gotten rid of them after the Justice Department shut him down?" Maisy wondered.

"That would be illegal—spoliation of evidence. He was under a court order to preserve them." Jordana explained.

"Could Sasha have them?" Deanne asked.

"No, because I would have been the one to index something like that, and I didn't."

The three of them sat in mutual confused silence until Deanne declared in a decisive, confident tone, "Then he still has them. Somewhere."

"Let's put that aside for now. What about the printer paper?"

Deanne shook her head. "He didn't print out much. I mean, you don't print code. And he liked physical books and magazines. If he wanted to read a study or something, he'd go to the university and borrow the print journal. And he wasn't much of a fiction reader. He had a handful of beloved books that he read over and over. I'm sure you saw his collection of the classics. He re-read those books every year."

"Not before ..."

"No. After Josh died, Landon donated most of Josh's books to the library. That shelf in his office? Those were Josh's books. Landon kept those six titles."

"They definitely follow a theme. Well, with the possible exception of the Sherlock Holmes mysteries," Maisy noted.

"Do you know what's funny? Sherlock Holmes inspired the whole Cesare debacle. Some scholars suggest Conan Doyle based his Professor Moriarty character on Cesare Lombroso's theories. When Landon was grieving hard, he read all the books and then all the scholarship about the books. Somehow, he overlooked the articles that argued Doyle was refuting Lombroso's ideas. He latched onto them and, well, you know the rest."

"And the other five books?"

"Let's see, the meaningless of life, obsession and revenge, criminality and guilt, isolation and alienation, and the punishment of evil." She ticked them off on her fingers. "Did I forget any?"

"That about covers it."

"I tried to talk to him about healthier ways to deal with our loss, but I never got through to him. And eventually, I gave up. I wonder what would have happened if he'd kept six more optimistic books from Josh's collection?"

They'd never know.

Jordana straightened up. "This is out of left field, but could Landon have used the printer paper as scratch paper? If he wanted to write notes but not keep them, especially after the consent decree, he might have scribbled things down and then shredded the pages."

Deanne raised her shoulders. "It sounds like something he might do."

"There's an industrial shredder in the lobby of the office building," Maisy recalled.

"Three cases of paper is a lot of shredding, though," Jordana mused.

"He was in that space for, what, three years?" Deanne countered.

Maisy summed it up. "Okay, that's our working theory. He shredded his grocery lists or whatever so they wouldn't end up in a court filing. And he has a laptop, somewhere. And notebooks, somewhere."

"None of this points to who killed him or why, though," Deanne said.

"It's only been a day. Give me some time. I *will* find out what happened to Landon. But right now, I have one more question for you."

"Shoot."

"Did Landon buy a fountain pen and letter opener when Josh was born and have his initials and birthdate engraved on the set?"

"No, I did. It was a gift for his first Father's Day, when Josh was just a baby."

Maisy hesitated, but she had to ask. "Did you give him the other set, too?"

Deanne grimaced. "He still has those?"

"Well, he had an identical pen at his office—with a different date."

She nodded. "That's the date Josh was murdered. Landon got them for himself. I told him it was morbid and unhealthy."

"What happened to the letter opener?"

"What do you mean?"

"There wasn't a full set, only the pen. But I can't imagine he didn't get the letter opener, too."

"He did. I'm positive he did."

"It's not in the apartment or the office. And I went through the inventory of personal property that the police turned over. They didn't have it."

"Where is all this stuff?" Deanne's voice rose in frustration.

"This is all okay. Better than okay," Jordana reassured her. "It gives us something to ask listeners. Maybe someone out there knows something, and hearing about the missing laptop, cell phone, or letter opener will jog their memory."

Deanne's shoulders relaxed. "Okay, that's good. When will the first episode go live?"

"Oh, it's gonna be awhile. We have to write a script and record, then edit. Maybe the middle of next month or a bit—"

Jordana cut Maisy off. "Tuesday."

Maisy turned toward her producer, blinking furiously. "What now?"

"Well, I do have to go to my grandmother's for dinner tomorrow. I promised to make an appearance. But Tuesday's a better day to drop a podcast, anyway."

"There's no way—"

"We'll let you know when it's available, Deanne. On Tuesday," Jordana said firmly.

Deanne appeared to be biting back a smile. "Great. Can't wait to listen to it. Now, I'm sorry to cut this short, but I'm pooped from traveling."

Maisy interrupted her staring contest with Jordana long enough to say goodbye to Deanne. When the video call disconnected, Jordana stopped the recording.

"We can't rush the first episode out," Maisy insisted. "My viewers expect a certain level of quality from me."

Jordana looked up from fiddling with the recording program. "And we'll meet or exceed their expectations. Trust me. But, Maisy, a podcast—especially a true crime podcast—isn't a finished news piece. You aren't telling the whole story at once. Your listeners are going on a journey *with* you. They're gonna send you tips and share wild-ass theories. Why don't you do Deanne a solid and drink one of Landon's bottles of wine while I clean up this file?"

She narrowed her eyes at the intense and intensely confident young woman at the table. "That's probably the best idea you've had yet, sugar."

She swept out of the room with all the dignity she could muster.

CHAPTER TWENTY-TWO

TIM TRIED to put the pain-in-the-butt woman out of his mind after he turned off his notifications. But her call nagged at him after he dropped the kids off at Marlena's and drove home to his empty house.

Maybe he should've gone back to his mom's place. Folks would still be there, eating, drinking, and shooting the breeze. He could've played cards or talked Nolan into walking over to the basketball court at the recreation center for some winter one-on-one to take his mind off the phone call, the news that Maisy Farley was sniffing around Lewis' office, and the knowledge that the people who hired him to keep Lewis in line would sell him out without a second thought. But with nothing to distract him, all that mess settled in his gut like a slab of fruitcake—dense and unpleasant.

He knew he need to *do* something. Watch a movie. Go down to the basement and lift free weights. Hell, he could swing by some open bars and bust some sad, lonely drunks getting over-served. If he was lucky, some schlub would take a swing at him and give him an excuse to pummel out his aggressions.

But in the end, he did none of these. Instead, he picked up his phone and scrolled through his social media feed, barely paying attention to the endless pictures of smiling kids in matching pajamas standing in front of piles of presents under trees and dining room tables laden with turkeys, hams, and all the sides. They blurred together, one after the other. Then, on the kids' babysitter's page, he saw it.

She'd posted:

> 🔥 Check out this true crime podcast dropping soon. Shout-out to my girl Jordana on her new gig as producer of the Farley Files!

Attached to the post was a short video clip. The thumbnail image was unmistakably Maisy freaking Farley. She wasn't all done up in her news anchor look with the hair helmet and the makeup, but there was no question: it was her. She was dressed casually, her mess of blonde curls piled high on her head, a pair of sexy librarian cat-eye-shaped glasses on her face. She was chewing on a pen and looking down at a notebook. None of that was what made Tim freeze and clench his jaw.

What had his heart thudding like a drum was where she was. She sat at a table littered with takeout containers, her long legs stretched out on the chair beside her.

He recognized that dining room from searching the place in a futile quest to find a laptop. She was sitting in Landon Lewis' apartment.

His finger hovered over the play bar for a long moment before he manned up and hit it.

ZANE'S ARMS were loaded down with gift bags, boxes, and leftover containers as he trailed Jenna into the living room to say goodbye to her family. She turned and gave him a confused look.

"I parked in the alley." She removed the keys from her coat pocket and dropped them into his. "Why don't you dump that stuff in the car and then come back in to say your goodbyes?"

He shook his head and reversed course. When he reached the kitchen door, he said, "A little help?"

Amber, who was filling the basket on the coffeemaker, didn't even look up.

He gritted his teeth. He knew full well she'd heard him, but she wanted to make him ask nicely. He'd sooner head butt a goat.

He dropped the crap on the table with a loud thud, yanked the door open, and slid the washer on the arm that held the screen door ajar.

Then he hauled everything out to the car. When he returned to the house a minute later, the kitchen door was still hanging open, and Amber was still by the coffee pot. She had her hands tucked up inside her sleeves and was mumbling about how cold it was.

He scowled at her but kept his promise to Jenna not to tangle with her sister anymore today. Instead, he traipsed back to the living room where Jenna's mom was sitting in her reclining chair with the scarf Jenna had knitted proudly wound around her neck. She glanced up at Zane from her tablet, where she was watching a video compilation of cats batting at ornaments.

"You kids sure you have to leave so soon?"

Jenna leaned in to give her a peck on the cheek. "Yeah, Mom. I have work in the morning, and Zane needs to be at the gym early to train. He has a fight coming up." She beamed with pride at her husband.

For his part, he was steeling himself for Lori Gatt's response. She had three favorites she cycled through—isn't it time to get a real job, maybe you can't get pregnant because he keeps getting punched in the privates, and how much is the prize purse worth? The second refrain had worried him enough to run the possibility by Jenna's doctors, who assured him that wasn't the issue. But his sperm motility was also not a topic he cared to discuss with his mother-in-law, so he waited in stoic silence.

To his surprise, she didn't trot out any of her greatest hits. Instead, she jabbed a finger at her screen.

"Look!"

He looked, expecting to see a fluffy white cat knocking a Santa Claus figure to the floor or something equally dumb. But an ad was playing. He was about to explain that creators insert ads into the middle of their videos to earn a few bucks, but Lori was already shushing them and turning up the volume.

"It's that weather girl," she exclaimed.

He squinted at the screen. "Isn't that the WACB news anchor? Maisy What's-her-face?"

Jenna laughed and answered him over her mom's head, "Maisy Farley. Yeah, that's her. But when you and I were in middle school, she was the meteorologist on WPXI. She was Mom's favorite. So, she's forever the weather girl."

Zane snorted, and Lori turned to glare at them.

"Will you two hush up?"

They zipped their lips and listened to the ad, which turned out to be a trailer for an upcoming podcast. It sounded like some kind of cold case investigation. That wasn't his thing, but Lori Gatt seemed pretty excited—or maybe she just *really* liked the weather girl. Then he caught the victim's name, and his gut twisted.

"You okay?" Jenna asked, and he realized he'd groaned audibly.

"Uh, yeah. Babe, we gotta bounce."

"Yeah, okay. Bye, Mom."

"Bye," her mother waved without looking away from the screen. "Tell Amber to come in here and show me how to subscribe to this podcast."

"Sure thing."

As they breezed through the kitchen, Jenna stopped to hug her sister.

"Call me tomorrow," Amber told her emphatically, shooting Zane a look.

"I will."

"With an update."

It was Jenna's turn to give Amber a pointed look. "I *will*. Mom needs tech support."

Amber rolled her eyes but wiped her hands on a dish towel and headed into the living room.

As Zane and Jenna walked to the car, he tried to push the thought of Landon Lewis out of his head by focusing on Amber's weird behavior. "What was all that about? With your sister?"

Jenna waved a hand. "She wants me to try some tea. A lady she knows had twins after she drank it for a month."

He just shook his head. He started around to the driver's side of the car, but she snatched the keys out of his hand and pointed to the passenger seat. "Nice try. I had half a glass of sparkling wine hours ago. You, on the other hand, drank half a brewery."

He slumped in the seat and brooded about Maisy Farley for the entirety of the short drive home.

CHAPTER TWENTY-THREE

MAISY STARED in disbelief at the tiny box tucked into the far corner of Landon's temperature- and humidity-controlled wine cave. She would never have found it if she hadn't been searching for a carmenère that she knew from experience paired well with cold Chinese food. She found a bottle of the Chilean red on the bottom right rack, and when she pulled it out, she spotted something shiny in the corner.

She returned to the dining room with the wine, a glass, a corkscrew, and the small metal box. Jordana, who'd been hunched over her phone, straightened quickly and flipped the phone facedown on the table.

"Everything okay?" Maisy asked.

"Sure. What's that?" She jerked her chin toward the box.

"Landon's treasure chest, by the looks of it."

"That was in the wine fridge?"

"Yep."

"That guy was something else."

"Understatement of the year, kid."

"Well, open it!"

"Priorities, Jordana," she said as she uncorked the carmenère.

She set the bottle aside to breathe for a few minutes and turned her attention to the box. It was roughly the size of a small mint tin—with one important modification: a lock.

"It's locked," she announced.

Jordana groaned and pretended to bang her head against the table.

"The dramatics are cute and all, but let's think."

After a moment, Jordana raised her head. "Did you check the freezer? That's where he hid the key for Josh's treasure hunt."

"That's good thinking."

Before Maisy could walk back to the kitchen, Jordana sprinted out of the room. *Ah, youth,* she observed, pouring the wine into the glass and settling into the chair. She turned the little box over in her hand.

Jordana slumped into the room with a hangdog expression.

"I take it there wasn't a key in the freezer?"

"Nope. Nothing but frozen vegetables ... and this." From behind her back, she produced a miniature container of premium ice cream. More like a cup, really. But it *was* the good stuff. "We could share it?" She offered in a tone that suggested she very much did not want to share it.

"It's all you. I've got my dessert right here." She gestured toward the wine.

Jordana beamed and pulled a single spoon out of her pocket. "I was hoping you'd say that."

For the first time all night, Maisy realized how very young she really was. Just then, Jordana's phone began to vibrate wildly, dancing across the table. At the same moment, Maisy's notifications blew up. Texts, calls, emails all started to hit her device in a cacophony of chirps, beeps, and dings.

"Mais, you do know silent mode is a thing, right?" Jordana told her.

Maisy frowned. "Something bad must've happened. Or, at least, newsworthy."

Jordana spooned the sea salt caramel ice cream into her mouth, supremely unconcerned. Meanwhile, Maisy's chest felt tight as she swiped up, hoping she wasn't going to find an alert about a Christmas Day domestic murder-suicide, a devastating natural disaster, or a seven-alarm fire.

She stared down at the screen uncomprehendingly for several heartbeats. Then she turned the screen toward the young woman and said in a low, dangerous voice, "Jordana, what is this?"

Jordana's head snapped up at her tone. She abandoned the ice cream and looked at Maisy's screen. Then to Maisy's utter disbelief, she grinned.

"Holy moly! You went viral already?"

"I didn't ... when did you post this ... this ...? What is this?" she waved the phone, her voice going up an octave as she tried not to shriek.

"Okay, first of all, take a breath. And a sip of your wine. Good. This is great news, I promise. Just come over here, and I'll show you," Jordana said in a voice that she might use to coax a cat out of a tree as she pulled something up on the laptop screen.

Maisy plopped down in front of the device.

Jordana clicked a button. "This is a trailer. It's just a really short teaser to introduce your podcast."

"I don't have a podcast yet."

She grinned. "Looks like you do. Watch."

She stared at herself on the screen. She was sitting at the table, chewing on her pen and taking notes. Suspenseful music played. Then Jordana's voice came through the laptop speaker:

One hot evening last July, the body of a brilliant tech executive with a troubled past was found battered and bloodied in an alley in Pittsburgh's Bakery Square. The police would identify the man as Landon Lewis, and the medical examiner would later rule the death a suicide. The story the official documents tell is Mr. Lewis jumped from his office window and died on impact when he hit the ground. But veteran investigative reporter Maisy Farley has questions about this narrative.

Another snippet of music, and then Maisy heard her own voice:

Landon had just come into money—a lot of money. The very same day he took a header out that window, one-hundred-million dollars hit his bank account. Add in the fact that his phone and laptop were never found, and it's pretty clear someone helped him out that window.

Back to Jordana:

When Mr. Lewis' ex-wife realized the authorities weren't going to take a closer look at the circumstances surrounding his death, she reached out to someone who would: Maisy Farley. When Deanne Lewis spoke to Maisy, she shared the prevailing themes of her deceased ex-husband's life.

Deanne said:

The meaningless of life, obsession and revenge, criminality and guilt, isolation and alienation, and the punishment of evil. None of this points to who killed him or why, though.

Maisy's voice again:

Give me some time. I **will** find out what happened to Landon.

Jordana:

Anyone who knows Maisy Farley knows she'll keep her promise to Deanne Lewis. Season One of the Farley Files starts this Tuesday. Join Maisy as she digs for the truth about the dead tech exec. Listen wherever you get your podcasts.

As the outro music played, Jordana turned off the clip and grinned. "You can pretend you're mad, but it's good, and you know it's good."

"I'm not mad. I'm flabbergasted. When did you make this?"

"When you were getting the wine."

"That fast? You pulled those excerpts, pieced this together, and, what, sent it out into the world in five minutes?"

Jordana shrugged. "Give or take."

"Honey, that is high-quality work. I mean, this is better than some of the promos WACB runs. You're really good at this."

"Well, yeah. Oh, but if you don't like the name, we can change it. It's a placeholder. Well, it was supposed to be, but, like I said, you're going viral, so we might be stuck with it."

"The Farley Files is great. Alliteration is very memorable."

She grinned. "I know."

"Show me where you posted it." Maisy nodded toward the screen as her excitement built.

"I went low-key. I sent it to my project group in my digital media class and a handful of friends. I made some quick social media profiles for the Farley Files and posted it on those. And on the podcast networks, of course. Then I threw ten bucks at some promo placements through a podcasting ad agency and stuck it in some videos and on their influencers' profiles. You know, the usual."

Maisy hadn't the foggiest what the girl was yammering on about, but it all sounded good to her. "And people have already found it? On Christmas night?"

"Sure. Think about it. They've been up since the crack of dawn. They're stuffed, tired, and probably buzzed. And definitely tired of their families. They're all scrolling on their phones. Let's see the analytics." She opened a dashboard. "You're trending on three of the major social media sites, you already have two thousand subscribers to a podcast that hasn't even launched yet, and The Steelers social media team shared your info with their fans. You're on fire."

Maisy shook her head at this brave new world. "I'll drink to that." She raised her glass, and Jordana raised her ice cream spoon. Just then, Maisy's phone chirped again. She glanced down.

"It's Sasha."

"Don't answer it." Jordana's eyes went wide.

"Child, do I look like I'm too stupid to come in from the rain? Don't worry, I won't. I am gonna text her, though. If you want to talk to her yourself about working for me, you best stop by her house tomorrow before you leave for your grandma's place."

Jordana gulped. "I will."

Maisy thumbed out a message:

> Hey, Merry Christmas to my favorite family! Sorry I couldn't take your call. My podcast producer and I are celebrating the warm response to my new show. Search online for The Farley Files if you want to check it out! J was planning on talking to you first, but things are moving fast. She's gonna stop by tomorrow. Be nice to her.

Sasha's reply came right away:

> Of course, I'll be nice. I can't risk losing my favorite babysitter. And legal interns are a dime a dozen. Besides, Naya already prepped me. Enjoy your moment of viral fame. 😀 I just really hope you and Deanne Lewis know what you're doing.

So did Maisy.

CHAPTER TWENTY-FOUR

TIM WAS PACING in front of Zane and Jenna Novak's end unit rowhouse when the couple pulled up in their little blue beater car. He took a final drag of his cigarette, flicked the butt to the sidewalk, and ground it under his heel.

"About time," he snarled as they exited the car.

The wife gave him the evil eye, then picked up the cigarette butt between two fingers and held it out in front of her like it was a dead rodent. She marched over to the trash bin nestled against the side of the house and dropped the butt in. Then without another word, she unlocked the front door and walked into the house, leaving her husband to deal with the crap piled in their back seat.

"That can wait. I need to talk to you. Now," he ordered as Novak started gathering up the bags and boxes.

He saw the fabric of Novak's sweater stretch across his broad back as the boxer flexed his shoulders before dropping the items back on the seat.

He turned to face Tim. "What do you want? It's Christmas Day, Colchis."

"I know what day it is. And that's Detective Colchis to you."

His hand went to the waistband of his jeans in a warning. It was an empty threat because he wasn't carrying, but it worked. Novak spread his hands wide in a gesture of appeasement.

"Sorry, detective."

Tim flashed a smile. "That's better. We have a problem."

The boxer gave a heavy sigh. "That Maisy chick?"

"You saw the trailer?"

"My mother-in-law was watching it."

"It's all over the internet."

"So, she's going to investigate Lewis' death. She's not going to find anything." The big man shrugged as if it didn't matter.

Tim saw through his bravado. "Doesn't matter if she does. Either way, what happened that night is going under a microscope. You sure you're up for that level of scrutiny?"

Novak grimaced.

"That's what I thought. She mentioned the missing phone and laptop. Now, I'm going to ask you one more time—you destroyed the phone, right?"

Novak's eyes flashed. "And I'm going to answer you

the same way I did every other time. Yes. I demolished the SIM and pitched the phone in the river."

Tim nodded. "Okay. And one more time, there wasn't a laptop in the office?"

"For crying out loud, how many times do I have to repeat myself? There was no laptop. There was some fancy notepaper and a freaking fountain pen on the desk. No computer."

"Well, if the reporter says a laptop is missing, he must've had one."

Novak shrugged. "You checked the apartment, not me. Maybe you missed it."

"I didn't miss anything," Tim gritted out between his teeth.

"Okay, you didn't miss it. It's just gone. So? It's not gonna tie back to us." He made a 'who cares' gesture with his open hands.

Tim wished he had brought his piece. The urge to push this jackhole up against the brick wall and jam a weapon under his chin was strong. Just to watch him piss himself. Instead, he growled, "There is no *us*. There's you, and there's me. And let me make it clear: if anybody goes down for this, it ain't gonna be me, Zane."

Novak stared at him for a beat. "Did our—sorry, *your* —employer hear about the podcast?"

He scrubbed a hand over his face. "Dunno. They haven't reached out yet, but I'm sure they will. I got a call from my contact earlier—before the trailer dropped. Maisy Farley was poking around Lewis' office."

"Today?"

"Yeah."

"Crap."

"She's a problem," Tim stated the obvious in a neutral voice.

But Novak read between the lines. "Nope. I'm out."

"Just scare her. You don't have to hurt her."

Novak laughed bitterly. "That's what you said about Lewis. And look how that turned out."

"Nobody told you to throw him out a window, you moron."

"He came at me. I reacted. It's called self-defense." Novak shrugged. "Now, are we done here?"

Tim glared at him. "This isn't over."

"Yeah, it is. I'm not roughing up the weather girl or threatening her or whatever it is you want me to do." He brushed past Tim and walked into the house, slamming the door behind him.

WHEN THEY'D REACHED the house, Jenna had rushed inside and beelined for the basement. This was her chance. While Zane was outside dealing with the detective, she could retrieve the phone before she lost her nerve—or changed her mind. She pulled the door open and pounded down the stairs, more concerned with speed than stealth.

As she reached the bottom of the stairs, her heart hammered so loudly that, for a second, she thought she'd left the dryer running. She darted past the washer and silent dryer and sprinted to the furnace. The sharp, earthy smell of the basement filled her nostrils as she wrenched the box free from its hiding spot with shaking hands and flipped the latch open. She dug through the papers and grabbed the phone tucked away at the bottom of the box. She scanned the nearest shelves, looking for something she could wrap up in the butcher paper to approximate the size and shape of the phone. But that was a lost cause. She didn't have time to mess around creating a decoy phone.

Besides, if Zane came down here for the phone, he'd certainly unwrap it. So she'd only be delaying the inevitable. What were the odds that he'd come looking for his hidden phone before she returned it?

She'd charge it overnight, power it on so that it revealed its secrets, and return it to its hiding place tomorrow morning while Zane was at the gym. She'd put it back before he ever realized it was missing.

Her mind made up, she shoved the lunchbox behind the furnace, slipped the phone into her pocket, and hurried back upstairs. She paused at the top of the steps to catch her breath and listen for Zane's footsteps.

The house was quiet. She turned off the basement light and eased the door closed. She crept through the first floor, stopping to peek through the living room curtains. Zane was still at the car, arguing with Colchis. She hated the way the cop hassled Zane and lived in a perpetual state of low-level terror that, one of these days, Zane was going to snap and beat the dick into a pulp.

Not that it wouldn't be deserved, because it would.

But it would also ruin their lives. She studied Zane's clenched jaw and furrowed brow. He had a handle on his temper—at least for now. He might slug Colchis someday, but it wouldn't be today. She let the curtain fall aside and turned away from the window.

She jogged up the stairs to the second floor and followed the narrow hallway to the bathroom at the front of the house. She hurried inside, eased the door shut with a soft thud, and secured the hook and eye lock. Then she yanked open the door to the cupboard built into the wall beside the shower. She pushed aside stacks of washcloths and towels until she found what she was looking for in the jumble of the crammed linen closet. She hugged the economy-sized box of sanitary pads to her chest and bumped the door with her hip to close it.

She perched on the lid of the toilet seat with the big box wedged between her knees. She pulled a handful of wrapped pads out of the box and set them aside on the edge of the sink. She reached into her pocket and took out the iPad charger Amber had given her. Then she took a long, deep breath and removed the phone from her other pocket.

For the third time in two days, she unwound the rubber band securing the butcher paper and unfolded the thick paper. Just as it had the first two times, it fell open to reveal the red iPhone. She wasn't sure why the sight of the thing still surprised her, but it did.

She stared down at the cold glossy rectangle in her lap for a long moment. Then she swallowed and got busy. She got onto the floor and opened the cabinet under the sink. For reasons known only to whoever remodeled the house in the nineteen fifties, the sole outlet in the bathroom was behind the sink. She assumed that the bathroom had a pedestal sink at the time.

But now that the sink had a built-in cabinet, the electrical outlet was blocked. Zane's attempt to solve this problem had been to drill an access hole in the back of the cabinet using a spade drill. The hole did allow them to fish cords through the cabinet. Unfortunately, the actual act of plugging something into the outlet involved a lot of blindly trying to insert prongs into an outlet that was out of sight while bending your arm at an unnatural angle. Long story short, they didn't use the bathroom outlet.

Now, Jenna eased the charger brick through the hole and waved it around until it made contact with the outlet. She crawled halfway into the cabinet and, after several tries, managed to maneuver the prongs into the slots. She heard the front door slam.

She was running out of time. She threaded the charging cord through the flap on the top of the box of pads, then inserted the business end into the dead phone's port. The familiar empty battery icon appeared on the screen to confirm that the device was charging. She exhaled. Almost done now.

She placed the phone in the bottom of the box and covered it with the stack of pads. She closed the tab on the top of the box and pushed the box under the sink, directly beneath the access hole. She knelt and peered into the cavity. The thin cord was barely visible as it snaked out the flap in the lid and through the hole. There was an approximately zero point zero possibility that Zane would open the box. It wasn't that he was particularly squeamish about her bodily functions—that ship had sailed when they started their fertility treatments. But there was simply no reason for him to look inside the cabinet in the next twelve hours.

She splashed some water on her pale face and left the bathroom before he came looking for her.

CHAPTER TWENTY-FIVE

AFTER COLCHIS LEFT, Zane went down to the basement and whaled away at the heavy bag until his shoulders ached and his nervous energy was spent. He resisted the urge to get the lunchpail while he was down there. He had a plan, and he needed to follow it through.

The confrontation with the detective had convinced him that he had to get rid of Lewis' iPhone. If the police decided to reopen the investigation because of Maisy Farley, Colchis would send the police to Zane's front door in a heartbeat. The only thing that could connect him to Lewis was the blasted phone. He'd been a dope to keep it—he knew that now.

Tonight, after Jenna fell asleep, he'd creep back down here and get it from the lunch pail. Then, in the morning, he'd run to the gym, taking the route across the Bloomfield Bridge and throw the blasted thing in the river for real. The swirling worry that had taken up residence in his gut might disappear once the red phone was lying on the silty river bottom.

He wiped the sweat from his face and neck and tossed the towel into the open washer. He jogged up the stairs and grabbed a bottle of water from the fridge. Jenna was chopping veggies and portioning out chicken breasts for the coming week's lunches. He reached over and snatched a carrot from the cutting board. He bit into it with a satisfying crunch.

She eyed him. "Good workout?"

"Just needed to work off the meal."

"Oh? I thought maybe you were working off whatever happened outside with the cop."

He waved his hand and took another bite. "Don't worry about Colchis."

She placed the knife on the cutting board with a bang. "I'm not worried about him. I'm worried about you. What's he got on you, Zane?"

"What do you mean, what's he got on me? Nothing. He has a hard-on for me because he knows I used to be a brawler. He doesn't believe I'm on the straight and narrow. That's all. Just ignore him."

She locked eyes with him. "Are you on the straight and narrow?"

"What the hell, Jenn?"

"I want to hear you say it. Tell me you haven't gotten into any trouble. Tell me you're keeping the promise you made."

He dropped the carrot and grabbed her by the shoulders. "Baby, I swear. I'm not in trouble. I'm ready to be a father, and that means being a law-abiding citizen." He parroted the words she wanted to hear, the words he wished were true.

She studied him somberly. After a moment, she nodded slowly. "Good."

"Good." He leaned over and kissed her neck.

She wrinkled her nose and edged away.

He took the hint. "I'm gonna hit the shower."

"Good idea. I'll fix us some leftovers for when you're done."

After he took a quick shower, they had turkey sandwiches and an assortment of cookies. Jenna was quiet and wolfed down her food in a hurry. Then she cleaned up the kitchen while he went into the living room and turned on the tape of the Ali-Foreman bout. He pretended to doze off in front of the TV. She came in, unplugged the tree's lights, and aimed the remote at the VCR to turn off the tape. She smoothed his hair off his forehead and gave him a soft kiss before heading upstairs.

He sat, unmoving, eyes squeezed shut, until she used the bathroom, turned out the hall light, and went into their bedroom, closing the door with a soft click. Then he pushed himself up from the couch and grabbed his gym bag from its spot by the front door.

He prowled down the hall to the kitchen and eased the basement door open. He left it ajar rather than risk having Jenna hear it close and decide to investigate. He tiptoed down the stairs and hurried across the ice-cold floor on his bare feet.

When he got to the furnace, he frowned. The light

down here was bad, but he could have sworn he'd concealed the metal box better than this. A corner of it poked up from behind the filter panel. That wasn't right. He grabbed the pail and undid the latch with one hand while he unzipped the duffle bag with the other. He rifled through the stuff inside, shifting it all to one side to get to the phone at the bottom of the lunchbox. His hand hit bare metal.

Where was the phone?

Frantic now, he dumped the contents of the box on the cold floor and squatted, shuffling through the cards, programs, and letters. No thick butcher-paper-wrapped package. The phone was gone.

He rocked back on his haunches and tried to breathe through the tightening in his windpipe. Tried to think through the buzz saw of panic in his brain. It had to be here.

He forced himself to breathe deeply and use deliberate, slow movements as he picked through each item on the floor, one by one. He examined every scrap of paper, each piece of memorabilia, as if one of them held the answer and would reveal the phone. But after he'd carefully returned each item to the lunchpail, the phone hadn't miraculously materialized. He closed the box and stood up, focusing on not vomiting as sour bile rose in his throat.

What the hell?

And in a flash, the answer came to him. Colchis.

The bastard cop hadn't just been waiting outside to harangue him. While Zane and Jenna had been at her mom's place, Colchis must've broken into the house, searched it, and found the phone. It was the only explanation.

And there was nothing Zane could do about it. What could he do? Call the police and report a robbery? He could hear it now. The operator would ask what was taken, and what would he say? An iPhone was taken. An iPhone I stole from a man who died because I tossed him out a window.

Yeah, that wasn't an option. He had no options. Colchis was setting him up to take a fall.

Zane's blood roared in his ears, and his vision narrowed to a pinprick. Before he could stop himself, his right hand clenched into a fist and drove forward with all his force. He punched the stone foundation wall at high velocity. His fist hit the stone with enough momentum to shake a shower of pebbles loose—and to break three of his knuckles and a couple of bones in his hand.

The pain cut through his murderous rage instantly, and he dropped to his knees and opened his mouth in a silent howl. He stayed like that, open-mouthed, rocking in pain and fear, until the cold seeping up from the ground through his sweatpants chilled him through and he began to shake uncontrollably. After a long time, he dragged himself to his feet and trudged upstairs, leaving the gym bag and lunch box where they lay on the ground.

CHAPTER TWENTY-SIX

WHILE JORDANA FILLED a dead man's refrigerator with takeout containers, Maisy wiped down the counters with a damp sponge and finished loading the dishwasher. She scanned the kitchen for stray dirty dishes, popped a tab into the reservoir, and started a wash cycle.

"Kind of wasteful to run it half empty," Jordana observed.

"I don't disagree, but apparently, Landon didn't own kitchen towels. Or dish soap."

"Or he hid them somewhere, and we'll stumble across them in the trash can or something. Where the heck could he have stashed that laptop."

Maisy shook her head. "I wish I knew."

"We should take one more look around before we leave," Jordana suggested as she shut the fridge.

They'd already agreed to use the apartment as their base of operations and planned to return on Tuesday to record the first podcast episode. There'd be ample opportunity to scour the apartment again. But Maisy wasn't in any hurry to return to her own empty house, and she sensed the younger woman felt the same way.

"Might as well," she agreed.

After she said it, her tongue darted out to lick her lips, and she caught herself. The air in the apartment must have been dry because she could already feel her lips chapping. She reached into her sweater pocket for the lip balm she carried everywhere from October through April. Instead of the tube, she touched something metal.

"The key!" she cried. Then she pulled the small key ring from her pocket and dangled it triumphantly.

Jordana gave her a hopeful look and drew closer to inspect the key. "Is that the key to the box from the wine cooler?"

"No. At least, I don't think so. But, let's check."

She motioned for the case, and Jordana grabbed it from the kitchen island. Jordana held it out, and Maisy tried to insert the key into the lock.

"Aww, it's way too small." The college student's disappointment was evident. She was practically pouting.

But Maisy grinned. "I think I know what it will open, though."

Interest sparked in Jordana's eyes. "Really?"

Maisy jerked her head toward the back of the apartment. "Come on. I'll show you."

She headed for the home office with Jordana tripping

on her heels like a puppy. When they entered the office, Maisy turned on the lights, and Jordana surveyed the room.

After a moment, she shook her head. "There's nothing in here *to* unlock. Where'd you find that, anyway?"

Like the storyteller she was, Maisy answered the second question first to draw out the suspense. "It was hidden in the storage closet at Landon's office. And before you ask, there was nothing in that office to unlock either."

"So, it's a useless key? Fun."

Maisy raised one eyebrow and then crossed the room to pick up one of the bronze horse bookends. "Check this out." She turned the bookend upside down and pointed to the locked compartment hidden in the base.

"Whoa," Jordana breathed. A millisecond later, she demanded, "What are you waiting for? Open it!"

Maisy inserted the key and rotated it. The lock disengaged easily, and the door to the compartment fell open to reveal a navy blue mini-notebook, no more than three-and-a-half by five inches in size. She used a fingernail to pop it out of the recessed compartment. She handed the bookend to Jordana and paged through the notebook.

"What's it say?"

"Mmm, it looks like he copied down quotes from his literature collection," Maisy told her.

"And why did he find it necessary to hide passages

from a bunch of musty books that are probably all in the public domain now?"

Maisy flipped the book closed, tucked it into her pocket, and threw her hands in the air. "Your guess is as good as mine. Grab the other bookend."

Jordana passed her back the first bookend, and Maisy relocked the compartment and returned it to the shelf. Meanwhile, Jordana grabbed its mate and turned it over.

"Will the same key work?"

"It should."

It did. The second compartment held another key, a smaller one.

"Bet it fits the box."

"Let's find out," Maisy said.

As they walked back to the kitchen, Jordana said, "Is there any chance he was, like, a spy? Because this is not normal, right?"

"Anything's possible. But I think Deanne nailed it. Landon was paranoid, tortured, and mistrustful. I doubt he was James Bond masquerading as a mild-mannered criminologist tech genius."

"Okay. But you have to admit that would be cooler than whatever this is."

"No argument here."

Jordana picked up the box and extended it toward Maisy. "Here."

Instead of taking it, she handed Jordana the key. "You do the honors."

Jordana grinned and stuck the key into the lock. It fit, and it opened the case.

"Is that an external hard drive?"

"Sure is," Maisy said.

"Guess we found Landon's backup."

"All we need now is the laptop." Maisy sighed. "This is like one of those *matryoshka* dolls."

"The Russian nesting dolls?"

"Yeah. There's always another layer with this guy. Oh, shoot, we should have been recording this." Maisy smacked her hand against her thigh in disgust.

"Do I look like an amateur? We've been recording." Jordana removed a digital recorder from her pocket.

"But won't it be muffled and poor quality?"

"Not when I'm done," Jordana assured her.

Maisy laughed, and her giggle turned into a yawn. She flipped her phone over to check the time. "Gracious, it's getting late. Let's call it a night."

Jordana packed up her recording equipment, and Maisy grabbed her purse. She slid the drive and the notebook inside. Then she locked up, and they headed for the elevators.

As they waited for an elevator car to come, Maisy cocked her head. "I wonder—?"

"What?"

"Do we need Landon's laptop or *a* laptop? I mean, I assume the drive is formatted for an Apple device, but won't any Mac do the trick?"

Jordana gnawed on her lower lip. "I don't know. I think if it's encrypted, attaching it to a different machine might make it self-destruct."

"Is that based on something that happened in real life or a movie?"

Jordana pulled a face. "Okay, it was in a movie. But *if* it happens, we're fu ... ducked."

"Fiona got to you, too, huh?"

"She's like a living echo, Maisy. You can't say *anything* in front of that kid."

They laughed. The elevator arrived with a juddering lurch, and the doors stuttered open. Maisy gave it a suspicious look. But she was too tired to take the stairs, so she said a quick prayer and stepped into the car. Jordana followed and hit the button for the lobby.

"You know, August, the IT guy at the firm, is really good. He'd know."

Maisy turned to face her. "You can't talk to anyone at McCandless, Volmer & Andrews about our investigation. You understand that, right?"

Jordana massaged her temples as if she had a headache. "I mean, sure, I wouldn't talk about anything specific we found. But it's not like we have a duty of confidentiality to Landon's ex-wife. You're making a public podcast about the case. Couldn't I simply ask him if an external hard drive that's been encrypted can be attached to an unfamiliar computer? Like, no details."

She considered the point. "I guess that'd be okay. But there are two things you have to remember. One, the podcast only succeeds if we don't get scooped. So we have to hold some of our cards close to our vests."

Jordana bobbed her head. "Okay, that makes sense. What's the second thing?"

Maisy rubbed her tired eyes and chose her words with care. "Sasha's one of my best friends. Leo, too. And you're close with them, too. We can't let that cloud our judgment."

Jordana's jaw tightened, and Maisy raised a hand to forestall the argument the girl was marshaling.

"Let me finish. There's no question that Leo did not kill Landon Lewis. And I know Sasha had nothing to do with his death."

"I hear a 'but' coming."

"*But* you know as well as I do that they both had a history with Landon. They both talked to him the day he died. And they were the first civilians on the scene when the police found his body. Think of all the messes they've somehow ended up in the middle of."

She reluctantly agreed, "There have been a lot."

"An inordinate number," Maisy said. "And those are only the ones we know about. So, as much as it might feel gross or disloyal, we can't share any details with the dynamic duo. Got it?"

The elevator groaned, bounced, and finally came to a stop on the ground floor. Before they stepped out into the brightly lit lobby, Jordana said, "I get it."

"Good."

Maisy didn't feel great about the boundaries she was drawing, but it was important to make them clear, and she needed Jordana to understand. Neither one of them had to like it. They both needed to do it.

CHAPTER TWENTY-SEVEN

December 26
Before sunrise

JENNA WOKE up surprised to feel Zane's warm body next to hers in the bed. He was usually long gone when her alarm went off. He almost always drank his protein shake and set out for his run to the gym while it was still dark. He liked to watch the sun rising over the city as he ran. Sure, sometimes he got a later start, but not this close to a fight.

She was about to reach over and shake him awake when he shifted his weight. He rolled over in his sleep, and that's when she saw his mangled right hand. She gasped and then clamped her hand over her mouth to muffle the sound so she wouldn't wake him after all.

From the looks of his damaged hand, he wouldn't be going to the gym today. She leaned over for a closer look. But he might be going to the emergency room.

His hand was a misshapen swollen lump. Vibrant purple bruises and dried blood covered most of his fingers and snaked down the back of his palm. His fingers were puffed up like sausages and splayed at different crooked angles. His hand—his right hand, no less—was unquestionably broken.

She exhaled through her nose. Based on past behavior when he'd injured himself, she doubted he'd bothered to ice it or take any painkillers last night. So he was going to wake up miserable: angry and bereft at the lost training time and in considerable physical pain. She'd probably have to spend most of the morning convincing him to get medical treatment.

She stifled a sigh and rolled out of bed. Good thing she didn't start until ten today. It wasn't until she padded into the bathroom to brush her teeth that she remembered the phone. Her gaze slid down to the cabinet under the sink. Now she was going to have to wait to power it on and see what it revealed. She didn't want to risk doing it while he was in the house.

She considered her options while she brushed. She could take it to work and do it there. There would be a skeleton staff today with so many people out on vacation for the week. There would only be three of them to answer all the customer calls, and Mondays were always busy with calls. She figured everyone who found their cell phone bill in the mail when they got home on Friday had the whole weekend to stew about the charges. Today, in addition to the callers fuming about changes to their plan or overage charges, everyone who got a new phone for Christmas would be calling to add it to their plan. No, she couldn't take it to work with her. Besides, if she *did* find something on the phone, if Zane *was* cheating on her, she didn't need to find out in the middle of Cheaptime Mobile's phone carrier's call center.

She spat and rinsed, then reached for the dental floss. Maybe she should just do it real fast before Zane woke up. Her heart rate sped up at the thought, and the floss shook in her trembling hands.

It'll only take a minute. Get it over with. That's what Amber would do.

She dropped the floss in the wastebasket and bent to open the cabinet. As she gripped the handle, Zane moaned loudly from the bedroom, and she jumped.

His feet hit the floor with a thud, and then he howled in pain. She winced. She'd bet anything he'd forgotten about his injury while he'd slept and had just pushed down on the bed with both hands to leverage himself to his feet. Talk about a rough wake-up.

She rushed into the bedroom and ordered him to stay put while she ran downstairs to get him some ice.

The iPhone would have to wait.

ZANE'S HAND THROBBED. While Jenna clucked and fussed over it with a bag of ice, he tried to formulate a plan. But his brain was still fuzzy from sleep, and his thoughts were scattered by fear. He frowned.

Jenna saw his expression and misinterpreted it. "I know you're disappointed about the fight, but the promoters will have to understand. You can't box with a broken hand."

He stared at her for a blank moment, then he remembered the upcoming match with Melvin Greene. "Aw, crap."

Just one more bad roll of the dice for Zane Novak. No matter what he did, his sucky luck destroyed everything good or even promising in his life.

His gaze slid to Jenna, whose head was bowed over his busted-up hand while she gently dabbed at the dried blood with a damp washcloth. Well, almost every good thing.

Jenna had stuck with him. She loved him through his dead-end jobs, his bar fights and scrapes with the law, and his hardscrabble plan to make it as a boxer. She was steady and steadfast, loving him no matter what.

Out of nowhere, the urge to confide in her overwhelmed him. The secrets he'd been keeping, pushing them down, down, down, suddenly bubbled up, demanding to spill out.

"Jenn?"

"Hmm?"

"I have to tell you something."

She raised her eyes to meet his and stared at him with a stricken expression. "Not now, Zane. Let's get your hand taken care of first."

He shook his head no. Now that he'd committed to this course of action, he was a freight train without brakes. He barreled forward. "I did something bad, something really bad. I ... Ow!" She was pressing down on his broken finger bones with a lot of force. His face twisted in agony. "Jenna stop!"

She blinked and released the pressure on his fingers. "I'm so sorry, baby. I didn't mean to."

He panted through the pain. "Yeah, okay. But listen, I need to tell you—"

"We need to get you to a doctor. Let me call into work and tell them I'm gonna be late. Just stay put."

She left the room fast—like she was afraid he might try to stop her.

Watching her leave, running from his confession, he wondered if somehow she already knew. But that was impossible. Wasn't it?

GET A GRIP, Jenna ordered herself, as she reached for her phone with shaking hands. *No matter what, you'll get through this. People are unfaithful. It happens.* But she couldn't deal with hearing Zane's confession. Not now, not while she was helping him.

Could she find the strength within herself to forgive him for cheating on her? Her stomach turned. Who was she? What if Zane got her pregnant? Wouldn't that just take the cake?

Her stomach lurched again, more forcefully this

time, and she raced to the bathroom to puke. She vomited until she felt hollow inside, then she washed her face and brushed her teeth again.

She gripped the edge of the sink and stared into her watering eyes in the mirror. *Keep it together,* she instructed her reflection.

Then she picked up the phone and called her supervisor. The call rolled to her voicemail, and Jenna whispered a thank you to the universe. The last thing she needed was for Christina to pepper her with questions.

She waited for the beep, then said, "Chris, it's me. Jenna. I hope you had a good holiday. Listen, I'm probably going to be late. Zane broke his hand and needs to go to the hospital. He can't drive himself, so I've got to take him. Hopefully, there's not a long wait and I won't be too late. I'll call you when I'm on my way in. I'm really sorry."

She hung up and hurried out of the bathroom before she was tempted to check on the phone charging under the sink. She pasted on a wobbly smile when she walked into the bedroom.

"Let's get you dressed and to the ER," she chirped.

"What about work?"

"I left a message for Christina that I might be late. They can manage until I get there."

He started to protest but she talked over him. "You're not going to be able to drive, and you clearly need treatment. So instead of wasting time arguing, which is only going to make me later, let's get moving."

His shoulders slumped forward in defeat. "Okay.

Thanks."

"We should go to UPMC so they can call in a sports medicine doc to consult if they need to."

He gave his hand a rueful look. "I don't know, Jenn. This might be it for my boxing career."

"Don't say that. Don't even think that. You have to stay positive. How'd you do it, anyway?"

"Do what?"

She raised her eyebrows. "Break your hand."

"Oh. I woke up on the couch, but I was wired, probably from all the sugar. So I went downstairs to hit the bag until I felt tired enough to go to bed. I guess I missed."

She left her eyebrows kissing her hairline and cocked her head. "You missed the bag?"

"Uh-huh, yeah. And I hit the wall." He laughed. "Must've been more tired than I realized."

She stared at him. The speed bag hung from the ductwork in the middle of the room, and the heavy bag was in the corner near the hot water heater. There was no way a swing and a miss at either bag would end in punching the stone wall.

Was he that stupid? Or did he think she was that stupid? Either way, the fact that he could lie right to her face with no problem stung, and it made her even less eager to look at the iPhone.

After a heavy pause, she said simply, "Oh, okay."

Then she yanked open the dresser to look for a shirt she'd be able to ease over Zane's hand without making him pass out from the pain.

CHAPTER TWENTY-EIGHT

MAISY SAT in her favorite chair, the one by the big window in her living room, and savored a mug of hot chocolate while she watched the pale orange sun struggle up over the top of a neighboring parking garage. It wasn't the most scenic place to watch a sunrise, but it was convenient. And cozy, she thought, as she snuggled under her warm fleecy blanket.

Her phone rang. She rested her mug on the side table to reach for the phone. She blinked when she saw who was calling.

"Jordana? What are you doing up this early? And not texting? Is this one of those things where I'm supposed to guess you've been kidnapped because you're acting so strangely?"

"What? Are you okay?"

"Yeah, it's a joke, Like the meme? Never mind, what's up?"

"I'm calling and not texting because I'm in the car on my way to my grandmother's place. But this is important, so I wanted to catch you early."

"Okay, hit me."

"I stopped by Sasha and Leo's place this morning."

"How'd it go?"

"Fine. She was super nice about me quitting. But it was chaotic. Finn kept showing me his Christmas presents, and Mocha chased Java through the train village under the tree, causing a tragic derailment. I mean, it was a typical morning for them, but I couldn't hear myself think. Anyway, Sasha's not upset."

"Good. Is that what you wanted to tell me?"

"No. I mentioned the hard drive and our question about what happens if we put it in a different Mac."

"And?"

"And she called August at home and asked him, hypothetically, what might happen. He said that someone as paranoid as the guy she described likely encrypted the drive. We wouldn't be able to read it without the encryption key, but he doubts it would self-destruct if we tried."

"Okay, good. Then I'll go ahead—"

"No! That's why I'm calling you. While Sasha was telling me what August said, Leo wandered into the room and heard her. He said he's almost positive that Landon would have booby-trapped the drive and that it will destroy itself, and maybe your laptop, too, if you try to brute force your way into it."

There was a long silence.

"Maisy? Did I lose you?"

"I'm here. I'm thinking."

"What are you thinking?"

"How would Leo know that?"

"He doesn't *know*. But he has a very strong suspicion."

"Based on what?"

Jordana hesitated. "Okay, I see where you're going. He definitely acted like he knew something, but he didn't come out and say it. He made me promise to tell you ASAP, and he said, his words, he 'strongly advises' us not to try to access the data unless we find an encryption key first."

"Well, shoot."

"I know. But I was thinking maybe we don't need the drive if you can find his notebooks. They have to be squirreled away somewhere in that apartment. If Deanne's right, he probably kept his important notes in those notebooks."

"I'll head over there in a bit," Maisy said. "Maybe I'll stumble across more of his secret hiding places."

"And that's the other reason I'm calling. Record yourself while you investigate. Don't worry about the quality, just use your cell phone. I can fix it in post. But it would be a wasted opportunity if you find something and it's not recorded."

Maisy had to grin at Jordana's forceful tone. "Yes, ma'am."

"Am I being bossy?" she worried.

"Never call yourself bossy. There's no need—plenty

of men will do that for you. And, no, you're not being bossy. You're being competent and good at your job. There's a difference."

Jordana laughed. "Got it. I should be back by ten, ten-thirty at the latest. But call me if you find anything really exciting."

"Nope," Maisy told her. "You focus on your family dinner. We'll talk when you're back. And drive carefully."

"Will do. Talk to you later."

Maisy ended the call and returned to her no-longer-hot hot chocolate. She gazed out the window, but she wasn't seeing anything outside. Her mind was racing, wondering where Landon had stashed his laptop and notebooks.

She suddenly recalled her dad's old hunting hound, Lemon. When Lemon caught a scent, she was single-minded, indistractible, and focused solely on running down her prey.

"Be like Lemon," she told herself. Then she rose to get dressed and start the hunt.

CHAPTER TWENTY-NINE

THE LOBBY of Kaufmann's Grand on Fifth was buzzing with activity and people milling around. It reminded Maisy of how lunchtime shoppers would descend on the building when it used to house Pittsburgh's iconic Kaufmann's department store—and briefly, Macy's. (But, honestly, everyone, including Maisy, called it Kaufmann's until the day it closed its doors for good.)

It was disorienting to walk past the trappings of modern apartment living—the package room, the lounge, the game room—where she remembered a sea of cosmetics counters and perfume saleswomen. According to the signage, the residents were enjoying a holiday week morning mixer courtesy of building management. She lowered her head and hurried through the crowd, eager to get to the elevator without being recognized.

She was just feet from freedom when she remembered the drama and suspense of last night's elevator ride and her conviction that the elevator was going to get stuck between floors—or worse. She made an abrupt U-turn and set a course for the stairwell. She wove through a group of shiny young professionals chatting about an upcoming concert over mimosas in plastic flutes and circled behind an older couple who'd brought their two shih tzu puppies to the gathering. The husband was stealthily feeding the dogs small bits of his blueberry bagel when his wife wasn't paying attention.

She hid a smile and headed for the stairwell. A sign outside a room to the right caught her eye, and she detoured. She stood outside the Podcast Room and peered through the glass door. She spied a large microphone and acoustic tiling on the walls. She was wondering whether Jordana knew about the existence of this room when the concierge on duty approached her.

"Morning, Ms. Farley." He smiled warmly.

She read his name tag. "Hi, Alonzo."

He nodded toward the room. "You want to sign up for some time? Mrs. Lewis said you're staying in the apartment for a while, and I heard you're starting a podcast."

"I am starting a podcast, but I don't need to use the space. Thanks, though. I'm just surprised to see the building has a room devoted to recording podcasts."

He shrugged. "It's a trend, I guess. Everybody and their dog thinks they should have a podcast." His brown eyes went wide. "But not you. I don't mean you. You're Maisy Farley. You're a journalist."

She placed a gentle hand on his forearm and gave him a big, megawatt grin. "It's okay. I'm not offended. Who knows? My podcast might stink. Maybe you'll listen and let me know what you think? The first episode comes out tomorrow."

Alonzo's face reddened. "I know. I already subscribed."

She laughed as if he'd said something witty. Then she asked, "What other amenities are there? Like Deanne mentioned, I may be using the space until the lease is up."

She had no intention of actually staying in Landon's apartment. The idea gave her chills. But she might as well gather information from the chatty concierge.

"I can give you the tour if you like. There's the golf simulator, the fitness center, the dog wash, the movie room ...." He rattled off the options as if he were reading them from a brochure. "Up on the roof, we even have a swimming pool, a dog park, and a basketball court. We turn the court into a skating rink in the winter."

"Wow, that's a lot."

He nodded. "We strive to provide an urban living oasis."

She gave him a long look. That wording *had* to have come from the building's brochure.

His blush deepened. "Sorry, sometimes I get carried away."

"I get it." Then a thought hit her. "Do you mind if I ask you a few questions about Mr. Lewis on the record? You know, background for my podcast."

He straightened his shoulders. "Really?"

"Really." She pulled out her cell phone.

"Wait. I can't violate any of our residents' privacy or anything like that," he waffled.

"Of course not. I'm just going to ask a handful of questions about Landon Lewis. His ex-wife is in charge of his estate, and the series on his death was actually her idea. So she's not going to complain."

"Then I guess it would be okay."

"Great. What's your last name?"

"Germain."

She smiled encouragingly and hit record on her app.

"I'm at the downtown luxury apartment building where Landon Lewis lived. Today, I'm talking to Alonzo Germain, the building concierge and tenant relations specialist. Did you know Landon well, Alonzo?"

He stammered a bit before he got going. She figured his throat-clearing could be one of the things Jordana fixed in post.

"He moved in last January, so he was only with us for about seven months before ... it happened."

"Do you know where he was living before then?"

"I think he had a place out in Milltown, but I'm not sure."

"What was he like, as a tenant? Was he outgoing or did he keep to himself?"

Alonzo considered his answer. "Well, he worked a lot. He'd leave pretty early in the morning, and most days he wouldn't come back until late, after the front doors were locked for the night. As you know, Maisy, we have a full complement of recreational and lifestyle amenities here in the building, but as far as I know, he never used them. And I don't recall seeing him at any of the social events we organized." He waved a hand at the party happening behind them.

Maisy hoped her microphone would pick up the background noise. "Right now, the tenants are enjoying one of those social events while I speak with Alonzo. About two dozen people are gathered for a holiday breakfast," she explained for her listeners. "So, would you say Landon didn't get to know his neighbors?"

He nodded slowly. "Yeah, that's fair to say. I guess he knew the Hoffmans." He pointed to the couple with the shih tzus. "They're in the unit next to his."

She filed that away for future reference. "Were you surprised when you heard he'd died?"

"Well, sure. Surprised that he was dead. And then when we learned that it was suicide, I was stunned. He seemed so driven, you know? He had all the energy to take on the world. But, I guess you never know what's going on inside someone's mind."

"I guess you never do. Did you know he'd just come into a large fortune?"

Alonzo shook his head. "No. The police came and talked to us, asked us some questions, and gained access to his apartment. I don't remember them mentioning that."

"Do you remember the names of police officers you spoke to? Was it Officer Ilsa Evans or Sergeant Oswald Bass, by chance?"

The tip of his tongue poked out for a second, then he raised one finger. "Hang on." To her delight, he pulled a small calendar out of his breast pocket and flipped back several months to read the notes he'd scrawled into the date squares. "Uh, yes, I met with Officer Evans. And then a few days later, a Detective Colchis."

Maisy wrinkled her brow. She knew most of the police assigned to Zone Five, but she'd never heard of a Colchis. "Huh. A detective?"

"That's what I wrote down, so that must be what he said. We didn't talk long. He mainly just needed me to let him into the apartment even though the police had already released the crime scene." He shrugged.

"Did anyone from law enforcement interview the other tenants?"

"Not that I know of." He chuckled. "But the Hoffmans wanted to talk to them."

"They wanted to talk to the police about Landon?"

"Yep."

"Did they?"

"Not as far as I know."

"Thanks for your time, Alonzo."

"My pleasure."

She switched off the recorder and stuck out her hand. "I really appreciate it. Now you make sure you listen tomorrow."

"I wouldn't miss it," he promised, enthusiastically pumping her hand like it was a bike tire he was trying to inflate.

SHE LOITERED AROUND THE LOBBY, picking at an uninspired fruit salad and waiting for an opening to talk to the Hoffmans. When one of the pups began to whimper, she got her chance.

"Come on, girls. Let's go up on the roof and tinkle," Mr. Hoffman said. "Miranda, the girls have to potty."

Mrs. Hoffman abandoned her half-drunk mimosa on a catering stand and picked up a fresh one, then trotted toward the elevator with the dogs and her husband in tow. Maisy dumped her fruit salad and beat them to the elevator bank. She pressed the 'up' button as they rounded the corner.

"Are you going up?" she asked cheerfully.

"Yes, Minnie and Mimi need to visit the roof," Mr. Hoffman told her.

The elevator arrived with a great grinding of gears, and the doors shook open. Maisy gestured for the couple and their dogs to enter the car first. She followed them inside. *Please don't get stuck while I'm in here with two dogs who need to pee,* she silently begged the elevator.

She hit the number for the ninth floor, and Miranda Hoffman studied her in the mirrored wall. "You don't live on our floor," she informed Maisy.

"Miranda," her husband murmured.

"Well, Charles, she doesn't."

Maisy flashed her a smile. "You're right. I don't. I'm just visiting."

"Whom are you visiting?"

Maisy allowed her smile to falter. "Ah, that's a tough question. It shouldn't be, I guess. I'm a friend of Deanne's."

Miranda shook her head. "I don't know a Deanne. Charles, have you met a tenant named Deanne?"

Minnie, or possibly Mimi, whined while Charles thought. Finally, he said, "Yes, we both did. She's Landon's ex-wife, remember?"

At the mention of Landon's name, Miranda Hoffman stiffened.

"That's right. Deanne's his ex-wife and, unfortunately for her, the executor of his estate. She lives in California, so I'm helping her take care of some things," Maisy explained breezily.

Charles took a closer look at Maisy.

"You're the weather girl," he announced.

Weathercaster or, if you prefer, meteorology reporter, she mentally corrected him. *And I haven't done the weather in over a decade.*

But she smiled. "You caught me. Maisy Farley, formerly of WACB News and now podcasting the Farley Files."

Charles drew his eyebrows together. "Podcasting, like on the radio?"

"Something like that."

"Pretty gal like you? You should try to get back on the TV."

Maisy kept her smile in place but allowed it to dim several degrees. His wife shot him a frosty look.

"She's investigating Landon's death, Charles. She thinks he was murdered."

"Oh, no, honey. The police said it was a suicide."

"Did they talk to you? The police?"

"No, they did not. Despite my request," Miranda said instantly, biting off each word.

The elevator came to a stop on the ninth floor. While she waited for the doors to open, Maisy offered, "Well, I'd love to hear anything you have to say about Landon."

Miranda thrust the pink leash she was holding into her husband's hand. "Here, you take the girls."

Before he could respond, the doors parted, and Miranda trotted off the elevator behind Maisy and followed her to Landon's apartment.

Once inside, Maisy offered the woman a fresh drink, which she declined. They sat in a pair of comfortable armchairs that flanked a large window with a view of the skyline. Maisy requested and received Miranda's permission to record their conversation. She hit record and dove right in.

"Miranda Hoffman was Landon Lewis' neighbor. Mrs. Hoffman, did you know Landon well?"

"No. He kept to himself."

"But you requested a conversation with the police after he died, isn't that right?"

"Yes. That's correct," she said primly.

"Did you talk to the police?"

"No. They brushed me off."

"Do you have information about Landon's purported suicide?"

For the first time in their admittedly brief acquaintanceship, Maisy saw Miranda Hoffman hesitate. After a moment, the woman recovered her confidence and plowed forward.

"Not about his death, per se."

Maisy hid her disappointment. "Then what did you want to talk to them about?"

Miranda pitched forward and lowered her voice. "His criminal activity."

"Are you referring to the profiling program he built for law enforcement?"

"What?" Miranda threw her a confused look. "No. I'm talking about whatever he was doing in his closet."

Maisy had learned early in her career that when an interviewee went off the rails, trying to wrest them back onto the track took considerable energy and effort and virtually never worked. It was better to let her tire herself out babbling about nonsense and, then, when she was spent, gently guide her back. So she was perfectly willing to let Miranda barrel, full steam ahead, down whatever embankment she headed for.

"What was he doing in his closet?" Maisy asked mildly.

"Well, *I* don't know. That's why I wanted to police to investigate. Whatever it was, he made an unholy racket. His closet shares a wall with Minnie and Mimi's room. For two days, there was hammering and drilling and all sorts of noise coming from his closet. For hours on end. The noise bothered the babies something awful. They were barking and whining all day. And they have very delicate constitutions, you know? They were so high-strung and nervous. It was *dreadful*. I called building management, and they said there was nothing they could do because the noise occurred outside of quiet hours. Honestly!"

The woman had wanted to make a noise complaint against a dead man. No wonder the police had blown her off.

"So, the criminal activity was disturbing the peace?" Maisy ventured.

"Don't be ridiculous. I buttonholed one of the workers when he was taking a break and demanded to know what they were doing in there."

"What were they doing?"

"Installing a safe. Not just any safe. A hidden safe. A hidden, state-of-the-art, uncrackable safe. Probably for his drugs." She leaned back with a satisfied expression.

Maisy was fixated on the news that Landon had a safe, but she figured she'd better ask just in case. "Do you have reason to believe Landon was doing drugs or selling drugs or otherwise involved in the drug trade?"

"Well, not beyond the obvious."

"Which is?"

"What possible reason would someone need a safe like that other than drugs? Or money from drugs? Don't you watch television?" Miranda snapped.

Maisy rubbed her forehead. "When did this construction happen?"

"The last week of July. The same week Landon 'committed suicide.'" She used her fingers to put air quotes around the phrase 'committed suicide,' and Maisy dearly wished she had this interview on video.

"Are you sure about the timing?"

"Of course, I'm sure. It was miserably hot and humid that week. The way I struck up the conversation with the workman was to tell him nobody would mind if he and his colleagues were to take a dip in the rooftop pool. I mean, not during peak hours after work or on a weekend. But during the day, when nobody uses the pool anyway, it would be fine."

"Did he take you up on that?" Maisy didn't care about the answer, but she figured she might as well keep Miranda talking.

"No. He said they were almost finished and that Mr. Lewis was paying a premium to get the safe installed as quickly as possible, so they couldn't take time off in the middle of the day to swim." She sniffed. "Of course, that didn't stop him from taking time in the middle of the day to loaf in the lobby with a sports drink."

"Do you know if they finished the installation before Landon died?"

"They must've. They cleared out, but I was still upset. I wanted to talk to Landon about being a more considerate neighbor. So the first day after the workers finished, I stopped by his apartment twice. Once in the morning, and once in the evening. But if he was home, he didn't answer the door. The next day, I tried again in the morning." She paused and gathered herself, "And, again, there was no answer. That same evening, we learned that his body had been found in that alley." She shuddered.

"Thank you for talking to me, Miranda," Maisy said. She stopped the recording and stood up.

To her eternal surprise and gratitude, Miranda Hoffman took the hint and also stood. Maisy hurried her out the door, locked herself inside the apartment, and rubbed her hands together with glee.

She resumed recording. "And now, dear listeners, we go on a treasure hunt."

CHAPTER THIRTY

JENNA WAS HALFWAY home from the emergency room when Amber called. Jenna's phone connected to the car's speakers through Bluetooth, which, given the age of the car, was never a sure bet. But, this time, Amber's voice rang out loud, clear, and demanding as soon as Jenna answered the call.

"Well? I've been texting you all morning. Did you do it?"

Jenna glanced to her right. Zane reclined in the passenger seat, his head lolling back and his mouth hanging open, courtesy of the cocktail of intravenous pain medication coursing through his veins. He was dead to the world. Still, she chose her words with care and kept her answer brief and vague.

"I'm driving. Can I call you back?"

Undeterred, Amber peppered her with questions.

"Driving where? To work? Weren't you supposed to start at ten?"

"Zane broke his hand last night. It's a bad break, so I had to take him to the hospital to get it set. We're on our way home now. After I get him settled, I'm going to work. I'll call you later."

She kept one eye on Zane as she spoke, watching for a reaction. But he was conked out.

"What about that special project you were supposed to do today? You know, for work."

Subtlety had never been Amber's strong suit. But Jenna supposed it didn't matter much since Zane was unconscious.

"I should still have time to do it later. I'll call you tonight." She hit the button to end the call without giving her sister a chance to respond or probe further.

As the car rattled through Oakland and Bloomfield, she dodged as many of the potholes on Baum Boulevard as she could. Despite her care, the ride was a bumpy one, and Zane groaned with every jostle.

"Sorry," she whispered.

In response, he made a sound that wasn't immediately identifiable as a word. She realized he must be at least semi-conscious, and that gave her an idea. She'd once watched an episode of her favorite forensics show where the bad guy was a hypnotherapist who extracted personal information from his patients by asking them questions while they were in the liminal space between sleep and wakefulness. On the show, at least, people in that state weren't alert enough to lie or refuse to answer.

She pushed down the feeling that what she was about to do was wrong and said, "Zane?"

"Mmmm."

"Why did you hide a cell phone in the basement?" She asked. Her palms were sweaty, and she gripped the steering wheel as if it was a lifeline.

"Maisy."

It sounded like he'd said 'Maisy.' She wrinkled her brow. "Maisy? Maisy Farley?"

"Mmm."

"What does she have to do with this? Is that her phone?"

What would a local celebrity want with Zane? Jenna recalled that Maisy had been romantically linked to a Steeler, a Pirate, and two Penguins. So it was clear she had a thing for athletes. But none of those guys had been married. And, no offense to Zane, but a broke, aging amateur boxer wasn't exactly in the same league as the rich, famous professional athletes Maisy Farley dated.

She waited, holding her breath and hoping Zane would say something that would make her laugh off her worry about the reporter-turned-podcaster. But he said nothing at all.

"Zane?"

The only response was his whistling snore. She gritted her teeth, noted the time, and hit the gas. Christina was a decent enough boss, but the later Jenna arrived, the worse her day would be. Everyone would have directed the most miserable customers' tickets to Jenna's queue. It was the unspoken rule of the office: part punishment for whoever dared roll in late, part self-preservation for the agents who were working. When the office was short-handed, they couldn't spare the time to deal with the really sticky cases. And the longer an unresolved issue languished unanswered, the angrier the customer would become and the longer it would take her to resolve each problem, causing a cascade effect.

Her misery at the thought of the day ahead of her was only exacerbated when Zane snorted, snuffled, and croaked Maisy's name a second time.

She sighed. Today was shaping up to be the worst day in a long time.

Later, she'd look back on this in the car, fretting over work and an imaginary affair, with something like longing for her lost innocence. Because, at this moment, Jenna had no idea just how bad her day was about to get.

CHAPTER THIRTY-ONE

MAISY STOOD in Landon's underutilized walk-in closet and allowed her anticipation to build. She imagined how excited she'd be when she found the safe. Only time would tell if the safe held the answer to Landon's puzzling death. For now, she wanted to breathe in the possibility and savor it for a moment longer.

Finally, when she could bear the suspense no longer, she hit her recording app and started her search, narrating as she went:

"By all outward appearances, Landon Lewis' closet is an ordinary closet. A well-appointed, high-end, walk-in closet, but just a closet. But according to neighbor Miranda Hoffman, this is no run-of-the-mill closet. Miranda says it concealed a safe."

She paused and scanned the space. If she were hiding a safe in here, where would she put it? There were no obvious hiding places. The exposed shelves and racks didn't lend themselves to concealment.

She decided to start with the drawers in the island-sized dresser. She'd given them a cursory look the first time she'd checked out the closet. But she'd been more focused on Landon's monochromatic wardrobe of basics than any false bottoms or hidden panels that might be revealed on close inspection.

Now, she worked methodically, drawer by drawer, removing the items of clothing within, running her hands over the smooth wood of the drawers' bases, and shining her phone's flashlight into the corners. In the end, she had nothing to show for her effort save several neat stacks of clothing and a small mountain of black dress socks that had been carefully rolled into pairs. She returned the items to their designated drawers and plopped down on the leather bench to think.

She swept her gaze over every visible floorboard, looking for something that didn't belong, something that stood out or seemed off. But all she could see was plank after uniform plank of hand-scraped wood.

"I'm missing something," she mused aloud. "But what?"

Miranda had complained about the noise. Although Maisy had never personally installed a safe, she couldn't imagine that the typical installation was a cacophonous, multi-day job. What would make that much noise? Cutting into drywall? Ripping up floorboards? She had no clue.

She lowered herself to her knees and crawled around

the perimeter of the closet, feeling for raised panels or latches. She found none. She slumped against the wall in defeat and stretched out her legs, propping her feet on the leather bench seat. She applied a touch too much force and kicked the bench, moving it several inches with a screech that left her convinced she scratched the floor.

"Oopsie."

She leaned forward to inspect the damage, and her pulse ticked up. She shoved the bench several feet to the side and peered at the section of the floor it had originally occupied. Was this rectangle of wood ever-so-slightly darker than the rest? She was sure it was. The color differentiation was subtle—a shadow, at most. It was barely noticeable, but it was there.

"Hot dog!" She exclaimed. Then she laughed at her own corniness.

"The leather bench that sits alongside the oversized dresser appears to be more than a mere convenient place for Landon Lewis to sit while putting on his shoes. After moving the bench aside and performing a close visual inspection of the flooring upon which it sat, it's clear to me that a section of the floor—made up of three wide planks, each measuring roughly one foot wide and three feet long—has been replaced."

She paused the recording and studied the rectangle. She knew Jordana could edit out all the dead air time, but she didn't need the pressure of figuring out how to gain access to the safe in real time.

She saw no latch or handle, so how did Landon lift the floorboard? She narrowed her eyes to squint at the flooring. A small notch was carved into the board that abutted the dresser. It could've been a mistake—the slip of a jigsaw when the closet was built and the dresser affixed.

Or ...

She slid her fingernail under the edge of the notch and pushed down on the slight depression. The pressure activated a spring mechanism, and the entire rectangle of wood slowly, silently rose until it came to a stop perpendicular to the floor.

She let out an excited hoot, then she remembered the recording. So she pushed the panel back into place, hit record, and repeated the entire process, describing it as she did so.

When the false floorboards were lifted, the compartment underneath revealed a slim rectangular safe. Maisy rejoiced when she saw that it wasn't a biometric safe. Considering that the owner of the safe had been cremated, getting a fingerprint or a retina scan would've been a real problem.

Her exuberance was, however, short-lived. Ever since Miranda had mentioned the safe, Maisy'd been hoping it would have a keyed lock. She'd already found two keys that Landon had hidden and liked her odds of finding a third. Unfortunately, the glossy white safe recessed into the subflooring was secured by a combination lock.

"Well, shoot."

She rocked back on her heels to think. After a

moment, she pressed the backlit numbers on the keypad to enter Josh's birthdate followed by the date of his death. The safe didn't open. She shrugged, disappointed but not surprised: that combination was probably a bit too obvious for Landon's tastes. She reversed the order and tried the date of death followed by birth. Still no joy. She wasn't about to do the math to figure out how many combinations of digits the two dates could create, but she knew it was more than she had the time or the patience to attempt.

She walked out to the kitchen for a glass of water in case changing her perspective and getting her blood flowing jarred loose a better idea. Also, she was thirsty.

SHE LEANED AGAINST THE ISLAND, taking a long drink of Landon's imported water. She closed her eyes to clear her mind. When she opened them, her gaze landed on Landon's little notebook filled with quotes, which was sticking out of her purse. Suddenly, she knew how to get into the safe.

She abandoned her glass, snatched up her purse, and sprinted—not to the safe in the closet, but to the home office. She scooped up the books from the shelf by the door and continued down the hall to Landon's bedroom, where she grabbed the copy of *Moby-Dick* from his bedside table.

Then, she hurried back to the closet and dumped the armload of books on the top of the dresser. She opened

Landon's notebook to the last page with writing and read the quote he'd copied:

Who's over me? Truth hath no confines.

The short passage was from *Moby-Dick*, and Landon had been considerate enough to include the page number on which it appeared. By now, Maisy's understanding of the man and his psyche was sufficiently robust that she knew the page number wouldn't be part of the combination to open the safe. She pursed her lips. But the chapter might be. She paged through the book to the passage, then located the chapter. The lines appeared in Chapter 36.

She dug her own notebook and a pen out of her bag and flipped to a blank page in the notebook. She scrawled the digits '36.' She returned to Landon's mini-notebook of quotes and found the quote that preceded the *Moby-Dick* lines. Back and forth, back and forth. She switched from Landon's quotes to the books from which he'd pulled them and then scribbled down the chapter numbers in which the quotes appeared. She was sufficiently confident in her method to narrate for her eventual podcast listeners as she went. When she was done, she had six two-digit numbers.

She stared down at the page for a long, silent moment savoring the moment of anticipation. Then she keyed in the digits, beginning with the Melville passage and working her way back. As soon as she hit the final digit, the locking mechanism whirred softly, and then the safe door swung open in a slow, smooth motion. She whooped triumphantly and peered inside. A space gray

MacBook was nestled in the safe on top of three stacks of letter-sized notebooks.

She lifted the laptop out first and set it on the dresser. Then she gathered the notebooks. She counted fifteen identical black notebooks. She flipped the first one open and read the date range printed in neat block lettering on the inside cover: October 2007—September 2008. Each journal covered a twelve-month period beginning with the month of Josh's death. The fifteenth notebook was identified as October 2021—_____, with the ending month left blank.

Did Landon habitually wait until the twelve-month period had officially ended to write the end date in his journals? Or had there been a harbinger when he started the last one, an icy inkling that whispered he wouldn't be alive to see September 2022? She shivered, then expressed the thought aloud for her recorder.

She paged through the notebooks, stopping to skim random pages. They were a treasure trove of Landon's inspirations, fears, and doubts as he created and refined his Cesare program. But, they were more than that. They were diaries in the truest sense of the word. These journals were much more than business records. They were personal records that memorialized his feelings and his experiences. She imagined that's why he hadn't turned them over to the Department of Justice or to Sasha during any of the court cases. These bound pages contained Landon Lewis' heart.

CHAPTER THIRTY-TWO

MAISY WAS BURSTING to share the news with someone. She grabbed her phone and was about to hit the speed dial for Sasha's number when she realized: she couldn't tell Sasha or Naya about this. At least not yet. She *could* tell Jordana—and would—but she couldn't justify interrupting her Hanukkah visit. Not when her producer would be back from her grandmother's place later tonight. She stared at the phone in her hand, perplexed and a bit deflated.

She was a reporter. She reported news. It was what she did. More than that, it was who she was. Could she really not tell a soul what she'd just found? She sighed and stared down at the open safe, feeling indescribably lonely. But after a beat, she brightened. There was *one* person she could share her discovery with right now. She dialed Deanne Lewis' number, bouncing on the soles of her feet as she waited for Landon's ex-wife to pick up.

She flipped through the pages of Landon's latest journal while she waited for Deanne to pick up. The most recent pages revealed his struggle with the morality of Cesare. It was reassuring to see that he eventually came to question the impact his criminal profiling AI might have on society. But surely he'd started grappling with these questions in 2019, at the latest. She knew he'd shared his doubts with Sasha in the aftermath of the Milltown debacle. Why was he still asking if he was doing more harm than good as late as this past summer? She'd have to go back through the previous notebooks to see if something had prompted the final bout of soul searching or if he'd been perseverating. Just spinning his wheels like a farmer whose tractor was stuck in the spring mud.

"Maisy? What's up?" Deanne answered.

"So much. Do you have time to talk? I know it's a holiday."

"Are you kidding me? First of all, it's eight in the morning here, so I have ten hours before my dinner guests arrive. Second of all, I heard the trailer for your podcast. I am *dying* to know what you've learned."

"What? How? Did Jordana send it to you?"

"No. That's the wild part. It showed up in my recommended podcasts. And believe me, I don't listen to any true crime podcasts. It's mostly therapy and self-improvement podcasts." She paused, then specified, "Uh, for work."

Maisy laughed. "I don't judge."

"Are you going to make me beg, or what?"

"Oh, no, sorry. I talked to some people in the building, and Landon's next-door neighbor gave me an earful—"

"The couple with the little white dogs? That wife is a piece of work. I took the stairs when I left so she couldn't trap me in the elevator and complain, yet again, about how much noise Landon was making." Deanne snorted. "You didn't know Landon, so you can't know how utterly ridiculous that is. He would never disturb his neighbors."

"Mmm. Well, he might. If he had a good reason."

"Such as?"

"Oh, I don't know. Maybe having a hidden safe installed beneath his closet floor."

Deanne gasped. "Are you serious?"

"Oh, yeah. I found it and figured out the code to get into it." Maisy realized she sounded prideful, but, in fairness, she *was* full of pride about her investigative breakthrough.

"What's in it? Anything about the source of his fortune?"

"Nothing that jumped out, unless he wrote about it in his journal or there are relevant files on his laptop."

Maisy heard a faint drumming as if Deanne might be tapping her fingernails against a table or desk while she considered this possibility.

Then she said decisively, "I doubt there's anything about the Thor Trust on the computer. Maybe in his most recent journal, though."

"I'm going to read through them—all fifteen years'

worth. There must be something worth protecting in them and on the laptop. He went through the effort and expense of having a safe installed for them."

"When was the safe put in?"

"Two days before he died."

The answer landed weighty with significance.

"Interesting timing."

"I think so, too. I get that historically Landon didn't store anything crucial on the computer, but I also have the drive that was hidden in his wine cellar. So I'll pop that in and see if there's anything about his finances on that."

"Mmm. Oh, hey, you should try Find My Phone once you're logged into the laptop."

"Assuming I can log in. Any chance you know his password?"

"Unless he had a midlife change of heart, it'll be Josh's initials and birthdate: capital 'J' then lowercase double 'l', followed by 031190."

"You're not serious. All this cloak and dagger, and that's his password?"

Deanne chuckled. "It's been his password since 2006. If he was still alive, he'd tell you that he uses an easily guessable password deliberately. The files on his computer have always been more of a decoy than anything else. It was his version of carrying a one-hundred-dollar bill in his wallet in case he was mugged. The plan was to hand over the Benjamin and hope that satisfied his mugger. Sacrifice something small to protect the rest."

"I guess."

"But that's not the real reason, or at least it's not the only reason. He set that password months before Josh died. I don't think he had the heart to change it after the murder. It would have felt like he was denying Josh or forgetting him."

"That makes more sense than decoy mugger money," Maisy told her. "And using the device to search for the phone is brilliant. Assuming it's a newer iPhone, there's a recent update that will ping the phone even if the SIM's been removed."

"And assuming the thing hasn't been crushed into nothing in the bottom of a landfill by now."

"That, too. Do you want to stay on the call while I fire up the laptop and see what happens?"

"Definitely."

Maisy grabbed the computer and headed to the office to put the thing on its dock to charge.

CHAPTER THIRTY-THREE

JENNA MANAGED to haul Zane as far as the couch. She eased off his shoes, propped a pillow under his head, and draped a blanket over him. Then she poured a glass of water and left it on the coffee table next to his pain medication. Through it all, he mumbled nonsense.

"I'm going upstairs to get ready for work. I'll check on you before I leave." She spoke loudly and slowly as though that would somehow break through his brain fog.

As she started to walk away, he stretched out his good hand and caught her wrist. "I'm sorry."

She almost asked him what he was sorry about but decided not to go there right now. Instead, she eased her wrist out of his grasp and hurried upstairs. She went straight to the bathroom and dug the iPhone out from the box of pads. Kneeling on the floor, she swallowed hard and hit the power button before she could lose her nerve.

She crossed herself, then stared down at the phone unblinkingly waiting to see what would happen.

"YOU READY?" Maisy asked Deanne.

"Ready when you are," she replied, her voice tinny through the speakerphone.

Maisy perched on the edge of Landon's desk chair and leaned forward. So far, everything had gone according to plan. The laptop charged right away, Landon had, in fact, not updated his password, and the Find My app showed that the dead man had chosen the necessary settings that would enable her to locate the phone—if it was charged and intact. It hadn't been online since July, but there was still hope.

"Okay, here goes nothing." Maisy's finger hovered above the tracker pad. "Wait. I can mark it lost and then create a message to contact me if it's found."

"Oh, yeah, do that!"

Maisy changed the settings, typed in her contact information, and then crossed her fingers for a moment before clicking the icon to find Landon's iPhone. She held her breath, focused her unwavering attention on the screen, and waited to see what happened next.

THE IPHONE EMITTED A PIERCING SOUND. Jenna jumped and bobbled the device, nearly dropping it. She jabbed desperately at the volume button to turn it down before it woke Zane. To her horror, the tone's volume increased and continued to increase, despite her efforts. Just when she thought the earsplitting noise would never end, the phone suddenly went silent.

She exhaled and pushed her sweaty hair off her forehead. She needed to reapply her deodorant after that. She opened the medicine cabinet and reached for the tube, keeping her eyes on the phone. A message appeared on the lock screen: *Lost iPhone. This iPhone has been lost. Please call Maisy F.* Beneath the message was a phone number with a 412 area code.

Jenna gagged. She turned off the phone and yanked the charging cord from the port. Then she stared at the cold red rectangle. Now what? She closed up the box of sanitary pads, shoved the phone into her purse, and ran down the stairs and out of the house, not bothering to check on Zane before she left.

"HOLY CRAP," Maisy breathed.

"What?" Deanne demanded.

"The phone's in East Liberty."

"Why do I know that name?"

"Bakery Square, where Landon had his office, is a development in East Liberty."

"So it's at the office?"

Maisy shook her head, studying the screen. "No, this

is a residential street. But I know where this is. It's only a few blocks from my townhouse, actually. Walking distance."

She zoomed in on the map, then enabled satellite view and zoomed in even further. The residence in question was a red brick row house. It was an end unit, so it was attached only on the right side. An alley ran along the left side of the structure. Maisy could make out a chain-link fence surrounding the side yard and a blurry blue sedan parked in the alley.

"Maisy ...." Deanne's voice held a warning.

"Hmm?"

"You put your name and phone number in as the contact info."

Maisy put the laptop into sleep mode and tucked it into her bag while she answered Deanne. "Right. But I don't think I need to wait to see if they reach out. I'll just pop by and—"

"No! It's not safe."

Maisy blinked at the urgency in Deanne's voice. "It's eleven a.m. on a Monday. I know the neighborhood like the back of my hand."

"The person who has Landon's phone might be a perfectly nice human who found it in a dumpster or something."

"Right," she agreed. She cradled the phone between her neck and shoulder and walked back to the closet, packing up her bag while she did so.

"Or," Deanne continued, "they might be a murderer. They could be the killer. You can't go traipsing over there, especially not now that you've given them a head's up that you, Maisy Farley, are looking for the phone."

Maisy made a *tsking* sound. Deanne had a point. She considered her next best play while she returned twelve of Landon's journals to the safe and put the three most recent volumes in her bag along with the laptop and the copy of Landon's file that the police had given to Deanne.

"Maisy?" Deanne prompted.

"I hear you." She added Landon's quote journal and her reporter's notebook to the cache of materials in her bag, but removed the hard drive and placed it in the safe. Then she closed and locked the safe, replaced the cover, and dragged the bench over to position it on top of the concealed door.

"So, tell me you're not going there."

"I'm not going to the house. You're right. That would be foolish. I'm going to the police station. Landon died in East Liberty. His phone's in East Liberty. This seems like something Evans and Bass should handle."

"Good. That's an excellent plan," Deanne affirmed eagerly.

Maisy returned the books to their spot on the floating shelf, adding *Moby-Dick* to the collection. Then she surveyed the apartment, put her glass in the dishwasher, and turned out the lights.

"I'll call you when I have an update," she promised Deanne before ending the call, stepping out into the hallway, and locking the door behind her.

Unwilling to press her luck with the elevator, she headed for the stairwell instead.

CHAPTER THIRTY-FOUR

Zone 5 Police Station
11:45 AM

MAISY FLASHED the officer behind the front desk her most winning smile. "Hi, there."

He didn't smile back. "Can I help you?"

She poured on the sugar. "I sure hope so, officer. I need to speak to Sergeant Bass right away, please. It's *urgent*."

He pointed to the clock on the wall behind him without turning to look at it. "Bass is at lunch."

"Is Officer Evans available?"

"Lunch."

Her sweetness slipped. "I really need some help here. Is there anyone who's not at lunch?"

"I'm not at lunch. Clearly."

She took a moment to muster her empathy. She, too, knew what it was to be hangry. "Well, I guess I'll run up to Park Bruges and grab some takeout. Maybe they'll be back from lunch by then. Can I pick something up for you?"

He eyed her suspiciously. "Why would you do that?"

Because my mama always told me the way to a man's heart was through his stomach.

"I'm going anyway. Looks like you're stuck here, so, why wouldn't I?"

"Hmmph. What do you like there?"

This was clearly a test. Luckily, she loved getting gold stars. "Oh, the goat cheese salad and the soup of the day." She waited for a beat, then leaned over the counter to whisper, "Just kidding. The mac & cheese with a side of pomme frites."

He nodded his approval. "There's no shame in that chèvre salad, though. It's legit. But do yourself a favor and try their tofu bahn mi. You'll thank me."

It was her turn to give him the side-eye. "Really? A vegan twist on a Vietnamese sandwich from a Belgian/French joint?"

"Trust me."

"What's your name?"

"Officer Thune. Frank Thune."

"Okay, Officer Thune. I'm counting on you not to lead me astray. I'll be back with two tofu bahn mi sandwiches." She turned to leave.

"Hey, wait."

She pivoted to see what he needed. "Yeah?"

"What's *your* name?"

"Maisy."

His eyes went wide. "I thought you looked familiar. You're the reporter."

"Former reporter, yeah."

"I didn't recognize you without all the crap on your face."

"Stage makeup," she nodded.

"You look better without it. Younger."

She flashed a smile and hurried to leave so she wouldn't ruin their tenuous connection by tearing into him.

When she returned twenty minutes later with the sandwiches, she was glad she resisted the urge to let him have it. A bemused Oswald Bass was leaning against the counter.

"Here, you go, Officer Thune." Maisy slid him his bag.

The officer jerked a thumb at the sergeant. "I put out a call over the radio for the sarge and Evans to come back. She's on her way."

"Thanks."

Frank Thune shrugged and raised his sandwich in a salute. "I'm taking my break," he bellowed to the room in general before disappearing down a hall.

Bass shook his head. "Did you just bribe Frank Thune with a tofu sandwich?"

Yes?

"I wouldn't call it bribery."

Bass barked out a laugh. "Come on, you can eat that thing while we wait for Evans."

He led her down a long hallway to a cramped, but tidy office. He pointed to a chair jammed up against a metal desk and handed her a paper plate and a napkin from a stack on his filing cabinet.

She dug into the sandwich and made a mewl of approval. He raised an eyebrow.

After she wiped her mouth with the napkin, she said, "I was a skeptic, too. I'm now a convert."

"Hmm."

Before she could delve into further detail about the merits of the sandwich, a loud, quick rap sounded at the door.

"Come in," Bass called.

The door opened and Ilsa Evans' confused face appeared in the doorway. "Did something happen, sarge? I got a call to come back."

"Yeah, Maisy here bought Thune a sandwich, so now he's her personal valet. She told him she needed to speak to us *urgently*. Thune stressed the urgency."

He leaned back in his chair and folded his hands over his stomach while the junior officer pulled the door shut and stood at attention.

"Aw, perch yourself on the filing cabinet," her boss told her.

"You need another chair in here," Maisy said.

"Where would I put it? On top of the desk?"

He had a point.

"So?" Evans prompted. "What's so urgent."

Maisy set the sandwich aside reluctantly and pulled Landon Lewis' laptop out of her purse. "This is Landon Lewis' MacBook."

"Where'd you get that?" Bass demanded.

"I don't know if you heard, but his ex-wife asked me to look into his death."

"Suicide," Evans corrected. "And yeah, we heard. Everybody heard. My sister wouldn't shut up about your podcast at dinner."

Maisy smothered a smile. "Deanne gave me access to Landon's office and apartment."

"We searched both of those," Evans insisted. "There was no laptop."

Maisy shrugged. "Guess you didn't look hard enough. It was in his closet."

"What are you playing at, Maisy? I thought you were gonna look into that nuisance bar thing we gave you."

"The lead with no names or other information? Sorry, I'm a reporter, not a magician."

"Are you, though?" Bass asked.

She cocked her head. "Am I what?"

"A reporter. I thought you were a podcaster."

She bristled. "Listen, I have something. I brought it to you two first because I like you. And because you caught Landon's case. But if you don't want it, maybe I'll see if what's-his-name is interested."

"Who?"

"Coltrane? No, that's not it." She snapped her fingers. "Colchis."

Evans and Bass stiffened in unison. They exchanged a look, then Bass said, "Who told you about Colchis?"

"The concierge at Landon's building."

"What?" Bass demanded.

"He said a few days after the original interviews, a detective came by to go through the apartment and talk to some staff. I'm pretty sure he said the guy's name was Detective Colchis." She pursed her lips. "I don't know anyone in this station with that name, though?"

"He's not assigned to Zone Five," Bass said woodenly.

"Then why was he working Landon's death? Is he homicide?"

"No, he's not homicide, because—as Evans just explained—Landon's death was a suicide. And as for why he went to the apartment building, your guess is as good as mine," Bass told her.

"So, you found the laptop," Evans said. "Anything on it?"

"I don't know yet. Deanne thinks probably not."

The two officers exchanged an exasperated look.

"Then what's so urgent?" Bass wanted to know.

"I also found his cell phone. Well, technically, I located his phone."

"You found Lewis' missing mobile phone?" Evans asked.

"Well, I know where it is."

"And where is it?"

Maisy pulled up the map on the laptop, turned the device so the screen was facing the cops, and pointed a finger at the row house with the blue car parked beside it. "As of an hour ago, it was right here. A rudimentary search of publicly available tax records tells me this is the home of Jenna and Zane Novak. That's enough to get a warrant for possession of stolen property, right?"

"Probably. Thanks for bringing it to us, Maisy," Evans said. She held out her arms as if Maisy might be clueless enough to hand over the laptop.

Instead, she slipped it back into her bag. "Nice try. Here's the deal. You get your warrant *and* I get to tag along on the search of the house to record it for my podcast. Then, we'll talk about access to the laptop."

Evans gave her a look that suggested there was no way they'd go along with her demands. But Bass didn't get to be a supervisor by being shortsighted.

He pointed a meaty finger at her. "Stay right there. Don't talk to anyone. We'll be back in a few minutes. Eat your sandwich."

Maisy grinned and pulled the plate back in front of her. "Don't have to tell me twice."

Evans hopped down from the filing cabinet, and the pair left the room in a hurry while Maisy savored her lunch.

CHAPTER THIRTY-FIVE

ZANE DREAMED he was in the ring. His right hand hurt like hell as he pummeled his opponent. In a distant corner of the gym, somebody was hitting a heavy bag. Over and over, rhythmic punches echoed off the walls.

He moaned as he shifted onto his side. The movement jostled the splint the ER docs had put on his hand to immobilize it until the swelling abated and they could put his hand in a cast and shook him out of his dream. He remembered the instruction to keep his hand above his heart, so he raised it above his head and let it hang over the edge of the armrest.

He blinked his eyes open. He was about to reach for the water and pills on the coffee table when he realized the punching noise hadn't stopped. Dopey from the pain meds and bleary from sleep, it took him another twenty seconds to realize nobody was punching anything. Someone was hammering at the front door.

"Jenna," he croaked. "Door."

He listened for a response, but the house was silent. She'd probably gone to work. He shoved a pillow over his face and ignored the knocking. For a beat, it stopped. He removed the pillow. Then whoever was out there jabbed the doorbell like it owed them money—a dozen fast, long presses that made his head throb. He growled and got to his feet.

As he shuffled to the door with his right hand propped on his left shoulder, he heard a male voice followed by a burst of static. By the time his dulled brain connected the dots to realize that was a police radio, he'd already fumbled with the lock and yanked the door open.

"You Zane Novak?" A uniformed officer demanded.

"Uh ... yeah."

"We have a warrant to search your residence." She handed him a sheet of paper. It slipped through his fingers and floated to the floor.

"Anyone else here?" The male cop standing behind her craned his neck to peer inside the house.

"I don't ... no. I think Jenna went to work. I was sleeping on the couch." He pointed groggily to his splinted hand. "I just got back from the hospital. I'm kinda out of it."

"Sir, is there an iPhone 13 belonging to Landon Lewis on the premises?"

Plead the Fifth, his brain demanded.

"There was until last night. Now it's gone," his uncooperative mouth said.

The officers exchanged a look.

"Where is it?" the female officer asked.

Plead the Fifth.

"Hell if I know. Ask your boy Colchis." How could he make his dumb mouth stop yammering?

"Colchis. Would that be Detective Tim Colchis from the Nuisance Bar Task Force?"

He nodded yes and tried to focus on the blonde woman standing down on the sidewalk, holding her phone up like she was at a concert. She looked familiar.

"Who's that?"

The police ignored the question. Instead, the male officer said, "Are you admitting you did have the iPhone 13?"

"Yeah, sure."

"Where'd you get it?"

Zane's brain finally took control of the situation. "I don't want to talk to you anymore."

The female officer shrugged. "S'okay. We have enough to bring you in." She removed a set of handcuffs from her duty belt.

The woman on the sidewalk coughed to get the cops' attention. "His hand is clearly injured. Is that necessary?"

The police exchanged a look.

Zane placed the woman's voice and exclaimed, "Hey, you're Maisy Farley!"

The male officer jerked his head. "Why don't you wait in your car? We'll get Mr. Novak nice and comfy in the cruiser. While you're waiting, check your app and see where the phone is now."

"Are you going to take him at his word that it's gone?" she asked.

"No, Maisy," the guy officer said in exasperation. "We're gonna do a thorough search, but it would be stupid—even for this numbnuts—to admit he had it and not turn it over if it's here. Will you just see if it's still on the map?"

She pulled a face but crossed the street to a little hybrid that was parked behind a black-and-white. Zane lowered his head as his neighbors started poking their heads out their doors and pulling aside their curtains to see what the commotion was about. Jenna was gonna *kill* him when she found out.

CHAPTER THIRTY-SIX

BELLA MASSAGED her temples as she listened to the word vomit pour from the mouth on the other end of the phone. When the speaker finally wound down, Bella allowed her eyelids to flutter closed for a beat. Then she summoned a smile. Even through the phone, a listener could tell when someone was smiling. As smiles go, hers was insincere. But then, this call *had* interrupted her post-holiday-party pedicure. Her crucial 'me time.'

"Thank you for your report, Frank."

Frank Thune stammered something indistinct, and she knew he was dancing around whether the information was good enough to earn him a break on February's rent. It was. And ever the gracious landlord, Bella didn't make him ask.

"We appreciate your help. So just as we agreed for next month, it won't be necessary to remit February's rent, either."

He thanked her, then thanked her again.

She had things to do. "I have to go, Frank. Be well."

She ended the call and glanced down at her ruby-red toes as Georgio swiped the last brush full of color onto her pinkie toenail. "They look great, but I have to run. Please put the little foam separators between my toes and swipe my card." She pulled out her Amex Black Card.

He protested, "No, Miss Bella, let them dry, please. Sit for a few minutes and relax. I'll bring you another glass of sparkling wine."

"Georgio." When he raised his head at the sharpness of her tone, she flashed him a flat smile. "I need to leave. Now."

"You work too hard," he told her as he closed his hand around the credit card she pressed into his palm. "I'll be right back with your receipt."

She slipped her feet into her open-toed sandals and shrugged her arms into her cream-colored coat. Georgio returned with her card and a complimentary bottle of the hand lotion she liked.

"Thank you, love." She leaned in to give him an air kiss and took the opportunity to slip a fifty-dollar tip into his hand to make amends for her shortness. "Happy New Year."

She returned her card to its slot in her wallet and nestled the wallet and the lotion into her purse. Georgio walked her to the door and held it open for her as she found her sunglasses and her keys. As she walked to the Tesla, taking small careful steps in case the lot had iced over, she dug out the untraceable cell phone she used for her more unsavory contacts and placed the call to Tim Colchis.

TIM HUNKERED down in the unmarked car, mostly concealed from view by a rusted dumpster. He'd gotten a tip that a dishwasher was selling rail booze out the back door of B.J. McPickles' Pub. The clientele for the cheap liquor came from the parochial school a few blocks away, from which Vinny Spatz, the entrepreneurial dishwasher, had graduated just three years earlier. According to Tim's informant, Vinny was running a weeklong sale so his underaged customers could stock up on booze for their New Year's festivities.

Tim had a grudging appreciation for the kid's hustle. Depending on how Vinny reacted to the eventual bust, he figured he might let him off with a warning in exchange for a partnership. Tim would look the other way for fifteen percent.

When the call came in on the burner, he was tempted to ignore it. But he remembered the woman's veiled threats and figured he'd better not. So he dug the phone out of the car's center console.

"Colchis."

"Yes, I know. Who else would be answering this phone?"

He rolled his eyes. Technically, she was right, but

who cared? He could answer it 'PoPo the Clown' for all it mattered.

"I'm working," he told her.

"What a coincidence, so am I."

"What do you need?" He turned his neck to the right and used the heel of his palm to push against his chin until he heard a satisfying *pop*. Then he repeated the motion on his left side.

"What I *needed* was for you to have done your job competently in July. But that ship has sailed, so what *you* need now is to clean up your mess."

He waited for a beat, but she didn't elaborate.

"Is this about that chick's podcast again? Why don't you wait until the first episode drops tomorrow and see if it's worth getting your panties in a twist?"

"I assure you, my twisted panties are the least of your worries. Zane Novak was just arrested."

He grimaced at the news. "Crap. What's that mouth-breathing moron done now?"

"It's not what he's done now that should concern you but what he did last summer. Despite your repeated insistence that Mr. Novak disposed of the cell phone, it appears he did not."

"No disrespect, but someone's giving you bad intel."

"Yes. You are."

He squinted through the dirty windshield, smeared with the remnants of yesterday's snow. B.J. McPickles' kitchen door opened, and Vinny slunk into the lot. He cast a furtive look in each direction, then reached behind him and picked up a cardboard box.

"Listen, I'm literally at work. On a stakeout. I need to pop this—"

"Novak was arrested because Maisy Farley tracked Lewis' phone to the Novak home. And then, like a good citizen journalist, she took it to the police. Sergeant Bass and Officer Evans just took Zane into custody because, allegedly, he admitted having the phone."

Tim forgot all about Vinny.

"What? That can't be right. Who's your source?"

"I'm not doing this with you. I have a well-placed source within the Zone Five station. I'm confident in the information. Where I lack confidence is whether you can clean up your mess yourself or if I need to do it."

He didn't like the sounds of this at all. "Just relax. Give me a few hours to sort this out." He forced himself to add, "Please."

After a brief delay, she said, "You have twenty-four hours."

"Thank you."

"Don't thank me. I'm not doing this for you, I'm doing it for me. I don't want to have to report this massive screw-up to our employer. But, if it comes to that, I will. And you'll wish I hadn't."

"I understand," he assured her, clenching his teeth so tightly that his jaw began to ache.

He ended the call and peeled out from behind the dumpster. He drove through a group of teenagers skulking through the parking lot. He didn't even take any pleasure in seeing them scatter.

CHAPTER THIRTY-SEVEN

THE DOOR to the bathroom creaked open, and a pair of heels clicked across the floor. From her perch on the toilet seat lid, Jenna watched the scuffed navy pumps move over the discolored white tile.

The feet came to a stop just outside her stall. She held her breath and twisted the shredding square of rough toilet paper that she'd used to dry her tears.

"Jenna, I know you're in there. I can see your shoes."

Belatedly, she pulled her knees up to her cheeks and propped her feet on the front edge of the lid.

Christina laughed and rose on her toes to peek over the top of the stall. "Very slick." Then she caught a glimpse of Jenna's swollen, puffy face, and her laughter died. "Come on out."

Jenna pressed her wobbly lips together to keep from crying as she slid off the lid, opened the stall door, and stepped out to stand in front of her supervisor.

"I'm sorry, Chris. I'll pull myself together and get back out there. Just let me splash some water on my face." She took a shuddering breath that ended in a hiccup.

Chris rolled her eyes. "For Pete's sake, Jenna, we're not curing cancer. We're explaining people's phone charges to them. You shouldn't even have come in."

"No, I can't use all my personal time up. I need to roll it over, in case."

Her boss studied her closely. "Look, I know it's none of my business. But we're friends, right?"

She nodded.

"Are you *sure* you want to go through all these procedures, all this expense, to have a baby? With Zane, I mean?"

"Chris-*tina*," Jenna gasped.

"Oh, come on. Don't act so scandalized. He broke his hand on Christmas night. You spent the morning in the ER. This is after he almost got his sorry ass arrested last summer. I mean, Jenn."

"That's not even the worst of it," Jenna whispered, staring at her own scuffed shoes.

"Sonofa—I *knew* it."

The venom in Chris' voice sliced through Jenna and made her drag her eyes up to meet Christina's. "You knew? How?"

"Because I'm not a moron, that's how. You come in here with some story about him punching a stone wall by mistake, you're a hot mess, and my cousin calls to tell me the cops are crawling all over your house. That piece of crap hit you, didn't he? I'm glad you called the cops." She rubbed Jenna's shoulder. "Let me know if you need a place to stay."

Jenna's mind was clunking around like she had a busted gear. She was several steps behind. Chris wasn't talking about an affair with a local celebrity. "Wait. What? The police are at my house? Why?"

"You didn't file a protection from abuse order against Zane?"

"No, of course not. He's never lifted a finger against me."

Chris pursed her lips and threw her a skeptical look. "Really? With that temper? And his boxing training? I don't believe you."

"I can't help that, but I'm telling the truth," she said simply.

"Never? He's never hit you?"

"No, never. One, do you really think I'd stick around if he did?"

Chris shrugged with a sick expression.

"Okay, jeez, no. And, two, his boxing training makes him less likely to be violent with me. Or anyone outside the ring. It's controlled violence. He doesn't hit people unless there's a paycheck behind it." *Well, usually.*

"Mmm, I don't know. Didn't Mike Tyson bite off that guy's ear like forever ago?"

Jenna stared at her. "Yeah, and he was also convicted of raping a woman. But, Chris, Zane is no Mike Tyson. Forget that. Why are the cops at my house?"

She shrugged. "Lucy didn't say. I just assumed—"

"You assumed they were there to arrest my abusive husband."

"Well, they did. Arrest him, I mean. She saw them take him out and put him in the back of a squad car. She said a reporter recorded the whole thing. You know, the one who's starting a podcast. The blonde with the curly hair?"

"Maisy Farley," Jenna supplied in a dull voice.

"Right, her."

"Chris, I hate to do this—"

"Go."

Jenna managed a sickly smile and a 'thank you' over her shoulder before she raced out of the bathroom.

"Hang on. If you didn't know about the cops, why were you in here crying?" Chris called after her.

But Jenna was already halfway to the elevator.

CHAPTER THIRTY-EIGHT

THE POLICE OFFICERS sent Maisy home. Evans explained that it would take a while to get Zane processed through central booking and promised to call her when they had an update. She also tried to wheedle the laptop out of Maisy, claiming their tech people could trace the cell phone more easily than Maisy could.

But Maisy held firm, secure in her confidence that she knew how to press a button just as well as some Zone Five IT guy or gal did, and well aware that, at present, the laptop—and her ability to use it to track the iPhone—made her valuable to the police. If she handed it over, they wouldn't need her, and she wouldn't have any leverage. No thanks.

So she headed home, laptop in tow, to make herself a cup of tea and start reading through Landon's most recent journals. She'd wait to try to find the iPhone again until she needed an excuse to call Evans to exchange updates.

When she opened the door that connected her attached garage to the mudroom outside her kitchen, she immediately knew she wasn't going to need an excuse to call the police: she'd walked into one.

She froze in the doorway. Her heart banged against her ribcage and her hands shook as she pulled out her cell phone.

"9-1-1. What's your emergency?"

"I just walked into my house. Someone broke in," she whispered.

"Ma'am, are they gone?"

"I ... I don't know."

"Are any other family members, roommates, or pets present in the home?"

"I live alone." She forced the words out as her throat tightened.

She could hear her breath, fast and shallow, as she scanned the mudroom. Someone had pulled down her file boxes of materials from old stories. She'd stored the files in a neat row on the shelf above the beadboard panel of coat hooks and shoe cubbies that she, as a single, childless person, had no real use for. The lids had been flung off, and the contents of the boxes were scattered underfoot.

The operator spoke in a clear, calm, but unmistakably firm voice. "Leave the premises right now. Go straight out the door you came in and get as far away from the house as you can. Run."

"I—"

"Now."

Maisy backed out through the open doorway, pulled the door shut, and hit the button on the wall to raise the garage door. Then she ran.

She gave the operator her name and address and asked for Bass or Evans to be alerted in addition to whoever caught the call. Then she sat on the damp cold retaining wall in front of the pediatric dentist's office at the end of her block on the other side of the street and shivered until a black-and-white cruiser rolled by. The car slowed to a crawl, then stopped. The passenger window buzzed down, and Sergeant Bass's pale jowly face stared out at her. Evans leaned over the steering wheel to peer at her, too.

"What happened?"

"Someone broke in. How are you here? Shouldn't you still be getting Zane Novak processed?"

"We sent Thune over to the jail to babysit. Hop in."

She hesitated for a beat. As long as she stayed where she was and didn't move from this admittedly uncomfortable wall, a part of her could pretend that her private space hadn't been violated, that her home hadn't been breached. But the melting ice was seeping through her pants and her shaking was becoming more violent. Another few minutes, and it would be uncontrollable.

"Come on," Bass told her. He got out of the car and opened the back door to usher her inside the vehicle.

She pressed herself against the seat and squeezed her

eyes shut. "It's the townhouse across the street, halfway down the block."

"The one with the garage door hanging wide open?" Evans asked.

"Yeah," she confirmed with her eyes still tightly closed.

The passenger seat creaked in protest when Bass twisted around to talk to her. "You see anyone coming out?"

She opened her eyes and shook her head. "No."

"And you didn't go any further than the hallway from the garage?" he confirmed.

"Right."

"Good."

She dug her keys out of her purse with trembling hands. "Here. The gold one goes to the front door. The silver one opens the back. In case you need them." She dropped them into Bass's palm, and he closed his hand around them.

"Did you lock the door from the garage to the house when you got out of there?"

"No. I just closed it and ran."

Evans pulled into Maisy's driveway. "Stay in the car," she ordered as she killed the engine.

Maisy nodded mutely. She watched as the pair got out of the car and communicated through a series of hand gestures. Evans walked into the garage bay, skirting Maisy's car with her hand resting on the butt of her gun at her hip. Bass disappeared through the alley to circle around to the back door. Maisy shoved her hands under her thighs to warm them up and maybe still the tremors.

She stared unblinkingly at her front door, waiting for someone—the bad guy—to come bursting through. In her mind, he was straight out of central casting for a cartoon. He wore a black mask with eyeholes, a black cap, and all-black clothes and had a canvas sack slung over his shoulder like some sort of anti-Santa Claus. The absurdity of the image made her burst into laughter. And that's when she knew she'd be okay, cackling to herself in the back of the squad car.

After several painfully long moments, Evans emerged through the front door and stood on Maisy's stoop. She gestured for Maisy to get out of the car and come into the house.

As she approached, Evans called to her, "The house is clear. He's long gone. But prepare yourself, he tossed it pretty thoroughly. It's a mess in here."

She nodded and ran up the stairs. When she reached the threshold, Evans stepped aside to let her pass. She hurried inside, then skidded to a stop when she saw the utter shambles inside her home.

"Son of a biscuit eater," she breathed.

Evans' eyebrow shot up. "Come again?"

"My Georgia comes out when I'm emotional. How am I gonna clean this up?"

Her townhouse—what she could see of it, at least—had been reduced to rubble. Piles of broken glass, feathers from cut-open pillows, papers, overturned drawers, and furniture cushions were strewn across the floor.

The officer bobbed her head once and pressed her lips together in a tight line. "The whole place looks like this. It's gonna be hard to tell if anything's missing, but let's walk through together."

Maisy didn't trust herself to speak, so she nodded and followed the police officer through the wreckage of her home in a daze. When they'd completed a full circuit of both floors, she plopped down on her cushion-less love seat and stared at nothing.

Bass came in from the kitchen.

"Was anything taken?" He asked Evans in a low voice.

"Not that she saw. Her jewelry's all here, so are all her electronics, some expensive clothes. Credit cards are in a desk drawer, along with the checkbook. Everything's accounted for." She gave a confused shrug.

"He came in through the back," Bass said.

"It was locked," Maisy mumbled numbly.

"He picked it. It's a decent-enough lock but nothing that'd stop an experienced thief," the sergeant explained.

Maisy snapped out of her trance with great effort. She got to her feet. "Okay. Do you all need to take fingerprints or something, or can I start cleaning up?"

Bass and Evans exchanged a look. After a moment, Evans said, "Don't worry about cleaning up right now."

"Oh, are you sending a forensics team over?"

"Well, we'll have to talk about that," Bass waffled. "But, you know, if nothing's missing, that means whoever did this didn't find what they were looking for."

Maisy blinked at him until she realized what he was

getting at. She hugged her purse closer to her body. "You think they're looking for Landon's computer."

"Could be. Why don't you give it to us for safekeeping?"

She narrowed her eyes and lowered her chin. "Sergeant, assuming just for the sake of argument that you're right, the police are the only people who know I found it."

He frowned. "That can't be right."

"And yet, it is."

"Hang on. Didn't you tell Deanne Lewis you found it?" Evans interjected.

Maisy made a sour face. "Okay, yes. I did tell Deanne. So you think a grief counselor arranged—all the way from Carmel-by-the-Sea, let's not forget—for a local East End criminal with lock-picking talent to break into my house and steal it? All without knowing where I even live? That's your theory?"

"No," Evans admitted. "That seems unlikely, to say the least. But it isn't actually true to say that *nobody* knows except for us. That's all I'm saying."

"You didn't tell anybody else?" Bass pressed. "Are you sure?"

She was positive, but she went through the exercise of thinking about her day to satisfy Bass. Then she shook her head. "No. I didn't tell anyone else."

"Well, that's good."

"How do you figure?"

"The fewer people who know about the laptop, the smaller our suspect pool is," he explained helpfully.

She stared at the two of them. "You're currently Suspects Number 1 and 2."

"Now who's being ridiculous?" Evans asked. "We were at the county prison with Novak when you called 911. Remember?"

She raked her hands through her hair. "Okay, whatever. I don't know what's going on. But I'm dang sure I'm not giving you this laptop. No chance."

Bass exhaled heavily. "I'll put in for a crime scene team to come dust this place, but a residential break-in where nothing was taken isn't gonna be a high priority without some extenuating circumstances." He cast a meaningful look at her bag.

"No chance," she repeated.

He shrugged. "Suit yourself."

Evans thrust a business card into Maisy's free hand. "The number for the crime victim advocate's on there if you decide you need to talk to someone."

She slipped it into her purse. "Thanks."

"Do you have someone you can stay with?" Evans asked.

Maisy gave her a wide-eyed look. "Why?"

"You shouldn't stay here, Maisy. They could come back."

Her stomach tumbled at the thought.

Then, Bass added, "And you're gonna need to get a locksmith in to fix that door. I jammed a chair under the knob for now and put your deadlock on. You should use that all the time, you know. Anyway, it's a temporary fix, at best. Spend the night at a friend's place, huh?"

"Right." She swallowed her pride and asked for a favor. "Would you two mind sticking around for, like, five minutes tops while I throw some clothes in a bag?"

"Take your time," he told her.

She raced up the stairs to her bedroom.

CHAPTER THIRTY-NINE

AS SHE BACKED her car out of her garage and down the driveway, Maisy waved goodbye to Bass and Evans, who sat with their engine idling in the street in front of her townhouse. Evans nodded to her. Maisy checked that the garage door went all the way down and then drove to the stop sign at the end of the block.

Which way to go? Left to Sasha and Leo's or right to Naya and Carl's? Whose doorstep to turn up at? She stared at the setting sun, which was sinking low in the sky, and tried to decide.

She knew both couples would welcome her unannounced appearance with open arms. She'd have a better chance of getting work done at Naya's place. But if she was bringing danger to someone's door, the McCandless-Connelly household was better equipped to handle it. So, Sasha's it was. She bit her lip, palmed the wheel, and hit her left turn signal.

Then she spotted a little girl splashing through the slush on the sidewalk, her mittened hand swinging in her father's. She hit her brakes. The twins. If she had a target on her back, she couldn't in good conscience put Finn and Fiona in danger.

She blew out a long breath. The dad on the sidewalk gave her a confused look, and she managed a smile. He smiled back, and the little girl waved. Then she ran ahead of her father and skipped up the front steps of a house displaying a highly polished menorah glowing in the front window.

Maisy's heart stuttered, then skipped a beat. She pulled over to the side of the road, dug her phone out of her purse, and pulled up Jordana's phone number. As the call connected, Evans' black-and-white rolled up beside her.

Bass buzzed down his window just as he had when they'd come upon Maisy sitting on the stone wall. She pinched the phone between her ear and shoulder and did the same.

"You okay?"

"Just calling a friend. I'm good. Promise." She flashed a smile and raised the window.

"Maisy?" Jordana's voice sounded in her ear as Evans stopped at the corner and then continued down the block.

"Hey. I'm sorry to interrupt your dinner."

"It's not even sundown yet. Don't worry about it. What's up?"

"You should stay at your grandmother's place tonight."

Jordana pitched her voice low. "Are you joking? Believe me, another two or three hours of quality family time is my absolute limit. Besides, if I get back earlier enough, I can come to your place and we can work on tomorrow's podcast. I was able to sneak in some time to edit it this afternoon after the family hike."

"No!"

"Um, are you okay?"

Maisy's voice shook and she gripped the phone so hard her knuckles blanched. "Yes. This is important, Jordana. Listen to me. Do not, under any circumstances, come to my house tonight. Do you understand?"

"Jeez, okay. What? Do you have a hot date or something?" The younger woman snickered.

"This is serious. I need to know you won't go to my house."

"I won't go to your house. Swearsies."

Maisy let out a shaky laugh that, to her horror, morphed into a sob. "Good. Thank you."

"What's going on? You're scaring me."

She gathered herself. "I don't mean to scare you. A lot's happened today—on the Landon Lewis front."

"Like what?"

"Like a lot. The short version is I found Landon's laptop and his journals."

"No way! Where were they?"

"In a safe that he had hidden beneath his closet floor."

"How did you—? Never mind, did the journals tell you how to get into the laptop?"

"No. Deanne did. The tech genius hasn't updated his password since 2006."

Jordana snorted, and despite the adrenaline racing through her, Maisy had to giggle.

"This is fantastic. We're gonna have a lit teaser for the second episode."

"I've only scratched the surface," Maisy told her.

"Are you for real?"

"I was able to use the MacBook to track Landon's missing cell phone to a house in East Liberty."

"Holy sh—"

"I took the information to the police and got them to let me tag along when they went to the house."

"Hang on. I have to interrupt you. Please tell me you recorded all of this stuff."

"I did. Well, everything except the break-in."

"The what?"

"The police didn't find the phone, but the homeowner admitted he'd had it until last night—when it evidently vanished."

"Convenient."

"Not too convenient. They arrested him on the strength of that statement."

"Wow. But I'm confused. The break-in, if it happened, happened last night. You couldn't have recorded that."

"Not that break-in. So the police took him to the county jail to be processed, and I headed home. I planned to spend the night going through Landon's journals. When I got there ..." she trailed off.

"Maisy?"

"Someone broke into my house and absolutely trashed it."

"Oh, no. I'm so sorry. Did they get much?"

"They didn't take anything as far as I could tell. The cops think they were looking for the laptop."

"Or the phone."

Maisy hadn't considered the phone, but that could be a possibility. "Or the phone," she agreed.

"So, I'm not staying at the house in case they come back."

"Gotcha."

Maisy spoke slowly, "And you shouldn't go home either."

"Oh."

"Right."

"Wait. The teaser didn't have anything about any of this because it all happened today. So how could anyone connect me to this?"

"I don't know. But, Jordana, aside from Deanne and the police, nobody knows I found the laptop."

She let that sink in. After a long silence, Jordana said, "This is really bad. You should go to Sasha and Leo's place for the night."

"No. I can't, not with the twins. If something happened to them, I'd never forgive myself."

"Where are you gonna go, then?"

She hadn't known until Jordana asked the question.

But in that instant, the answer came to her. "Landon's apartment. Nobody will think to look for me there."

"Us. Nobody will look for us there."

"Jordana—"

"Don't even bother finishing your sentence. I'm coming back. We're going to go through those journals and get the second episode lined up. I'm not going to argue with you about it. I'm your producer. It's my job. Just take a few minutes before you drive over to the apartment building to record a piece about walking into your house and finding it trashed. Something short. Okay?"

"Okay," Maisy agreed. "If you do something for me."

"What?"

"Stay for the dinner and be careful driving back. Call me when you're leaving your grandmother's place."

Jordana huffed.

"That's the deal. If you want to come back and work tonight, you have dinner with your family first."

"Fine. Record that bit."

Jordana ended the call. Maisy pulled up her recording app, closed her eyes, and returned to her garage and the moment she opened the door to her mudroom.

CHAPTER FORTY

JENNA SAT in her car with the heat blasting her in the face and stared around the corner at her house. She'd been sitting like this for twenty minutes, waiting for the sun to set so she could pull around, park in the alley, and hustle inside before any of her nebby neighbors stuck their noses out their doors to shout questions at her.

She pounded the steering wheel in frustration. She hadn't heard a word from Zane. Wasn't he supposed to get a phone call? She knew he did, of course. What she didn't know was if he'd call *her*. After all, it wasn't like he'd forget what she'd told him last summer.

She closed her eyes as tears rolled down her cheeks at the memory. She'd been home alone, staring at the blood running down her legs—evidence of her fourth miscarriage in three years. She felt hollowed out, dead inside at the thought of losing another baby. She must've called Zane a half-dozen times. Every time, the call rolled to voicemail.

Finally, she'd dug a hard seltzer out from the back of the refrigerator and cracked it open. Then, she'd stood under the shower until the water ran cold, crying and drinking the fruity, boozy drink. She'd climbed out of the shower, cinched her robe around her waist, wrapped her hair in a towel, and padded down to the kitchen in search of another drink. What she'd found was her husband, sitting at the kitchen table with a bag of frozen peas on his cheek and his bleeding knuckles wrapped in a dish towel.

He looked up at her drunkenly when she walked into the room. "Hey."

"I called you six times." She didn't ask if he was hurt or needed anything because, at that moment, she didn't care.

"Sorry. I was scrapping with León, and the cops rolled up."

She chopped a hand through the air to cut him off. "You know what? Do me a favor, and don't tell me about it."

He furrowed his brow as he digested this request. Then he asked, "What did you want—when you kept calling?"

She walked across the room to stare out the window over the sink. With her back to him, she said, "I lost the baby."

He groaned and pushed the chair away from the table with a metallic screech. He came up behind her and placed his arm around her shoulders. "I'm so sorry, baby."

She twisted away from him and ducked out of his embrace. When she turned to face him, she felt like she was on fire. "You should be. I needed you, and you were out being a fool. You're damn lucky you didn't get arrested tonight. And let me tell you something right now: if you *do* get arrested, you better not call me. Because I'm not coming to bail you out. I'm gonna leave your ass to deal with it yourself, just like you left me alone tonight."

"Baby—"

"Don't," she gritted out between teeth clenched so tight she thought she might break one.

"Jenna, please," he begged desperately.

"What?" she spat.

"I promise you. I'm not gonna get arrested. I'm not gonna get into any more bar fights or scuffles on the basketball court. I'm not even gonna take the bait when your sister tries to get a rise out of me. I'm gonna be a man you'd proud to raise a child with. I promise." His voice cracked then, and the ice lodged inside her chest began to thaw and melt.

Then, like the colossal idiot she was, she'd forgiven him. Now, here she was five months later, about to face down her idiocy yet again. She opened her eyes to wipe away her tears and spotted Mrs. Haluski stomping toward the car. She put the car into drive and peeled away from the curb before the woman could rap on her windshield with her cane and demand to know what Zane had done now.

She parked in the alley and sprinted into the house. Inside, it was dark and eerily quiet. She walked from room to room and turned on all the lights. She'd expected to find a mess, like after a CSI unit was done with a place on television. But the house was more or less the way she'd left it. Zane's water glass and pain meds were still on the coffee table. She walked over to pick up the prescription bottle. He'd need these, assuming she could get them to him.

Some papers folded in thirds were being held down by the water glass. She moved it aside and grabbed the papers to scan them. The top document was a copy of a search warrant. She skimmed the legal language. The police had gotten a warrant to search Zane's person and the premises for a red iPhone 13 that was believed to have been stolen during the commission of a felony. She glanced at the other sheet. It was a probable cause affidavit that set out the factual basis for the warrant. A Sergeant Bass out of Zone Five had written that a red iPhone 13 was stolen from an office building back in July. Earlier today, a Find My Phone app had traced the device in question to the home of Zane and Jenna Novak.

Her stomach lurched. She ran upstairs and checked under the sink. The box of pads was undisturbed. She unplugged the lightning charger from the wall and returned the box to its spot. This wasn't Zane's fault. This was *her* fault.

She skimmed the small print on the bottom of the documents. They would have taken Zane to the Allegheny County Jail Downtown for booking and processing. Then, he'd be arraigned over at the Arraignment Court, where his bond would be set. According to the form, arraignments were held 24/7. She grabbed the checkbook from the top of the dresser and then opened her jewelry box, lifted the ring tray, and fished out the bank card she'd squirreled away underneath the tray. It was to an account Zane didn't know about. She'd started a secret savings account for when a baby finally came.

She stared down at the card for a long, resigned moment, then slipped it into her purse along with the checkbook. She peeked inside to make sure the stolen (really, Zane, *stolen?*) phone was still tucked into the bag's inner pocket. Then she ran down the stairs and out the door.

She'd make this right. She had to.

CHAPTER FORTY-ONE

ZANE LOOKED around the intake area. As his new friends in the holding cell had explained it, he'd stay here, in the intake processing unit, for up to three days until his preliminary arraignment in front of a magistrate, who would either set bond, dismiss the charges, or release him pending a hearing. That didn't sound too bad, if he was being honest. His hand hurt like hell, but he figured he could pass the time replaying his top ten boxing matches in his mind.

"Novak, do you want to make your phone call or what?" A guard came to the cell and eyed him.

"Uh, okay."

The skinny bald guy called Ward jerked his chin. "You get thirty seconds for free, so talk fast."

"Thanks, man."

As the guard led him through a series of locked doors, someone called his name.

"Yo, Novak!"

Zane and the guard turned in tandem in the direction of the voice. Tim Colchis was striding toward them. He nodded to the guard. "Hey, Martin."

"Tim. What's up, man? Good Christmas?"

"Sure. You?"

"Got a VR headset from my folks. It's wild."

"Huh. Listen, Novak here's one of my CIs. I think this whole thing's been a misunderstanding."

"Oh, yeah?"

"Yeah. Has he been processed yet?"

"He's on the list for a phone call, so I guess he has."

"Any idea when he'll be arraigned?"

Martin threw his hands in the air. "Your guess is as good as mine."

"I'm gonna call in some favors. Can you set us up with a video arraignment room? I think I can get him sprung tonight." Colchis turned to Zane, who was listening closely and holding his breath for fear he'd screw this up if he so much as exhaled. "What d'ya say, Zane? Instead of calling your old lady and pissing her off, why don't we try to get you out of here tonight?"

"Yeah. I mean, of course. Please."

Martin's eyes darted around the hallway while he thought through this departure from procedure. Finally, he nodded. "Here's what we'll do. I'll set you up in a video hearing room now. You can call your friend on the bench from in there and work your magic to get the arraignment going. How's that sound?"

Colchis stuck out his hand. "Sounds like you're the man, Martin."

The guard shook the detective's outstretched hand. Zane caught the folded bill pass from Colchis to the guard, who palmed it.

"This way."

He led them to a depressing room with a tv monitor on the wall and a wood laminate table and chairs. A telephone sat on the table.

"Enjoy that VR, pal," Colchis said as the guard turned to leave.

"Beats the hell out of my actual reality," he countered.

"Amen to that."

The guard walked out and closed the door. Colchis watched him disappear from view, then walked over to the door and locked it from the inside.

"Listen, detective, I appreciate your help with this."

Colchis flashed him a weird, tight smile.

Zane rambled on, "The warrant was to search for an iPhone, but they didn't find one, so I'm thinking it's no harm, no foul, right?"

"You think?"

"I don't know. You're the cop, er, detective. What do you think?" Zane didn't want to risk setting him off and having him decide not to help him out.

Instead of answering the question, Colchis nodded at Zane's hand. "What happened?"

He settled for the partial truth. "I got pissed off at

something Jenna's sister said at her folks and punched a wall."

Colchis eyed his mangled hand.

"A stone foundation wall," he clarified.

"You break it?"

"Yeah."

"You're a righty, aren't you?"

Zane nodded ruefully. "Stupid. I shoulda at least used my left. Now, I'm probably out of the ring for a month, maybe more."

Colchis closed the distance between them. "Definitely more."

Zane gave him a confused look. Colchis' hand snaked out fast and wrapped around his throat.

"Huh?" Zane sputtered. He clawed at the hand that was squeezing the life out of him.

Colchis spun him around and bashed his head against the wall.

"What the ...?" Zane coughed and gagged.

He got his feet under him and threw his left elbow back into Colchis' kidney, hard and fast.

The detective roared and punched him in the back of the neck with his free hand, smashing his face into the wall again.

Think, Zane begged his oxygen-hungry brain.

He lowered his head and tucked his chin, then reared back and drove the base of his skull into what he hoped was the shorter man's forehead. But he'd settled for breaking Colchis' nose.

The detective lost his grip on Zane's throat, and Zane spun around. He feinted left, then danced right.

"Come on, let's see what you've got. I'll take you down with a broken hand." He settled into a rhythm of bobbing and weaving just like the Champ himself.

But Tim Colchis was no George Foreman. He pushed up the leg of his jeans and pulled a knife out of his boot. He shoved the blade under Zane's right ear, pressing it against his jugular vein.

"Here's what I've got," he hissed in Zane's face. "I like my odds."

"Why?" Zane managed.

"Why what? Why am I going to take you out? Because you're trash, Zane, and that's what we do with trash."

"I don't ... I did everything you asked."

"Did you? Everything? Then tell me, why did those pricks from Zone Five get an arrest and search warrant, Novak?"

"I dunno." He swallowed, and the tip of the knife dug into his skin.

"You dunno? I know. Because that bitch reporter used Find My Phone to ping Lewis' phone and guess where she got a hit?"

"My house?" He shook his head, baffled, and the knife pricked him.

"You're not as stupid as you look. That's right. Your house. Now, tell me, how could that have happened when you threw the frickin' phone in the river in July?"

Zane pleaded with his eyes. "I'm sorry, man. I screwed up."

"Ya think? Where's the phone now, Zane? Why didn't they find it."

"Didn't you take it? Last night?"

"What?" Colchis spat.

"I thought ... when you were at the house when we got home, and then it was gone. I thought you heard the podcast trailer and freaked out."

"And broke into your pad and stole evidence I didn't know was there? Evidence that would connect me to a murder? Forget what I said. You are as stupid as you look."

"If you didn't take it, then—?" Zane cut himself off as soon as he realized there could only be one other answer.

Judging by the glint in Colchis' eye, he knew it, too.

Zane started to beg. "Please, don't hurt her. She doesn't know anything about any of this."

Colchis smiled and pressed the knife deeper. "Sure. Do you have any last words for her?"

"Tell her ... tell her ... she deserved better than me."

Colchis flicked his wrist and dragged the sharp blade across Zane's neck with a quick, sure motion. Hot blood spurted out, fast and heavy. Zane gagged and gasped as his legs gave out and he slid down the wall. Colchis looked down at him, expressionless. Then he raised his leg and stomped his boot down on Zane's broken hand.

The sadistic impulse turned out to be unintentional kindness because Zane passed out from the pain and slipped into death without regaining consciousness.

CHAPTER FORTY-TWO

JENNA FOUND a spot in the covered parking garage closest to the complex that was home to both the jail and the arraignment court. She and Zane liked to park here and take the T to the North Shore when he scored Steelers or Pirates tickets from someone at his gym.

She popped open the glove box, stuck the iPhone that had caused all this trouble inside, and locked the compartment. Then she pulled on her gloves and hat and exited the car. She hurried across First Avenue, her head bent against the wind.

After the short, two-minute walk, she stopped and stood between the jail and the court building, waffling. The paperwork was unclear and her quick Internet search hadn't provided any additional clarity. Should she go to the jail and ask to see Zane? But she wasn't an approved visitor and wasn't sure how to become one. Or should she go to the arraignment court building and see if bail had been set yet? That seemed like a long shot.

In the end, she decided to start with arraignment court—mainly because the thought of walking into the jail made her legs wobbly. A random bureaucratic office building was less intimidating than the massive jail. If Zane's bond hearing had happened, she was sure that bail could be paid at the arraignment court building on nights and weekends because she'd come once with Amber to bail out one of her crappy boyfriends.

Way to be judgmental. It's not like your taste in men is so stellar.

She reminded herself that although Zane had absolutely done something boneheaded, *she* had the phone the police were looking for. So maybe she should hold off on judging anyone.

She walked into the building and beelined across the quiet lobby to the bond window. The line was short, but slow-moving. While she waited behind a cranky woman with an even crankier kid in tow, she took off her hat and gloves and shoved them in her purse. Then she spent a few fruitless minutes trying to smooth down her staticky hair.

The older man at the front of the line got directions to the bank machine across the hall, which was plainly visible from where they stood. As he shuffled away from the window, the woman in front of Jenna snapped at him for being a dumbass and wasting everyone's time.

Jenna offered him an embarrassed, sympathetic smile. "It's okay. This place can be confusing."

He mumbled a thank you and headed toward the bank machine. The exchange earned Jenna the stink-eye from the woman. Jenna ignored her, and waved to the kid—a small boy, bundled up in a snowsuit, his nose running like a fountain. He smiled at her and ducked behind his mom's knee.

"Next," the woman at the window said in a monotone.

The snappish mom pushed her son forward and told the woman she needed to post bail and was in a hurry.

"Most people here are," the counter worker agreed languidly. "Not me, though. I'm here until twelve-thirty in the morning no matter what."

Jenna bit back a smile. She sensed this was payback for the mom's bitchy attitude toward the old guy. She wondered, not for the first time, why people seemed so intent on abusing the seemingly powerless workers who actually held the power to help them? It was a dynamic that she was intimately familiar with, as it played out daily at the Cheaptime Mobile call center.

She let her mind wander and waited patiently while the mom argued with the court worker over the fifty-dollar fee for posting bond. Jenna could agree that paying a fee to pay a fee was excessive, but she also knew it was set by statute or regulation or something and there wasn't a blessed thing the woman behind the counter could do about it. It was the exact same thing as the monthly 911 surcharge that the commonwealth required mobile plan providers to charge customers. It didn't matter how loudly someone screamed at Jenna over the dollar sixty-five, she couldn't remove it from their bill.

Finally, the woman in front of her wore herself out arguing and paid the bond, fee and all. The counter worker, who didn't seem to be the type to hold a grudge, offered the kid a candy cane from a jar behind the counter. Mom, who definitely held a grudge, smacked his hand when he reached for it and dragged him away, wailing.

Jenna waited to step forward until the woman said, "Next." Then she presented herself at the counter with a smile.

"Hi. I'm kind of confused and I'm hoping you can help me."

"I can try."

Jenna studied the woman. Tightly permed hair, glasses hanging from a beaded chain around her neck, sparkly poinsettia pin affixed to her cardigan. She was someone's grandma, for sure.

"Thank you. So, I came home from work today, and my husband was gone."

The grandma behind the counter inhaled sharply. "Hon, you need to report him missing to the police, not here."

"Oh, he's not missing." She smiled sadly and pulled the warrant and the affidavit from her purse, smoothed the pages, and pushed them across the counter. "These were on the coffee table."

She watched the woman skim the documents. "Hmm." Then she flashed Jenna a puzzled look.

"Where's the inventory of seized property? They're supposed to leave that."

"I don't think they took anything." She gave a little laugh. "Well, except for Zane."

"What about this iPhone? See here? This is what they were looking for."

"Yeah, they didn't find that. Zane doesn't have it."

The woman clicked her tongue. "Then they shouldn't have arrested him."

"That's sort of what I thought," Jenna said. "But, I don't know how to get this cleared up. Do I go to the jail or—?"

"No. They're not gonna tell you anything. Let me see if his preliminary arraignment is in the system yet." She turned her chair ninety degrees to the right, settled her glasses on her nose, and clacked away on her computer keyboard. Every few seconds, she made a '*hmm*' sound in her throat.

Jenna was the smiling embodiment of patience as she waited.

When the woman turned back to the counter, she wore a sad expression. "Sorry, hon. He's been processed, but the arraignment hasn't been scheduled yet."

She sighed. "Okay. Thank you for looking. I've been out of my mind with worry."

"I'm sure."

"I know this isn't really your area, but I don't know who else to ask. Since the police didn't find the phone they were looking for, is there any chance they'll just drop the charges without going through the hearing? Is that a thing that happens?"

"Mmm. It's something the procedures allow to happen. But, to be honest, it never does. Maybe once every couple of months, if that."

It was what she'd expected.

"I get it. One last question, and then I'll get out of your hair, I promise."

The woman waved an airy hand. "Like I told Miss High and Mighty, I'm here until after midnight. Ask away."

She rooted around in her purse while she explained, "Zane broke his hand last night. It's a bad break."

"Some Christmas."

"Tell me about it. I took him to the ER this morning and then left him resting on the couch because I couldn't call off work. Not the day after a holiday, you know?"

"Oh, I know."

Jenna dug out the bottle of painkillers. "He either didn't think to take his medication, or they wouldn't let him. If I go over to the jail and give this to him, will he get it?"

"Can I see?"

She extended her hand, and Jenna placed the prescription bottle in it. The woman sucked on her teeth as she studied the label. "I'm afraid not. There's a very limited list of meds they'll let you bring in, but you have to get preapproval. And this is a narcotic. That's definitely not on the list."

"But the doctors prescribed it," Jenna mumbled.

"Yeah. I'll be honest with you. If you take this over there, they should send you away. But most likely, they'll take it and tell you they'll give it to him. And then the guards will sell it pill by pill to the inmates."

Jenna blinked at her. "Seriously?"

The woman nodded and started to hand the bottle back. Then she hesitated. "I'm sorry I can't help you."

"Oh, you've been super helpful. My head's been spinning since I got home. At least now I know he's been through the intake process. It's more than I knew when I came in here." She ginned up a weak smile.

The woman's fist closed around the pill bottle. "Tell you what. My husband—Fred—had his hip replaced right after Thanksgiving. They gave him three days' worth of prescription pain meds. *Three days.* They told him he could manage the pain with ibuprofen after that. Well, between you and me, *I* can't manage his constant complaining. It's taken all my willpower not to smother him with a pillow in his sleep." She laughed to let Jenna know she was joking.

Jenna laughed, too. And she knew better than to make the woman come out and ask the question she was dancing around. "Well, they aren't doing Zane any good where he is. Maybe Fred could use them?"

She pretended to consider it. "That would be a blessing," she told Jenna.

"Then please, just keep them."

The woman slipped the bottle into her cardigan pocket with a furtive motion. "Thanks, hon. Why don't you give me your number, and I'll put an alert here in the system on your hubby's inmate number. That way, I'll get a notification the minute his arraignment is scheduled. I'll call you and let you know as soon as there's an update—even if it's after I leave tonight."

The woman pushed a pen and pad across the counter. Jenna scrawled her name and telephone number, then slid the pad back to the woman.

"I can't tell you how much I appreciate this ..." She trailed off so the woman would supply her name.

"I'm Dotty, hon. Dotty McDaniels."

"Thanks, Dotty. Please call no matter what time it is. I don't care how late or how early it is. I'm not gonna get any sleep until I see Zane."

Dotty squeezed her hand. "I know."

"You take care. And I hope Fred gets some relief."

Dotty flashed a wide smile. "Thanks, Jenna. Candy cane for the road?" She shook the jar at Jenna, who shrugged and plucked one out.

"I could use a little sweetness tonight."

"Couldn't we all?" Dotty observed. "Couldn't we all?"

CHAPTER FORTY-THREE

JORDANA AND MAISY once again made Landon's dining room table their base of operations. Maisy read through Landon's journal and snacked on the pile of crisp potato latkes that Jordana had brought back from her grandmother's while Jordana reviewed the recordings Maisy had made in her absence. They worked in companionable silence, which was punctuated every so often by the clink of Maisy's fork against the plate as she dipped a piece of latke into the little mounds of sour cream and homemade applesauce that Jordana insisted would elevate the meal.

Suddenly, Jordana removed her headphones and dropped them to the table with a soft thunk.

Maisy looked up from Landon's diary. "Did you find something?"

"No, but I'm wondering if we shouldn't ping the iPhone again."

"Now?"

"Yeah, so we can include it in the first episode."

Maisy chewed on her bottom lip for a moment, then placed her fork on her plate and marked her place in the journal with a scrap of paper. She sighed heavily.

"What?" her producer demanded.

"I feel responsible for Zane Novak's arrest as it is. Obviously, the app is malfunctioning or something. I don't want to get someone else in trouble with the police if it misfires again."

Jordana arched her right eyebrow. The single eyebrow raise was a mannerism Maisy had never been able to perfect despite her diligent attempts. It was an effortless way to communicate that someone was being a dope.

But, being a dope, she didn't know what Jordana was thinking, so she had to ask. "What am I missing?"

"We don't *have* to tell the police."

"Fair point. Except we probably should if the person who broke into my house was looking for the laptop or the phone—or the laptop as a means of finding the phone. We could be walking into danger or leading the break-in artist to an innocent person. We have to think this through."

"Just ping it. We can decide what, if anything, to do with the information if you get a hit. Like you said, the app could be going haywire. The phone might not even show up on the map this time. But, it's a loose end."

Maisy twitched her mouth. Jordana was right. As things stood, there was a gaping hole in the narrative.

"Okay. But if we get a hit, we don't chase after it tonight. We keep working on what we have here, and we can run it down tomorrow in the light of day."

"Deal."

Maisy fired up Landon's laptop and opened the Find My app. Jordana hit record on her software, then gave Maisy a nod.

"Having struck out at the Novak home earlier today, we regrouped. At approximately 8 PM, I initiated contact with Landon Lewis' missing iPhone for the second time," Maisy narrated. The phone icon popped up at the Novak home. Maisy sighed. This thing wasn't working.

Then, as she stared at the screen, the map faded and reformed. This time when she zoomed in, the phone wasn't in East Liberty. It was Downtown—just about a half-mile away from where they sat.

"Holy cow, that's over on First Avenue," Jordana breathed.

Maisy zoomed in further, then frowned. "It's right next to the Allegheny County Jail Building. That can't be right, though. The police took Zane Novak to the jail for processing, but he didn't have the phone on him."

"Maybe it was hidden, like in his shoe or something," Jordana suggested.

"In his shoe?"

"I don't know. Play the sound."

"Why?"

"Because if he did smuggle it in, someone might hear it. Or if it's in the bottom of a trash can near the T

Station, someone might hear it. That's the point of the sound," she urged.

"Okay, okay. Ready?"

"Ready."

Maisy pressed the button.

JENNA HUDDLED in front of the car's vents while the engine warmed up. She could almost hear Zane's voice telling her the air physically could not blow hot until the car was warmed up, but she didn't care. Psychologically, she felt warmer.

She unlocked the glove box and took out the blasted iPhone that had caused all this trouble and stared at it. Should she just run over to the T platform and throw it on the tracks? Technically, that would be a crime. But what was a little destruction of evidence for a girl who'd just given a controlled substance to a court employee?

She laughed darkly. If someone had told her that she'd illegally trade prescription narcotics for information, she'd have told them they were out of their mind. Yet, here she was: a drug dealer contemplating another crime. But if she didn't get rid of the phone, what could she do with it? Keeping it would only implicate Zane further when the police eventually, inevitably found it.

She wanted to hang on to it until she could confront Zane with it, though. So the thing was in her life for the next seventy-two hours or whenever Dotty called her.

For some reason—one she'd later be unable to articulate—she pressed the button to power the device on.

And, then, just as it had in the bathroom, it begin to emit its painfully shrill tone. It gradually grew louder, until Jenna was wincing. Then, after what had to be the longest one hundred and twenty seconds in history, the message from this morning popped up on the screen: *Lost iPhone. This iPhone has been lost. Please call Maisy F.*

This time, Jenna pulled out her own phone and did as she was instructed.

CHAPTER FORTY-FOUR

"I KNOW we agreed not to chase the phone tonight. But, Maisy, it's like a ten-minute walk to that garage. I don't even know how long it could take to drive there—three minutes?" Jordana said in a reasonable, not-at-all-pleading tone.

"It's not the distance. It's the danger."

Jordana didn't seem to have a response to that, so they returned their attention to the little icon on the map, tantalizingly close and tempting, and stared at it in silence. Then the cheerful tune of Maisy's ringtone tore their attention away from the screen.

She reached for the phone and cocked her head at the number on the display.

"Who is it?" Jordana asked.

"They're not in my contacts." She shrugged and hit the speaker icon to pick up the call. "Hello?"

A halting female voice said, "Is this Maisy Farley?"

"Sure is," she chirped. "What can I do for you?"

"Um ... I guess I found your iPhone. Or, at least, I found *an* iPhone, but the message on the screen says to call you. So, I'm calling."

Jordana grinned and pumped her fist in the air. Maisy gestured frantically for her notebook and pen. Jordana slid them toward her. '*Thank you,*' she mouthed.

To the caller, she enthused, "Thank you so much. You have no idea how grateful I am that you called."

The woman on the other end of the line cleared her throat. "Yeah. But, it's not your phone, is it?"

Jordana pressed her lips together and widened her eyes.

Maisy's cardinal rule as a journalist was to never lie to a source or subject. If she couldn't create trust, she couldn't build a story. Even if it meant spooking this woman, she had to be honest with her. She exhaled slowly, ending in a soft sigh, and said, "No, ma'am, it certainly isn't."

To her surprise, the caller also sighed. But hers was a sigh of relief, not resignation. "Oh, thank heavens. I thought he might be having an affair with you."

"Who?"

"My husband. Zane," she admitted.

Zane?

"You're Jenna Novak?"

"Wait ... how did ... what .... What's going on?"

"Jenna, I don't want to alarm you, but your husband has a dead man's phone. I'm investigating the circumstances surrounding his death for my new podcast and, well, I think someone very badly wants to get their hands on that phone before I do. My home was broken into this afternoon."

"Oh my gosh. Zane was arrested today, too. And the paperwork the police filed listed this iPhone as the basis for his arrest."

Jordana shook her head no. Maisy nodded her agreement. She was committed to honesty, but she wasn't a fool. She wanted to be looking Jenna Novak in the eye when she explained that she was the one who turned the police onto Zane and why she'd done it.

"Sugar, I think you may be in danger. Why don't I meet you somewhere so we can talk this through?"

"Uh, yeah. Okay. I'm Downtown right now. Where are you?"

"As it happens, I'm *also* Downtown. Do you know the bar in the William Penn?"

"The Tap Room?"

"Mmm, the other one. In the basement?"

"The Speakeasy?"

"That's the one."

"I'm not really dressed for that."

"Oh, don't you worry about that, sugar. They're not open tonight."

"Well, then, why are we meeting there?"

"I have a friend who works there. He'll let us in and make sure we have privacy for our conversation."

"Uh, okay. I guess."

"We'll meet you in the hotel lobby in five minutes."

"Who are you bringing with you?"

"My producer, Jordana. You can trust her. Us."

"Um. Give me ten."

'*She's going to walk,*' Jordana mouthed.

That was a hideous idea. Maisy shook her head. "Jenna, there's a parking garage in Mellon Square, right across from the hotel."

"It's twenty dollars," Jenna told her. "Maybe more."

"I'll reimburse you," she promised.

"I don't—"

Jordana leaned over the phone. "Hi, Jenna. This is Jordana, Maisy's producer. You know the apartments in the old Kaufmann's?"

"Yeah."

"We're working out of a friend's place here. Leave your car at the garage and take the T from First Avenue to Steel Plaza for free, and we'll meet you there to walk you back here. That way, we can talk in private."

"How do you know where I am?" she demanded.

"Because of the phone," Maisy explained. "Jordana's right. You need to get off the street."

"Fine, but you don't have to meet me. My sister works in the Steel Plaza building. Amber will walk me over to the apartment building."

"Perfect," Jordana purred. "Tell the front desk you're here to visit Landon Lewis' apartment."

"Isn't that the dead guy?"

"I promise you'll be safe with us," Maisy told her. "Give your sister my cell phone number so she can reach us if it'll make you feel better."

"Okay. I'm leaving now," she said in an uncertain voice.

Maisy ended the call and leveled Jordana with a look.

"What?"

"What? Why would you invite her here? As a matter of personal safety, I usually meet sources in public."

"Yeah, but we're not safe in public. And neither is she. You said so yourself."

Maisy blew out a loud breath. "But we don't know if we can trust her."

Jordana shrugged. "There are two of us. There's one of her."

"You've been working with Sasha too long. It's made you fearless."

"I'm not fearless. But she's not going to open up to us in a hotel bar, Maisy. Besides, it'll be easier to record here. Plus, we have potato pancakes." She lifted the plate and pretended to lure Maisy with the latkes.

Despite her misgivings about this plan, Maisy found herself laughing at Jordana's antics. If nothing else, she was more fun to work with than Maisy's last long-suffering producer.

AMBER GRABBED Jenna by the shoulders when they reached the corner under Kaufmann's iconic clock.

"Are you sure you want to do this?"

Jenna took a shaky breath. She'd spent the short walk

from the plaza to the apartment building filling Amber in on the highlights (more like lowlights) of the situation: Zane's broken hand; the message to call Maisy Farley when she'd powered up the phone; and Zane's arrest. She hadn't shared the dark seed of fear nestled in her chest, the worry that had made her call Maisy in the first place.

Only two years apart in age, Amber and Jenna had been best friends and sworn enemies at various stages of their lives. And Amber made no secret of how she felt about Zane. Of course, Jenna allowed, Amber's judgment wasn't perfect. The fact that she worked days as a medical transcriptionist and nights cleaning offices to pay off a credit card debt one of her exes had run up in her name was proof of that.

But Amber was also the one person Jenna could tell anything. No matter how frightening or sad or ugly. So she filled her lungs with cold air and car exhaust fumes and nodded.

"I'm sure. The phone belongs to that dead guy."

Amber's blue eyes clouded. "What dead guy?"

"That tech guy who jumped from his window last summer."

"The one Maisy's doing the podcast about?"

"Yeah. And I have this bad feeling that Zane might have been involved."

Amber, who'd been dancing from foot to foot to drive out the cold, stopped stamping. "Involved how?"

Jenna just looked at her.

Amber shook her head in a quick, decisive no. "Zane's a moron, but he's not a killer."

"Remember when he suddenly came up with the money for the fertility clinic?"

"Yeah, you said he cashed in those treasury bonds his granddad left him."

She swallowed around the rock lodged in her throat. "There weren't any bonds."

"Where'd he get the money then?"

She held her sister's gaze and shook her head slowly. "I didn't ask. It was right after I lost the baby, and ... and I didn't care," she admitted. "But the thing is, I checked the news articles while I was waiting for the train. That guy died the same week Zane gave me the money."

"And now he has the dude's phone," Amber said slowly.

"Right."

"Oh, Jenn."

Jenna's eyes filled with tears, and Amber grabbed her in a fierce hug. Jenna clung to her sister for a long moment, then pulled back and wiped her face with the back of her hand.

"So, you see why I have to talk to Maisy? If he did this—"

"Don't borrow sorrow from tomorrow," Amber insisted, deploying one of their mother's favorite sayings. It was a close second to 'what doesn't kill you makes you stronger,' which, Jenna thought, was equally applicable to the situation.

"I know. But *if*."

"Yeah, if. If he did, then you have to try to make it right as best you can."

"Right."

Amber sighed and glanced up at the clock. "You good?"

Jenna managed a wobbly smile. "Yeah. Thanks for walking me over."

Her sister waved away her gratitude, then pulled her in for another hug. "Call me tomorrow."

"I will. Love you."

"Love you more."

Jenna watched Amber jaywalk across Grant before she turned and walked into the lobby of a dead man's building. A dead man whom her husband might have killed.

CHAPTER FORTY-FIVE

THEY HEARD the groan of the elevator arriving, then light footsteps in the hall. There was a soft knock on the door, and Jordana pulled it open to reveal Zane Novak's wife standing in the hallway with a sick expression and a faint green cast to her skin.

"Jenna?" Maisy asked unnecessarily.

The brunette nodded, twisting her hands around one another in a nervous gesture.

"Come on in. I'm Maisy, and this is Jordana."

Jenna stepped inside, and Jordana closed and locked the door. At the *snick* of the lock, Jenna's eyes flew up to meet Maisy's.

"Safety first," Maisy explained.

"Here, let me take your coat." Jordana held out her arms, and Jenna struggled out of her bulky winter coat.

"Thanks." Her voice was soft and uncertain. Then, after a moment, she straightened her spine and pulled back her shoulders. She dug into her bag and pulled out the iPhone. "Here." She extended it to Maisy, who took it with a grateful bob of her head.

She led Jenna to the living room. Maisy and Jordana had agreed they should start slow with an informal conversation in the living room, building rapport and getting Jenna comfortable with them before moving to the dining room and recording a conversation about how her husband came to have Landon Lewis' phone.

Jenna Novak apparently had other plans. She held Maisy's gaze and said, "Did my husband kill that man?"

Maisy revised her first impression of the woman from *mousy* to *fierce*.

"I don't know. Do you think he could have?"

She caught Jordana's eye and tilted her head toward the dining room. Change of plans.

"Let's talk in the dining room," Jordana suggested smoothly.

Jenna followed them through the conversation pit to the dining room table. Maisy cleared the dishes from the table, and the three of them settled into chairs.

Jenna cleared her throat. "If you'd asked me a week ago, I would have said no, of course not."

"And now?" Maisy asked in a gentle voice.

"Now I'm not sure. They arrested him today. The police must think he did something, right?"

Maisy and Jordana exchanged a look. Then the producer asked, "Can I record our conversation, Jenna?"

The woman hesitated. Maisy leaned forward and gave her an unwavering look. "I promise we won't air anything without getting your permission first. This is just for background."

Jenna nodded slowly. "Okay."

Jordana cued up the software and clipped a microphone to Jenna's blouse. Maisy rattled off the details of who she was interviewing, where, and when so they'd have a record. Then she paused for a beat trying to decide the best way to answer Jenna's question. After a few seconds, she decided to just rip the bandage off.

"Zane was arrested because I contacted the police."

"*You* did?" Jenna gave her a baffled look.

"Landon's ex-wife asked me to look into his death. She felt that the police made up their minds that it was a suicide and ignored anything that didn't support that theory."

"Like the missing phone and laptop?" Jenna asked.

It was Maisy's turn to express confusion. "How did you know about the laptop?"

"I heard your trailer last night. We were at my mom's place and she was messing around on her tablet." Jenna snorted softly. "She's a huge fan."

Maisy managed to smother her grin. Jordana didn't even try to hide hers.

"Right. Well, I found the laptop today."

Jenna's eyes widened. "Wow, really?"

"Yep. And Deanne—that's Landon's ex—knew his password, so I was able to log on and search for the phone."

Jenna laughed. "Today's the first time you tried to find it? Using that sound?"

"That's right. And the map that popped up showed the phone at your house. I called some officers I know, and they got a warrant."

"Because they think Zane killed Landon?"

Maisy frowned. "The basis for the search warrant should have been that they believe he was in possession of stolen property."

"Stolen when he killed him, though, right?"

This woman seemed committed to getting Maisy to say she thought her husband was a killer. But Maisy wasn't sure that was true.

"The police really do think Landon killed himself—or at least did. Deanne and I are the ones who have questions. The phone was missing when Landon's body was found. But it's possible your husband just came across the phone somewhere, right? Someone else could have dumped it and he found it."

"Maybe." She thinned her lips. "But ..."

Maisy waited. It was never smart to fill in the pauses during an interview. She didn't need to hear the sound of her own voice.

"A few days after Landon died, Zane gave me fifty thousand dollars. Cash."

Maisy blinked. "Are you sure about the timing?"

"It was the very end of July. We've been trying to get pregnant, but my insurance doesn't cover IVF. That money paid for two rounds. We did the first one at the end of September. I'm positive about the dates."

"Did he say where he got the money?"

"No." She looked down at her hands. "And I didn't ask."

Maisy pursed her lips. "Okay, it doesn't look great for your husband, but don't jump to the worst possible conclusion."

"You mean don't borrow sorrow from tomorrow?" Jenna said in a soft voice.

"Somethin' like that, yeah. Listen, I was there when the police went to your house today."

Her eyes snapped up. "You were? When they arrested Zane?"

She nodded. "I was. And he was kind of out of it, but he told them right away that he'd had the phone at one point, but he didn't know where it was. That's a strange thing to own up to if he killed the guy."

"He was on pain meds," Jenna explained. "I took him to the hospital this morning because he messed up his hand pretty bad last night. Also, you have to understand something about Zane."

Maisy waited again.

"He's not ... smart."

Jordan's eyebrows shot up.

Jenna hurried to elaborate. "I'm not trying to be mean, okay? He's a good man. But he doesn't always think things through. He's a boxer, and he's physically gifted. He has what they call spatial intelligence, and I guess he's smart about the physics of boxing. But, when it comes to daily living stuff? He's sort of a dope. So, I'm just saying even if he hadn't been on meds, he wouldn't have been the most strategic. Like, what should you do when the police ask you a question?"

"Keep your mouth shut," Maisy and Jordana said in unison.

Jenna raised her palms in a wide gesture. "Exactly. Everybody knows that. But, Zane?" She shook her head.

"I get it." She switched gears. "How'd he hurt his hand?"

"He says he went down to the basement to work out, accidentally missed the heavy bag, and hit the stone wall. As further evidence that he's not that bright, that's literally impossible. He had to have punched the wall intentionally. I think because he was pissed."

Maisy wanted to ask if Zane routinely expressed anger through violence, but she needed to keep the focus on recent events. There'd be time later to gather background.

"Why was he mad?"

"He started acting weird at my mom's place. Right after she played your trailer, as a matter of fact. He said we had to get home. Oh, back up, you need to know this: I found the phone hidden in the basement on Christmas Eve. I didn't know where it had come from." She laughed without humor. "I thought it was one of my presents, so I put it back. But when he didn't give it to me yesterday, Amber said maybe he was cheating and that was his burner phone. It was dead, but I wanted to see what was on it. So I borrowed a charger from my mom's place. Are you with me?"

"I am."

"We got home from my mom's place, and that jagoff was waiting outside."

"What jagoff would that be?" Maisy managed not to trip over the word. Even after a decade and a half in Pittsburgh, *jagoff* didn't roll off her tongue.

"Colchis. Second time in less than a week that he showed up at our house. But, Christmas Day? I mean, come on. It worked out for me. I ran down and grabbed the phone while they were outside arguing. But I think Colchis turning up like that set Zane off."

Maisy frowned and turned to Jordana. "Can you pull up the recording from this afternoon at Jenna's place?"

Jordana nodded. Her fingers flew across the keyboard. A few seconds later, the audio file was on the screen.

"Thanks. Fast forward to about the eight-minute mark."

Jordana did as she asked. Then she hit the play button. All three of them leaned forward to listen:

"Sir, is there an iPhone 13 belonging to Landon Lewis on the premises?"

"There was until last night. Now it's gone."

Jordana paused the audio.

Jenna shook her head. "What'd I tell you?"

"Yeah," Maisy agreed. "He should have kept his mouth shut, but the part I want to hear is coming up." She gave her producer a nod.

"Where is it?"

"Hell if I know. Ask your boy Colchis."

"Colchis. Would that be Detective Tim Colchis from the Nuisance Bar Task Force?"

"Pause it," Maisy said. Jordana did. "I'll check my notes, but I know Zane nodded yes."

"Okay. That all tracks. I told you Colchis showed up."

"Zane seemed to think the detective knew about the phone. Does that track?"

Jenna screwed up her forehead. "I honestly don't know. Why would he?"

"I don't know either, but my sources on the force mentioned an unnamed member of the Nuisance Bar Task Force who recently took an unusual interest in Landon's case."

"Why would Colchis care about a suicide?" Jenna asked. "He mainly breaks up bar fights. That's how he knows Zane."

Her voice was heavy with judgment, and Maisy made a note to definitely follow up on the boxer's propensity for violence.

"I don't know what his interest in Landon's case was, but I can't imagine it's a coincidence."

"There are no coincidences," Jordana interjected.

Maisy turned to her. "What?"

"It's something Sasha says all the time."

Jenna coughed. "Could you play the rest, please? I've been thinking about it all day, wondering what happened when the cops showed up."

Jordana waited for Maisy's signal, then hit play. Zane's slurred voice came through the speakers:

"Who's that?"

"Are you admitting you did have the iPhone 13?"

"Yeah, sure."

"Where'd you get it?"

"I don't want to talk to you anymore."

"S'okay. We have enough to bring you in."

They heard the jangle of handcuffs and then, louder, a cough.

"His hand is clearly injured. Is that necessary?"

"Hey, you're Maisy Farley!"

Maisy nodded to Jordana. "You can stop there. They sent me to my car after Zane recognized me."

Tears brimmed in Jenna's eyes. "Thanks for looking out for him."

Maisy tried to smile, but her mouth wouldn't cooperate. "I'm the one who brought the cops to your door, Jenna. I hardly looked out for him."

The woman raised her chin. Her eyes blazed. "No. Zane brought the cops to my door. I want to believe Colchis got him mixed up in something stupid after the fact. I hope that's what happened. But I need to be sure. If Zane killed someone, I have to know. So what can I do to help?"

CHAPTER FORTY-SIX

JENNA CURLED up on the couch with the dead man's diaries. Maisy and the producer—who looked like she wasn't a day over eighteen, especially with that red and black split-dye—suggested that she look through them. For what, none of them knew. But Maisy was going through the phone, and Jordana was editing the first episode of the podcast so she could drop it right at midnight. Jenna figured her job was mainly busy work.

Maisy had insisted they all spend the night at the apartment. That was fine by Jenna. There was safety in numbers, and she knew if she went home to her empty house all she'd do was lie awake and worry until Dotty called.

She'd explained to Maisy and Jordana that she hadn't been able to see Zane or talk to him yet, but that she had a 'friend' at the arraignment court who would let her know when his preliminary hearing had been scheduled. They all agreed the best, easiest way to find out what Zane had done was for Jenna to come right out and ask him.

He'd tell her if she asked. He was dense but fundamentally honest. She just had to be patient until she could talk to him.

And what if he tells you he chucked the guy out that window? Don't borrow sorrow from tomorrow, she scolded herself. She'd worry about that when and if Zane told her he'd done it.

For now, she just needed to focus on Landon Lewis' word vomit. Like, she hated to think ill of the dead, but this guy's journals were the most boring thing she'd ever read. Jordana had given her the broad strokes—his kid was murdered, his marriage fell apart, and he became obsessed with creating an artificial intelligence program that could predict who would commit crimes. It sounded like a tragic, but interesting, life. These journals said otherwise.

She propped her chin on her hand, flipped the pages, and hoped Maisy was having more luck than she was.

MAISY SHIFTED in Landon's stupid desk chair. For an allegedly ergonomic chair, the thing killed her lower back. But they'd agreed to spread out so they wouldn't distract one another. Jordana needed the dining room table to edit the podcast episode, and Jenna was camped out in the living room with Landon's journals. So it was either the thousand-dollar torture device chair in the office or the bench in the closet.

She squirmed again and peered down at the phone. She'd unlocked the thing with Landon's sixteen-year-old password, but the result had been anticlimactic. Landon wasn't a texter. There were no photos on the phone's camera roll. He didn't even have any games or social media apps installed.

Think. Somebody wanted this phone badly enough to break into your house. Why?

She shook her head. It beat the heck out of her. She scrolled through his emails again. It was possible some smoking gun was hidden in his email inbox, but nothing jumped out at her.

She had a suspicion Landon had been an inbox zero enthusiast. The allure of an empty email inbox was lost on her, but her former co-anchor, Chet, had been obsessed with zeroing out his inbox at the end of every week. He used to display the results to her like a fourth-grader looking for a gold star sticker.

Given that all the emails on the device post-dated Landon's death and were largely news alerts, journal renewals, and ads, she wasn't expecting much. But, investigators investigate. So she was investigating.

Tomorrow, when Jenna could talk to her husband, maybe they'd figure out Detective Colchis' role in all of this. Part of Maisy wanted to reach out to Ilsa Evans and ask about Colchis, but she'd been around long enough to know that if she was going to accuse a brother in blue of malfeasance, she'd better have solid proof. Thinking of Evans reminded Maisy of her trashed townhouse. She'd try Bass, too, to see if he'd had any luck getting a crime scene team assigned to the break-in. She wasn't going to leave her place in disarray indefinitely. She scrawled a note to call a locksmith and a cleaning service in the morning.

Focus.

Okay, maybe this weirdo used his phone to make actual phone calls. It takes all kinds, after all. She blew out a breath and pulled up his call log. Maybe she'd stumble across a call from her killer, but she wasn't banking on it. She hoped Jordana was having more luck than she was.

AS IF MAISY had summoned her with the power of her mind, Jordana appeared in the doorway to the office.

"Are you at a stopping point?" she asked hopefully.

"Absolutely," Maisy groaned. "What've you got?"

Jordana beamed. "The episode's done. And I ginned up a trailer for the second episode. Jenna's ready for a break, too. Apparently, Landon's journals aren't the most engrossing reading. So, if you can put the phone aside, I thought we could all listen together."

"That sounds a million times better than scrolling

through Landon's email spam," Maisy told her. "Deanne wasn't kidding. I don't think he stores anything important on his devices."

Jordana gave her a sympathetic look. "Maybe we'll find something on the hard drive."

"Maybe. First things first, though. I can't wait to hear the podcast." She used the top of the desk to hoist herself out of the blasted chair and followed Jordana out of the room.

"Do I smell popcorn?" she asked as she entered the living room.

Jenna came out of the kitchen, cradling one of Landon's glossy white bowls in the crook of her arm. "You do. He didn't have any butter, though. So, I hope everyone likes melted coconut oil."

Jordana grabbed three bottles of mineral water from the refrigerator, and the three of them arranged themselves cross-legged on the living room rug in front of the coffee table that held Jordana's laptop.

"Everybody ready?" she asked.

Maisy popped a piece of popcorn into her mouth. "Hit it."

Jordana hit play, and the intro music filled the room. Maisy closed her eyes and listened to the story unfold. She didn't open her eyes until the outro music cued up.

"Well?" Jordana was watching her with an expectant expression.

"It's got good structure."

Jordana had used the first ten minutes of the episode

to lay out Landon's sad history, the initial reports of his suicide, and Maisy's interview with Deanne. After a break that Jordana explained would eventually be a message from a paid sponsor, the story continued with Maisy finding the laptop, going to the police, and recording Zane Novak's arrest. There was a second break, then the final ten-minute segment started with Maisy's reaction to the break-in at her place, followed by Maisy and Jordana pinging the phone again, and, finally, the call from Jenna to report she had the phone.

Jordana turned to Jenna. "What do you think?"

Jenna nodded enthusiastically. "It's completely engrossing. It starts off with a puzzle, then Maisy digs up all this information, and, at the end, boom, the stakes go up. People will be *hooked.*" Then her expression changed. "Oh, no, my mom is gonna hear this. *Everyone's* gonna hear it."

Jordana raised her hand. "Don't start freaking out. Listen to the trailer first, okay?"

"Okay." She gulped her water.

Jordana opened a second file and pressed the play button:

Next week on the Farley Files, Jenna Novak works with Maisy to learn how her incarcerated husband, Zane, got his hands on Landon's cell phone and what role a Pittsburgh Police detective played in the puzzling events.

Music played, and then a snippet of Zane's arrest from episode one:

Sir, is there an iPhone 13 belonging to Landon Lewis on the premises?

There was until last night. Now it's gone.

Where is it?

Hell if I know. Ask your boy Colchis.

Colchis. Would that be Detective Tim Colchis from the Nuisance Bar Task Force?

Maisy's voice broke in:

Zane nodded yes.

Then Jordana's:

According to Jenna Novak, Detective Colchis was a frequent visitor to the Novak home in recent days, including turning up uninvited on Christmas night.

Jenna said:

Second time in less than a week that he showed up at our house. But, Christmas Day? I mean, come on. It worked out for me. I ran down and grabbed the phone while they were outside arguing. But I think Colchis turning up like that set Zane off.

Maisy:

My sources on the force mentioned an unnamed member of

the Nuisance Bar Task Force who recently took an unusual interest in Landon's case.

Jenna:

Why would Colchis care about a suicide? He mainly breaks up bar fights. That's how he knows Zane.

Maisy:

I don't know what his interest in Landon's case was, but I can't imagine it's a coincidence.

Jordana said:

Jenna bravely offers to help with the investigation.

Jenna's determined voice:

Zane brought the cops to my door. I want to believe Colchis got him mixed up in something stupid after the fact. I hope that's what happened. But I need to be sure. If Zane killed someone, I have to know. So what can I do to help?

Finally, Jordana closed with:

Find out next Tuesday on the Farley Files. Listen and subscribe wherever you get your podcasts.

Jordana stopped the program as the trailer ended,

and she and Maisy both turned toward Jenna. The woman had her knees pulled up to her chest and her arms wrapped tightly around her shins.

"What do you think, darlin'?" Maisy asked in a neutral tone.

She took her time answering. "It's good. But it makes me sound like a hero, when I'm not. I took that money from Zane and never asked where he got it. You don't even have anything about the money in the first episode."

Jordana opened her mouth, but Maisy said, "Let me. Listen, Jenna. I've worked in television for a long time, and one thing I've learned is people need someone to root for. I'm gonna assume a podcast is no different. They may tune in because they know me. But this isn't my story. I'm just telling it. They're not gonna root for Landon. And Deanne's too far removed from the situation. Depending on what Zane tells you tomorrow, they may root for him. Or they may not. But right now, you're the closest thing this story has to a hero."

She chewed on that for a long moment. "Okay. I guess."

"So, am I good to drop the episode? And the trailer?" Jordana confirmed.

Jenna nodded.

"Maisy. Do you want to run anything by Zone Five? Or Sasha and Naya, to make sure we're not opening you up to a slander complaint from the detective?"

Maisy played back the episode and the trailer in her mind. "No need. I stand behind my reporting. Evans and Bass knew I was recording the arrest, and we don't claim anything about Colchis as fact except for things that we know are true. He did show up at Jenna's house. Zane did say his name. What's the saying? Ship it."

Jordana giggled. "I think that's for software. Maybe drop it?"

"Drop it." Maisy raised her water bottle in a toast to their inaugural episode.

CHAPTER FORTY-SEVEN

December 27
Entirely too early

BELLA WATCHED as her private Pilates instructor sprayed down the mat before rolling it up to take it away.

"Good session today," Laura said. "Why don't you come into the studio later this week and we'll get you on the Reformer?"

Bella put down her cucumber-infused water to shudder dramatically. "The torture machine? Am I being punished for something?"

Laura laughed politely and pulled out her calendar. "I have an opening on Thursday. Same time?"

"Oh, you sweet child. No, it's one thing for you to

come to me before sunrise. But it's entirely too early for me to drag myself to the studio. How about eight?"

"You're the boss, Bella. See you on Thursday. At eight."

Bella walked the instructor to the door, taking pains to mirror the younger woman's dancer's carriage and regal posture. Laura handed her the newspaper from the porch, and Bella quickly closed the door to keep out the chill. When the phone rang on the kitchen counter, she thought she must be imagining it.

She hurried to the kitchen and saw that her phone was, in fact, silent. But she still heard the unmistakable sound of a ringtone. When she realized what it was, her confusion turned to indignation. How dare *he* call *her*. And at this hour, no less. She picked up her beloved purple bag from the kitchen island and pulled out the burner phone.

"It's six-thirty in the morning," she hissed.

Tim Colchis' rough voice was loud in her ear. "You're welcome. I waited this long to call out of courtesy."

"I don't think you know what that word means," she told him. "Unless this is a dire emergency, it's entirely too early to be calling. And if it *is* an emergency, you really ought to call someone who'll help you."

"Listen up, you old bat. I'm not in the mood for high-society trash talk. We have a problem. I searched the reporter's place yesterday. No phone. So I went to see Zane, who confirmed he didn't dispose of it after all."

"Well, ask him where it is. Don't you have to take a course or something to call yourself a detective?"

He laughed sourly. "Zane won't be answering questions from me or anybody else about the phone."

His tone chilled her more than the winter air ever could. "Why not?"

"He's dead."

"You—"

"I took care of him."

She closed her eyes. "Where?"

"In the jail."

"Please tell me you're not being serious."

"Simmer down. Have you ever been in the county jail? That place is a zoo. They probably haven't even found him yet. And if they have, let's just say, nobody's going to go to extraordinary lengths to figure out what happened to him."

"Fine. Whatever." She didn't care one way or the other if he killed his co-conspirator. From a mitigation of risk standpoint, it was probably the safer move. But it did have other consequences. "But now how do you intend to find the phone?"

"His wife has the phone. I spent most of last night sitting on her house, but she never came home. So then old Tim, he had a stroke of genius."

"You're referring to yourself in the third person now? Delightful."

He ignored the jab. "I went back to the prison complex and found her car parked at the First Avenue garage."

"So, she went to visit her husband?"

"She couldn't have. It was outside visiting hours. Besides, Zane was … terminated … before he added anyone to his approved visitor's list, so she couldn't get in to see him if she tried."

"Well, where is she, then?" Bella snapped. She didn't enjoy puzzles, but she especially didn't enjoy them before she was fully awake.

"Maisy Farley dropped her podcast. It's a doozy. And the trailer for the second one is already going viral."

"I don't have time to listen to a podcast, detective. Summarize it for me."

"Jenna—that's Zane's old lady—is working with Maisy now. Maisy has the phone, and she's probably protecting Jenna, too. She needs to be dealt with."

Bella swore softly under her breath. Then, "Which she?"

"Maisy. Both of them, actually. And probably that producer, too."

"I want to make sure I'm understanding you correctly. You want to dispose of three civilians?"

"Do you have a better idea?"

This man has antisocial personality disorder, she realized with a start. She could never remember the difference between a sociopath and a psychopath. The bloodthirsty detective was the one that lacked a conscience and the capacity for remorse.

"Well?" he demanded.

"No," she finally said. "I suppose I don't."

"Okay, then. I need you to lure Maisy to the office

building at Bakery Square. Make up some story, just get her there within the next hour."

"I can barely get there within the next hour," she protested.

"Seven-thirty," he told her, unmoved. "You get her there, and I'll take care of the rest."

"What about the other two?"

"We need to prioritize. She's the one with the big mouth."

"Fine." She ended the call and rushed upstairs to get dressed.

She was doing her eye makeup when she remembered the difference. Sociopaths were the rash hotheads. Psychopaths were cold and calculating. She put down her mascara wand and removed her Smith & Wesson from her vanity drawer. She confirmed that it was loaded and that the thumb safety was engaged before tucking it into her purple purse.

Tim Colchis was a sociopath. She checked her hair in the mirror and smoothed a stray lock behind her ear. She was the psychopath.

MAISY, Jordana, and Jenna were celebrating the enthusiastic reception to the first episode of the Farley Files with fresh-squeezed orange juice, pastries, and coffee that Alonzo, the building's concierge, had brought up after Maisy called down to ask where a girl could get a cup of coffee nearby. She'd invited him to stay and have a Danish or croissant, but he had to hurry back to his station and bask in his sudden internet fame.

Jordana had connected her laptop to the flatscreen television on the wall, and they were watching the download numbers tick up and the comments fly in on the various podcast services. Jenna was multitasking, monitoring social media comments about the podcast on Landon's laptop and shouting out the ones with the most engagement. She'd already talked to her supervisor, who'd okayed another personal day so she could deal with the Zane situation.

Maisy bumped Jordana's shoulder with her own. "We're off to a good start."

Her producer grinned. "You can say that again. We have a waiting list of sponsors."

"Are you serious?"

Jordana showed Maisy her cell phone screen, where she was keeping a running list of sponsors who'd contacted her since midnight. She was serious.

"I feel giddy," Maisy confessed.

"Let's chase that feeling," Jordana said.

Just then, Maisy's phone rang. "Oh, that might be the locksmith. I better take this."

She hurried into Landon's office, where the squealing and whooping would be less audible.

"Hello?"

"Ms. Farley?"

She frowned. She almost recognized the polished voice on the other end. Almost, but not quite. Her brain itched. "Yes."

"It's Bella Steptoe. The listing agent for the Bakery Square office? We met on Sunday."

"Of course. Hi, Bella."

"I apologize for calling at such an ungodly hour."

"No apology needed. I'm up."

"Reveling in the warm reception your podcast is enjoying, I imagine?"

Maisy chuckled. "Well, actually, yeah. Are you calling about the office furniture? I confirmed with Deanne Lewis that you're welcome to sell it to the next tenant and take a finder's fee, of course."

"Wonderful," Bella murmured. "Although that's not why I'm calling."

"Oh? What can I do for you?" Maisy didn't want to be rude and rush the realtor off the phone, but she *was* dying to see how many more downloads the podcasts had received. The dopamine hits were addictive.

"It's about your podcast."

Maisy was suddenly one hundred percent more interested in this conversation. "Oh?"

"Yes. I found something at the building that I think might help you piece together what happened the night Landon died."

"Really? Have you contacted the police?"

Bella hesitated. While Maisy waited for her to respond, she listened to the distinctive sounds of the morning commute. Honking, brakes squealing, and trucks idling.

Finally, Bella said, "No. What I found is somewhat

sensitive. I thought Mrs. Lewis might not appreciate my taking it to the authorities. So I reached out to you."

What kind of kink were you into, Landon?

Maisy looked around the sterile room as if she'd missed something and gave a slight shiver.

"I'm sure Deanne would appreciate your discretion. I can meet you somewhere to talk if you have time today."

"I'm on my way to Bakery Square right now. I have a very busy day, but if you could get here by seven thirty or so, I'll show you what I found, and you can decide what to do next."

Maisy checked the time. 7:07. It'd be tight, but she could make it.

"I'll leave right now," she told the realtor.

"Wonderful."

"And, Bella?"

"Yes."

"Thank you for calling me first."

"It's my pure pleasure, Maisy."

Maisy ended the call and raced through the apartment, shouting instructions to Jordana and Jenna while she pulled on her boots and ran a brush through her tangle of curls. She grabbed her car keys and mini-cinnamon bun from the platter on the island and then dashed out the door.

CHAPTER FORTY-EIGHT

7:20 *AM*

JENNA WAS CREATING a spreadsheet so Jordana could track sponsorship slots when her cell phone vibrated on the table. Amber had already texted her to say she'd heard the podcast, and her mother slept until ten most days. She didn't recognize the number.

"Hello?"

"Jenna?" The voice on the other end was thick with tears as if the caller was choking back emotion.

Her chest tightened. "Yes, this is Jenna. Is this Dotty?"

"Oh, hon. I'm so sorry."

It was definitely Dotty, and she was definitely crying.

"Dotty, are you okay? Did something happen to Fred?"

The concern in Jenna's voice caught Jordana's attention, and the younger woman drew closer as if she knew Jenna was going to need moral support.

"Not Fred; Zane."

"Something happened to Zane? Is it his hand? Will they take him to the hospital?"

The barrage of questions went unanswered for a long minute while Dotty sobbed.

Finally, she wailed, "There's no good way to tell you this, so I'm just gonna say it. Your husband's dead."

"No!" Jenna shouted and threw the phone on the table.

Jordana gave her a startled look and picked up the phone. She hit the speaker button and said in a clear voice, "Hi, Dotty? My name is Jordana Morgan. I'm a friend of Jenna's. Can you repeat what you just said, please?"

Dotty made a guttural noise. Then she said, "Zane Novak is dead."

Jenna gripped Jordana's arm, unable to form words.

"What happened?" Jordana asked.

"I've been on the phone since four in the morning trying to find out. Here's what I know for sure. I got an alert just before four o'clock. I figured the preliminary arraignment had been scheduled, but that's not what it was. A death in custody had been reported for Zane's inmate number."

"A death in custody," Jordana repeated. "What does that mean?"

"It can mean anything from a fatal car crash while a prisoner was being transported somewhere to a drug overdose to a heart attack to ... what happened to Zane."

Jenna found her voice and croaked, "What did happen to Zane?"

"He was stabbed. They found him after the shift change. He was in a video hearing room. He'd bled out hours earlier. They have to do an autopsy, of course, but the report says rigor mortis had already set in, so he'd been dead for at least a few hours when they found him."

Jordana was shaking her head. "I don't understand. Nobody noticed he wasn't in his cell or whatever?"

"Honey, the intake pod is usually chaotic on a good day. And right after a major holiday, they were probably short-staffed and over capacity. But it doesn't make sense that he was in that room. Those rooms are exactly what they sound like: spaces where an inmate can participate in an arraignment or hearing by video. Zane didn't have any reason to be there. And he couldn't have gotten in there by himself."

Dotty let that sink in.

"So, someone took him there to kill him?" Jenna asked to make sure she was understanding correctly through the persistent loud buzz in her brain.

Dotty answered carefully. "Someone took him in there. And someone killed him in there. It doesn't necessarily follow that they were the same someone."

"But there'll be an investigation, right?" Jordana pressed.

Dotty cleared her throat. "There always is. They rarely come to any useful conclusion."

"What do *you* think happened, Dotty?" Jenna begged.

"I can't say for sure, and I can't ask any more questions because I've already poked my nose in way more than I should have. But if I had to guess, someone paid off a guard to get them some time alone with Zane in that room."

Jenna and Jordana's eyes met over the table. '*Colchis,*' Jenna mouthed.

Jordana nodded, her mouth twisted into a sneer of disgust. "Would there be a log of police officers who entered the prison last night?" she asked Dotty.

"There should be. Like I said, sometimes it's chaotic, but a FOIA request would get you a copy of the log. I'm sorry can't help you more than I have."

"I understand, Dotty. Thanks for calling me. And take care of Fred," Jenna said dully.

"You take care of yourself, honey." Dotty was sobbing again when she hung up.

Jordana sat with Jenna in silence for a long moment. Then she asked, "Can I call your sister for you?"

Jenna nodded dully. Then her eyes sparked with fear. "Oh my God, we have to call Maisy first. If it was Colchis, she's not safe."

7:25 AM

THE PHONE RANG through Maisy's Bluetooth connection. Jordana's contact info and photo popped up on the radio display.

"Hey, how's Pittsburgh's premier podcast producer?" Maisy asked, amused by her own alliteration.

"Where are you?" Jordana's voice was frantic, but Maisy assumed she was buzzing from adrenaline and strong coffee.

"Ugh. I'm trapped behind this bus. I'm gonna be a few minutes late, but, oh well. So what do you think Bella's got on Landon? A fetish? A lover? It definitely sounded scandalous, judging by her tone. But then, she does seem like a pearl-clutcher. I wonder if—"

"Maisy. Zane Novak was stabbed to death."

Maisy's heart thumped and her stomach lurched. "What?"

"Jenna's friend from arraignment court just called. His death was reported in the system around four o'clock this morning, but they think it happened last night."

"Oh, my stars. How's Jenna?"

"A mess. I'm going to call her sister, but listen, whoever killed Zane was able to get him in an isolated room where he should *not* have been. So, not another inmate."

Maisy's mouth dried up. "You're saying a guard did it?"

"Or a cop."

"A cop," Maisy repeated. "Like Tim Colchis, for example."

"For example."

"Did I just get a man killed?"

"Let's not get ahead of ourselves," Jordana said calmly. "According to Jenna's friend, he was probably dead before the podcast dropped, so do *not* jump conclusions. Okay?"

Maisy made an indistinct noise that Jordana chose to interpret as 'okay.'

"But if it was Detective Colchis, there's a chance this meeting with this Bella person is a set up."

"Bella Steptoe doesn't strike me as the type of person to hang out with dirty cops."

"If working for Sasha taught me one thing, it's that there is no type of person when it comes to criminals."

Maisy nodded. "That's a fair point."

"Maybe call Bella and tell her you have to reschedule?"

Maisy craned her neck to see around the bus. "I'm almost there."

"Maisy." Jordana's voice was a warning.

"Let me pull over and call her. I'll see if she gives off any kind of vibe."

"Maisy, this is serious!"

"Look, if we're going to have a successful true crime podcast, we're going to have to take the occasional risk."

"I agree. A reasonable risk was inviting Jenna to meet us in the apartment without knowing anything about her.

Walking into an ambush isn't a reasonable risk. You can see that, right?"

"I'm going through a tunnel," Maisy told her.

"Maisy!"

"Okay, I'm sorry. I'm not going to do anything foolhardy. I can't kill a person with my bare hands, unlike your last boss. So I'll act accordingly."

"What does that mean?"

"It means I'll be careful."

Jordana huffed out a long, agitated breath. "You're an adult."

"I am indeed."

"Just do me a favor, and don't get killed. Oh, and don't forget to record it."

Maisy laughed. "You've got a deal on both counts. I'll call you back when I have something to report."

She pretended not to notice her hand shaking when she jabbed the screen to end the call. The bus finally turned, and she zipped up the street and turned into the alley behind Landon's office building. As she turned into the parking lot, her throat threatened to close.

Pull it together, princess.

She drove past Bella's silver status symbol. At this early hour, the Tesla was the only car in the lot, but she didn't pull into the next spot. Her instinct was to park out of view, and Maisy always followed her instincts. So, she drove around to the side of the abandoned warehouse and parked the car where it wouldn't be visible from the street or the office windows.

She killed the engine and dug through her purse

until she found the card Evans had given her yesterday. It did have the victim advocate's number printed on it, just as the officer had said. It also had Ilsa Evans' personal mobile number scrawled on it. She wasn't sure why Evans hadn't wanted Bass to know she'd given Maisy her number, but she was sure she needed to talk to someone she could trust. And Evans was close enough.

She punched the digits into her cell phone and stared at the building while the call connected. From her vantage point, she could only see the metal emergency exit door, the alley where Landon had died, and a sliver of the glassed-in lobby on the side of the building visible from the green space.

"Evans." Evans answered her phone exactly how Maisy imagined a police officer wrested from sleep would. Alert and ready to roll.

"Evans, it's Maisy."

"Why are you whispering?"

She hadn't realized she was, but she answered at normal volume. "Sorry. Did I wake you?"

Evans cackled. "No. My shift started at six. I'm sitting in the car waiting for Bass to pick up his bagel. Why? You calling to gloat about your podcast? My grandma said the first episode was, and I quote, lit."

"Ha. Did you listen?"

"No, I just told you. I'm working."

"Right. Did you hear about Zane Novak?"

Suspicion crept into Evans' voice. "What about him?"

"He was murdered in jail last night."

"What the—are you sure about that?"

"No, but my source is reliable. There should be a, what's it called, death in custody report in the system." What system? She had no idea, but she figured Evans would know.

Evans was cursing a blue streak. Maisy heard a car door slam. And what may have been a shoe or boot kicking something metal.

"Evans?"

"What a frickin day. First Thune, now this."

"Thune? Frank Thune?"

Evans laughed bitterly. "Yeah, your lunch buddy was suspended without pay. And this is *off* the record, Maisy. He's been giving out information about active investigations to somebody. Internal Affairs isn't sure who yet, but can you believe the balls on that guy? Now we're all under the microscope."

A man in a leather jacket exited a car parked illegally across the street from the office building. He scanned the road in both directions for traffic, then sprinted across the street. As he pulled open the glass lobby door, the wind caught his jacket. It billowed out to reveal a holstered gun on his hip. Maisy sucked in a breath and slumped below the windshield.

"Evans?"

"You're whispering again."

"What does Tim Colchis look like?"

"Like a jagoff."

"That's not helpful. Does he have dark hair that he wears a little too long in the back?"

"Yeah."

"Tall, ugly guy?"

"Yeah. He wears a beat-up leather jacket everywhere."

Maisy's heart hit her knees. "Does he drive a brown Tercel?"

"I don't know. Let me ask Bass."

A muffled conversation ensued. Then Evans returned. "Bass says yeah. It's either a Tercel or a Camry."

"It's a Tercel."

"Okay, it's a Tercel. Why?"

"I think he's here to kill me."

"What are you talking about? Where are you? You didn't go back to your place, did you?"

"No. Landon's landlord called me right around seven and asked me to meet her at The Joshua Group's office. She said she found something there that might be related to Landon's death, but she didn't feel comfortable calling the police about it."

"So she called a flippin' podcaster?" Evans's disdain oozed through the phone.

"Evans, can we focus?"

"Yeah, sorry."

"Anyway, I was supposed to meet her five minutes ago, but then I got the call about Novak. And I just had this feeling that maybe this was an ambush. So I called you. And a guy who looks like Colchis just got out of a brown Tercel and went inside the office building. He's got a gun on his hip."

"For the love of … did he see you?"

"No."

"Where are you?"

"In my car."

"Stay," Evans ordered as if Maisy were a golden retriever.

"Okay."

"I mean it. We're on our way."

"Maybe don't call this in? You know, just in case Thune isn't the only leaker?"

"Thanks for telling me how to do my job, Maisy."

"You're welcome. Hurry, please."

Evans' tone softened. "We will. Just hang tight."

"Okay." Maisy breathed.

"We'll be there in ten minutes, tops."

CHAPTER FORTY-NINE

IN THE END, Maisy waited four minutes.

She thought about the way Jenna Novak had jutted out her chin and vowed to find out the truth about her husband even if it was painful. She thought about the way Deanne Lewis was fighting to learn what had happened to her ex-husband even though it was undoubtedly painful. And then she thought about something her mama had told her way back when she was appearing on live television for the first time, making her debut on Spanish Oak's cable access channel.

Baby, being brave doesn't mean you're not scared. It means you're scared witless but you still do the thing. So get up there and do the thing.

She'd done the thing that day, and now, scared as she was, Maisy did the thing. She turned on her recording app and pulled up her call log. She found the incoming call from Bella and called the number.

"Hello?"

"Hi, it's Maisy. I'm running late. I should be there in ten minutes."

Bella let out an exasperated sigh. "I have appointments."

"I'm sorry. I got stuck behind a bus. Do you want to reschedule?" Maisy called her bluff.

"No, just hurry. Please."

"Ten minutes," Maisy promised.

She ended the call, then crept out of her car and circled the building, running in a low crouch. She narrated in a loud whisper as she ran. When she reached the lobby, she slipped inside soundlessly, skirted the elevator, and took the stairs.

Her heart drummed so loudly she couldn't tell if her feet made any noise on the floor, so she hoped for the best. She was tempted to try the supply closet, but she already knew that the sound wouldn't travel well through the wall. But a bullet would. So hiding in the closet would only give her the illusion of security. It was better to just do the thing.

She sneaked right up to the door and pressed her ear and her phone against the surface and listened hard.

Bella said, "She'll be here in ten minutes. What's the plan?"

Colchis replied in a gravelly voice. "I figured I'd shoot her, take her purse so it looks like a robbery. You call it in, and wait for the cops. Tell them you found her in here when you came in to do some realtor bullshit."

Bella sighed. "Can you try to make sure there's no

exit wound? Blood is exceedingly difficult to remove from this blonde wood."

Maisy grimaced, but Colchis apparently found humor in the gruesome request.

He barked out a laugh. "I'll do what I can."

"I appreciate it."

After a beat, Bella spoke again. "And the other two?"

"The so-called producer is a college kid. Easy enough for her to get in a drunk driving accident in a few days. I don't think Jenna Novak will be a problem. She's gonna have her hands full dealing with her sudden widowhood."

"Mmm. Speaking of widows, what about Deanne Lewis?"

"Jeez, lady, how many people do you want to kill? Once the reporter's gone, nobody's gonna give two craps about Landon Lewis' supposedly suspicious suicide."

"I suppose."

"What about our employer?"

"What do you mean?"

"I mean, you said they don't like messes or loose ends. I think this cleans everything up pretty well. But am I missing anything?"

"There is *one* thing," Bella told him.

"What's that?"

"You."

"What the hell? Put the gun down," Colchis ordered, his alarm forcing his voice up to an unnaturally high pitch.

Oh, holy moly, they *both* had guns.

"I can't do that, detective. You have failed repeatedly to carry out the simplest instructions. Stage a suicide. Dispose of a phone. Retrieve a laptop. No, I can't in good conscience allow you to continue to wander around, making more messes. So here's how it's going to go. I'm going to shoot you now. When Ms. Farley shows up, I'll shoot her, too."

"Then what, genius?"

"I'll tell a variation of your oversimplified story. I walked in on a robbery in progress. Ms. Farley was, tragically, already dead. I screamed for help, and a brave officer of the law—that'd be you—came running to investigate. The criminal shot and killed you and fled the scene. I'll dispose of my gun and then call the authorities. You will get a completely unjustified hero's burial, and I believe your ex-wife and children will get additional death benefits because you died in the line of duty. So, you're welcome."

Colchis gave a long, slow clap. "Points for creativity, but I really don't think you can get the drop on me."

"Let's find out, shall we?"

Do the thing.

Maisy filled her lungs with air, sent up a quick prayer that she wouldn't pee her pants and that Evans and Bass would hurry up already, and then pushed the door open. "Let's not."

Colchis was standing by the window. Bella stood behind the desk, her Hermes bag still draped over her elbow, and her gun aimed at the detective's chest.

Colchis took advantage of Maisy's entrance to unholster his weapon, which was now aimed at Bella's head.

Maisy was marginally surprised nobody was aiming at her, but then, again, she was the only one who wasn't armed.

"What's your plan, doll?" Colchis asked.

"Doll? You know, three different people have called you a jagoff in the past few days. I get it now," Maisy fluttered her eyelashes at him.

Bella snickered. Maisy ignored her. She flicked her eyes toward the window behind Colchis.

Finally. A police cruiser pulled into the lot with its light flashing but no audible siren.

Just a few more minutes, Maisy promised herself. How many times in her career had she looked over at her producer on live television and seen him miming stretching dough or a rubber band? She must've ad-libbed a hundred and fifty times. She could do it once more.

"Here's what I don't understand," she said now.

Bella arched a perfectly groomed brow. "What?"

"How did *you two* end up working together? I could see you and Officer Thune. He's a decent enough guy—I mean, except for the whole divulging information about active investigations thing. But Colchis? Look at him. He really is a jagoff. You had a harpist playing at your Christmas party. Your kid's in an MBA program at an Ivy League school. You have a freaking twenty-thousand-dollar purse. Colchis strong-arms bar owners and blackmails drunks into doing his dirty work. You're not exactly a match made in heaven."

"That's an understatement," Bella told her.

Maisy heard footsteps in the hallway. *Just another minute.* She widened her eyes and pointed at the window behind Colchis.

"Look, the police are here. The non-corrupt ones, I mean."

"Nice try, blondie." Colchis gave her a cold smile.

But Bella followed her finger and gasped. "She's not lying."

Colchis whipped his head around to check and turned back with a growl. Maisy ducked behind the credenza and screamed as Bella took a shot at him. He returned fire. Luckily, they both had lousy aim. Her shot went wide. His hit Bella's oversized bag and ricocheted off the metal clasp.

Before either of them could try again, Evans kicked the door open, and she and Bass pounded into the room, shouting instructions. Bass launched himself at Colchis. Evans covered Bella. Maisy stayed right where she was, cowering beside the piece of storage furniture, and confirmed that her app was recording the arrests of Tim Colchis and Bella Steptoe.

LATER, much later, after the detective and the realtor had been taken to the county jail for processing, Bass and Evans walked Maisy to her car.

"Why did you go in there?" Bass asked her. "Evans specifically told you to stay in the car. What was your thought process?"

She tilted her head and considered the question.

He misinterpreted the gesture. "I'm genuinely asking."

"No, I know you are. I figured they wanted to kill me to keep me quiet, but it's like the saying: three can keep a secret, if two of them are dead. Colchis killed Zane so that we'll never know his side of what happened the night Lewis died. So it stood to reason he'd also kill Bella so she wouldn't be able to tell anyone what happened when they killed me. Do you follow?"

Bass nodded. "Sure."

"What I hadn't expected was that Bella was *also* planning to kill Colchis. When I went inside, I was just gonna listen at the door and record until you two got here. But they started sharing their various murderous plans, and it got my dander up."

"Got your dander up?"

"Her Southern comes out when she's upset," Evans cracked.

Maisy smiled despite herself. "But it did. It made me furious that if they succeeded in killing each other, then we'd have no way to get to the truth about what happened to Landon or Zane."

"Or, in this hypothetical, you," Bass pointed out.

"I didn't go inside until the eight-minute mark. So as long as Ilsa was accurate in her time estimation, I knew I'd be okay."

"One, never rely on an ETA that *any* cop gives you," Evans said. "And, two, you're damn lucky it all worked out."

"I was born under a lucky star," Maisy told her, deadpan.

Evans narrowed her eyes and studied her. "I believe that, actually."

"But how do you plan to get around the Wiretap Act? You must know that Pennsylvania is a two-party consent state," Bass said.

Maisy pulled a face. "And *you* must know that one of the exceptions to the consent requirement is that a witness may record a conversation if she reasonably suspects the parties she's recording are committing, or are about to commit, a violent crime. That little tête-à-tête definitely falls under the exception."

Bass laughed. "Just testing you."

"Mmm."

"What the sarge means is that we can't wait to hear next week's episode of the Farley Files."

"That's right," Bass said. "Oh, and don't clean up your house. If Colchis did break in, we should be able to get some DNA evidence that will link him to the scene and, with any luck, to Novak's murder."

"Ugh, okay. I guess I can stay at Landon's weird bachelor pad for a few more days." She popped the locks on her car.

"Drive safely," Bass told her.

She nodded and got into the car. Evans leaned on the door frame. "You do know that Colchis and Steptoe both being alive is still no guarantee that either one will ever talk, right?"

Maisy smiled up at her. "Sure. But if they'd both died, it would have guaranteed that neither of them would ever talk. As long as they're alive, I have a chance to get one of them to tell their story. I wouldn't bet against me on this."

The police officer shook her head. "Don't worry. You won't catch me doing that. When I met you, I thought you were a Southern belle, all frilly and sweet. But you're not. You're one of those steel magnolias. Soft outside, but tough as hell inside."

"Nah," Evans interjected. "She's lived in Pittsburgh forever. She's a steeltown magnolia—a rusty steeltown magnolia."

Maisy was laughing when she drove away.

CHAPTER FIFTY

Eleven days later
The first Saturday of January
Law Offices of McCandless, Volmer & Andrews

MAISY LOOKED up as Leo Connelly came into the spare office and dropped a pile of boxes on the floor. "Is that the last of them?"

She stood and dusted her hands on the seat of her jeans. "Yep. Thanks for helping. When Sasha said she could lend me some muscle, I didn't realize she meant you."

"Neither did she. She and Naya were planning to help you move all these files over, but then she went and scheduled both of the twins' dentist appointments for the same time."

"I'm not following."

"She thinks it's more efficient than taking them separately."

She frowned. "Isn't it?"

He snorted. "You might think so, but that's a rookie mistake. I told her she could take them and I'd help you. We'll see how efficient it was later."

"You're evil. But you are helpful."

He gave her a lopsided grin and surveyed the boxes. "So all this stuff is Landon's?"

"Most of it. I've got all of his journals, the files from his office, and the printouts from his hard drive. Then there are the police files, and all the public information requests that Jordana's put in about Zane Novak's murder. There's also a pile of background research on Bella Steptoe and that dirty detective. So, it's all related to Landon at least tangentially. We've got enough material for an entire season of the podcast."

He flipped the lid off a box and peeked inside. "And what about this collection of depressing classic books?"

"Also Landon's. Deanne asked me to store some things from his apartment until she comes back to town next month."

"So you still don't know who wired him all that money?"

"Nope. Her financial team hit a dead end at Thor Trust International." She shrugged. "It'll all come out. It always does."

"Yeah, it tends to. And what's Deanne's plan for all this stuff?"

"I'm not sure. Jordana and I are still working through the criminal angles for the podcast, but Deanne wants to retain Naya to help her set up some kind of foundation to help violent crime victims' families. I don't know the details."

"And she's hiring Jenna Novak to help run it? That's what Sasha told me."

"That's the plan."

"Even though Jenna's husband most likely killed Landon?"

"Even though. Actually, that's probably a big part of her reason. She wants to end the cycle of recrimination and pain. Or something like that."

He shook his head. "She's a bigger person than I am."

Maisy cocked her head. "Is she? You didn't seek revenge against Landon for what he did to Sasha. And you could've."

"Maisy, if I tried to get revenge against everyone who ever threatened or hurt my wife, it would be a full-time job. I'm not particularly evolved. Just practical."

She laughed. "You seem pretty interested in him, though. Landon, I mean."

He shrugged. "I think I was the last person to see him alive. Well, except for Zane Novak. And it was such a weird interaction. It stuck with me."

"I can see that." She checked the time. "Oh, I have to run. My ride to the airport should be here any minute."

"That's right. You're going back to Georgia for a visit, right?"

"Yeah. Just a few days, but it'll do my soul good."

"I would have given you a lift. You didn't have to call a ride share."

She felt her face heat. "I didn't."

"Oh?"

"No, um. Jake offered to drop me off." She blushed even deeper and stared at her feet.

"I know. Jordana told me. I'm just giving you a hard time." He cracked up at himself.

She drew herself up. "You're incorrigible."

"Thanks." His grin faded. "Listen, I was planning to wait until you left and then sneak this into one of the boxes. But that's not sitting right with me. So, I'm going to give this to you, but I can't answer any questions about it. Deal?"

"Leo, I'm an investigative reporter."

"True crime podcaster, according to your producer," he corrected her.

"Either way. I can't agree to that. Especially when I don't even know what the 'it' in question is." She fisted her hands at her hips.

"Sorry, Mais. That's the deal." He gave her a rueful look.

She relented. She knew she wasn't going to be able to bluff a man who could make up an entire fake federal law enforcement agency on the fly. "Fine."

"I knew your curiosity would win out," he said as he took a slim rectangle wrapped in butcher paper from his pocket and handed it to her.

She unfolded the paper and stared down at a pewter letter opener. She knew before she turned it over that the other side would be inscribed with the initials JLL and the date 10.13.07. And it was. She ran her fingers over the engraving.

"Where did you get this?"

She looked up, but he was gone.

THANK YOU!

I hope you enjoyed this Maisy-centered mystery! Long-time readers know that Maisy Farley has been popping up in my Sasha McCandless thriller series since 2011. I was so happy to give her a book of her own. She's a fun and feisty character to write.

Although *Steeltown Magnolia* stands on its own as a complete book, it takes place within the context of my existing universe. In *Insidious Threats*, Sasha and Leo pick up where Maisy left off. You can join them by ordering a copy wherever books are sold.

If you're new to my books and want to read more about the events that led up to *Steeltown Magnolia*, go back and read *Independent Sources*. In *Independent Sources*, Sasha is working with Landon Lewis on a case when he dies, and Maisy is investigating allegations that someone's trying to influence the outcome of that case.

If you want to know even more, you can go back to

THANK YOU!

the Sasha McCandless book where Landon Lewis makes his first appearance. That's *Inevitable Discovery*.

I write in several other series, too. You can always find an up-to-date list of all my books, on my website, www.melissafmiller.com.

ALSO BY MELISSA F. MILLER

Thanks for reading *Steeltown Magnolia!*

You can always find an up-to-date list of the titles in this series, as well as my other books, on my website: www.melissafmiller.com

Sign up. To be the first to know when I have a new release, sign up for my email newsletter at my website. In addition to new release alerts, subscribers receive notices of sales and other book news, goodies, and exclusive subscriber bonuses.

Share it. Please lend this copy to a friend.

Review it. Consider posting a short review to help other readers decide whether they might enjoy it wherever you purchased this book.

ABOUT THE AUTHOR

I've always wanted to be a writer. Ever since I was a little girl, reading and books have been my life. I'm so happy to have realized that childhood dream. Thank you for coming along with me!

I was born in Pittsburgh, Pennsylvania. My family lived in a house overlooking the Pittsburgh Zoo. On quiet nights you could hear the lions roar from our backyard. My parents supported my love of reading, until I crashed my bike because I was trying, unsuccessfully, to read and cycle at the same time.

I studied Medieval English Literature in college. You're not going to believe this, but there was not an enormous job market for Medieval English Literature majors when I graduated college. I worked as an editor for several years before heading back to Pittsburgh and law school.

After law school I took a job in Pittsburgh. I would meet and marry my husband David there before we moved to Washington, D.C., and then to central Pennsylvania, where we started a small law firm together.

Confined to hospitalized bed rest with complications during my third pregnancy, I started writing *Irreparable Harm* to fill the time, and the rest, as they say, is history. In 2015, I retired from the practice of law to focus on my writing. I've now written more than three dozen novels!

When I'm not writing, I enjoy gardening, yoga, and, always, coffee.

Connect with me:
www.melissafmiller.com

Made in the USA
Monee, IL
10 May 2023

33442476R00239